BILOXI LIGHTS

by

Tom Ellis

LOOSE CANNON ENTERPRISES
Paradise, CA

2016 Edition
1.01
ISBN 978-1-944476-09-0

Cover art design by Harper By Design

-Also available as an ebook -

www.loose-cannon.com

Author's Notes

The disclaimer at the front of this book states it is a work of fiction. This is a story, a tale. It is not true. Everything is a product of my imagination. The story fit the Gulf Coast and the geographical locations are real. And that is all. Literary license has been liberally applied to Baldwin County Alabama, Biloxi Mississippi and the Biloxi Police Department.

Thank you for reading *Biloxi Lights*. Look for another Hadfield-Burns novel soon. If you like the story I would appreciate your leaving a review on Amazon. And if you would like to comment directly to me, go to my webpage :

www.Brokenspurs.com

Tom Ellis
St Clair County, Alabama
December 2015

Contents

CHAPTER ONE

AFTER several hours of practice the fly line *finally* looped perfectly across the placid lake. Andrew Burns watched the fly settle gracefully on the water and slowly sink below the surface. Andrew or Andy as he was sometimes called was not a fisherman. He was a totally inept novice with a nine-foot fly rod. At 49 years old teaching himself to fly fish was exasperating. He'd thrown tangled rods and reels into the lake and could even get the line on a cane pole snagged under water. So far his frustration level with the fly rod remained below the chunk it in the drink point. As he began to strip the line back he felt the hook catch on something unseen. He yanked sharply on the line to free the snagged barb. The late afternoon light provided enough illumination for a good view of a body when it surfaced. As he reeled the corpse toward the bank the stench of decomposition assailed his senses.

Andy's fly was hooked just below the lapels of the dead man's double-breasted suit coat. The fly line was tangled across a dark striped tie. Underwater weeds and debris on the clothing made it difficult to judge the colors of the tie. The handle of a large knife protruded below the man's jaw. Ironically the Windsor knot in the necktie was undisturbed by the violence inflicted. Andy suspected the blade was protruding out the back of the skull. The turtle population of the lake had eaten all the skin, the lips, and the eyes from the face leaving a gray grinning skull staring at Andy. The teeth were so perfect he wondered if they were the work of an orthodontist or natural.

Andy Burns' reaction to the gruesome sight was not shock or revulsion. It was disgust. It had been over four years since he retired from more than two decades in law enforcement. And for the last twenty four months things had been going well. A body floating in his lake was the last thing he needed. His two dogs began sniffing at the corpse. Andy snapped his fingers and the animals immediately sat awaiting his next command. Andy looked at the brush-faced dogs and said, "Truck." They bounded for the nearby red all terrain utility vehicle and jumped into the cargo bed.

Burns knelt and looked closely at the knife handle. As he suspected the workmanship on the handle and hilt was familiar. He secured the fishing line so the body would not float back into the lake and walked to the ATV. As he started the engine he looked back at the body and said "shit." The dogs barked in agreement.

Ten minutes later Andy was sitting in his workshop. He considered the state of the emergency before dialing 911 and dialed it anyway. The dispatcher for the Baldwin County Alabama Sheriffs Department answered.

"Baldwin County Nine One One what is your emergency?" A female with a nasal southern accent answered.

"My name is Andrew Burns I live on Raifield Trail, near Foley. I just pulled a dead body from my lake." Burns said, knowing the woman was looking at a screen that displayed his name and address.

"What?" Came an astonished reply.

Andy sighed once more and drew a breath. "I was fishing in my lake and I snagged what appears to be the body of a male human being."

"Are you Andrew Burns of number one Raifield Trail?"

"Yes." He wondered how many times the woman got calls about bodies in lakes.

"Did he drown?"

Andy considered that question for a moment. "I think the knife sticking out of his neck might have prevented him from drowning. But I'm not a pathologist."

After a silent pause the dispatcher told him to direct the responding deputies to the scene and they would handle the rest. Andy hung up the phone. Hopefully this would not get too screwed up. He went out to the ATV. The dogs had waited patiently in the back of the little vehicle. Burns drove the quarter-mile to the front of his property and unlocked the gate. He was not looking forward to what he knew would be a long evening and night. There wasn't that much daylight left. And the Alabama Gulf Coast insects wouldn't be too bad this early in the spring. Still he reached for the can of insect repellant he kept in the dash pocket of the ATV. He would much rather be drinking a beer than dealing with what was about to happen.

Sergeant Jolene Hadfield's cell phone rang. It was her week on call for the detective division of the Biloxi Mississippi Police Department. As she answered the first call a second call beeped in. It was from her boss Lieutenant Alan Busby. From dispatch she learned a missing person case victim had possibly been found dead in an Alabama lake. When she answered Busby's call on his third try he rudely ordered her to proceed to the scene in Baldwin County Alabama forthwith. Busby was a jerk.

Having just finished dinner Jolene was glad for the call out. She didn't like her dinner date. Being on call was a handy device for Jolene. On the rare occasions she dated she would always feign being on call even if she wasn't. It always provided an excuse to leave if she didn't like the situation. Tonight's date looked crestfallen by the turn of events as he paid the check and followed Jolene out of the casino restaurant where they had dined.

Like all casinos you couldn't enter or leave without passing a gaming table or slot machine. Jolene watched the craps tables she passed with a practiced eye. She hoped her sudden stop at a hot table would not cause her date to crash into her butt. Which she correctly surmised he was ogling as he walked behind her. Statements made by her late second husband and her ex first husband, many male cops as well as her own observations had convinced her that her derriere was exceptional. Only lately she was beginning to think it was exceptionally large also. Jolene was only a few months short of the big four oh, a birthday she planned to ignore.

At the moment her worry was not the size of her butt, it was just squeezing it and the rest of her five-foot-seven-inch-one-hundred-and-thirty-five pound frame into position at a crap table so she could get a bet down before the next roll. She dropped a ten dollar bill on the come line just as the shooter rolled. The dice were making the numbers. Her late husband had taught her well. The cubes produced an eight and she dropped another ten on the number eight and the number six. This time the shooter rolled a six. The table action was fast and Jolene pressed her bets. The shooter finally made his point, and she made over one hundred and fifty dollars in less than five minutes. Her vibrating cell phone stopped her from placing bets on the next come out roll.

After she cashed in her chips, Jolene's date followed her to the entrance where a parking valet asked for his claim check. Hadfield's unmarked police car was parked in a nearby limousine parking area. As her cell phone begin vibrating the second time she handed her date a twenty for her share of the dinner check and waved by as she walked to her unmarked Ford. She answered her cell phone.

"Sergeant Hadfield."

The sarcastic voice of Alan Busby came through loud and clear. "It's about time answered your phone Hadfield. Your ass had better be on the way to Alabama unless you want to report to night shift patrol as a relief supervisor in a couple of hours."

Jolene ignored the remarks as she opened the door on her car. "What do you want Lieutenant?" Her tone just short of being insubordinate.

"The victim in the lake has been tentatively identified as Nigel Hoffman and it is apparently a homicide. Make sure we are in that Sheriff Department's loop on everything pertaining to this case. I want a report first thing in the morning." Busby hung up the phone before she could reply.

Ten minutes later she was traveling east on I-10 the unmarked Ford Crown Victoria cruised effortlessly at eighty-five. She briefly considered the ethics of her excessive speed and justified it by being on police business. Ironically the dead man was the CEO of the casino she had just left. The lieutenant's remarks angered her. The only reason she wasn't the relief supervisor on the night shift, the worst sergeant's job at Biloxi PD, was that Busby wanted to bust her back to police officer rank. That had not happened because her work was done to perfection and her mentor was Captain Lyle Thigman Busby's boss. And it didn't hurt that Thigman had once served in the Mississippi Highway Patrol with her now retired father. Unfortunately Thigman was slated to retire at the end of the year.

So far she had lasted twelve years in the Biloxi Police Department. They hadn't been easy years either. Her professional abilities kept the harassment down. Still she was hit on in subtle ways. 'Sure you can go to this school. Let's go to lunch and discuss it.' The implication was always there even in 1999. The world of good old boy cops was far from changed. Something she learned the hard way as a member of the Jackson Mississippi Police Department. It was her first law enforcement job and she hoped a stepping stone to bigger and better things. It wasn't that. She had filed a sexual harassment complaint four years into her career. It didn't have the effect it would have in another work environment. Police officers, particularly those with high rank know how to retaliate. The complaint had cost her a divorce and her first police job. Lyle Thigman had been instrumental in her getting hired at Biloxi PD. The chief wasn't exactly subtle when he told her she wouldn't have the job long if she filed anymore harassment complaints. And she would not get a badge any place else either.

Six of her twelve years at Biloxi had been wonderful. She was married to Major Thomas Jefferson Hadfield, United States Air Force. Tommy Hadfield was a newly promoted major in a non-flying assignment at Keesler Air Force Base. The lack of a jet fighter to strap into had caused the crap-shooting pilot to mope around like a kid who had lost his puppy. Non-flying jobs were part of the career path for rated Air Force officers, and the Gulf Coast casinos had helped ease the pain for Major Hadfield. They also helped him get acquainted with some F-15 pilots stationed at Tyndall Air Force base in the nearby Florida panhandle, which made Tommy Hadfield's new assignment much more palatable. He could cage stick time in the F-15 with a couple of hours driving and prior planning. He met his future wife while he was in route to one of these rides.

Jolene's mood brightened as she recalled the incident that led to her meeting her future husband.

While working uniformed patrol she was in pursuit of a robbery suspect driving a stolen car. With siren blaring emergency lights flashing and adrenalin pumping Jolene maneuvered her Ford cruiser too close to the stolen vehicle. In an effort to allude the cops the crook wheeled his car into a casino parking lot. Jolene followed and promptly realized she could not stop before crashing into the suspect's car knocking it into a parked BMW.

The Beemer was the smallest car in the wreck and the stationary kraut can didn't stand a chance. Neither did the bad guy.

Jolene slightly rattled from the impact and the abrupt restraint of her shoulder harness and air bag thought the first things cops always did after wrecking a police car. 'How am I going to explain this?'

That thought didn't last long when she saw the suspect bail out of his wrecked car and run. It was a short lived sprint. He ran straight into a fist.

After cashing in his chips from a successful trip to the tables Tommy Hadfield was walking rapidly to his car. He had just enough time to make Tyndall AFB for his scheduled flight when he saw demise of his BMW. Jolene wound up rescuing the hapless robber from the angry fly boy. The crook would spend more than a couple of hours in the emergency room having the damage inflicted by Major Hadfield repaired. When she snarled at Hadfield that not only would she have to explain the wreck. She would have to explain why the suspect was a victim of assault. Tommy Hadfield looked at her and said that the least she could do was have dinner with him. There was an awkward moment when she realized they shared the same last name. That was put aside when he assured her he was from Pacific Northwest and it was high unlikely they were even remotely related.

Two months later Jolene married Tommy Hadfield. She had just been promoted to sergeant when Tommy got back in the cockpit with a squadron officers job at Tyndall. She took vacation leave and followed him to Las Vegas Nevada, where he was participating in a large training exercise.

After a wild weekend of lovemaking and gambling Tommy died in a crash. He rolled dice like he flew, fast and faster. When you lose with dice it is only money. Losing in a jet fighter is usually forever.

Jolene wondered if she could ever put Tommy Hadfield behind her. She accepted his death. Still after three years it wasn't over for her. Police officers always make a point of saying goodbye to their families when they go to work. They might not come home. She had been sound asleep when Tommy had left for the air base. *She didn't hear him say good bye.*

Her father was supportive. A widower of ten years he lived on his pension from the Mississippi Highway Patrol.

He encouraged her to keep up with her police job and hang on till retirement. She could retire in few years. The question was just how much could she tolerate between now and then. If she had the nerve and the capital Tommy Hadfield had taught her how to make a living rolling dice. As the casinos multiplied along the Mississippi Gulf Coast she polished her skills. Still she was scared to play with the big chips always settling for the five-dollar minimum bet tables. Her crap shooting skills had netted enough money for a down payment on her bass boat.

Bass fishing and pistol shooting were two of her daddy's loves in life. Jolene could shoot a pistol as well or better than any cop and catch bigger fish. The women's professional bass tournament trail interested her more than shooting craps. She could win money bass fishing.

The interstate turned into a long bridge crossing Mobile Bay. Jolene saw the lights marking the USS Alabama. A World War Two battleship permanently moored near the interstate. She was always awed at the size of that ship.

Her exit would appear in minutes. She wondered if she could get off from work in two weeks for a fishing tournament in Louisiana. She could afford it because tonight's winnings would make the payment due on her Ranger bass boat. Jolene looked south into the dark sky over the black waters of Mobile Bay.

"Thanks Tommy," she whispered, smiling.

CHAPTER TWO

THE directions included Walmart as a landmark prior to turning onto a county road identified only by a number. The Supercenter parking lot provided a place to stop and change her dress shoes for a pair of hiking boots she kept in the car. After a quick trip inside for a much needed potty break Jolene started her car and turned onto the county road. She wondered if it were possible to go anywhere without having Walmart included in the directions.

Soon the only light was from her headlights. There are no streetlights or other cars on the rural county road. Several minutes passed before she spotted the sheriff's cruiser waiting as promised at a country store. She followed it for fifteen more minutes on three different county roads before they turned into a dirt driveway. Jolene thought about how she was going to get out of this place when they passed through an open gate. The cruiser stopped and its driver motioned her to pull alongside.

The young deputy didn't bother to get out of his cruiser. He turned on the interior lights so she could see him better.

"Detective Hadfield, if you just keep right toward the flood lights you can barely see from here.' He was gesturing in the direction he wanted her to go. 'You can get to the scene without any problems. Just follow the tire marks in the grass. It is solid so you won't get stuck. When you get closer to the lights it will be easier to see where you're going. Our detectives and Deputy Rabun our evidence tech are there. He's a good guy he'll help you out. I've got to go back and meet the ambulance that is coming to pick up the body. You be careful where you step down there at the scene. The guy that owns this place says there's snakes all over." The young deputy said.

Jolene smiled, "Thanks for your help. Are you going to be here to lead me back to civilization?"

"I can. But all you gotta do is turn left at every paved road you come to. Once you see Walmart you can get back to Mississippi without any trouble."

Jolene thanked the young deputy again. She'd thought about asking him if he were old enough to drive. The driveway she was on continued off to her left into the darkness. She spotting some dim lights in that direction. Off to her right the glare of floodlights was only slightly brighter. She turned on the high beams as she followed the dirt and grass track toward the lights.

The trail or what passed for a trail continued deeper into thick woods and wound away from the lights. For a moment she could only see them in her rear view mirrors. When the track turned left Jolene realized she had made a one hundred and eighty degree turn when the flood lit scene appeared ahead.

She found a parking spot near a collection of marked an unmarked police cars and a van emblazoned with sheriff stars crime scene unit logos and the current sheriff's name. Opening her car door Jolene immediately searched the ground for snakes. She quickly donned a light weigh raid jacket with police insignia. Twisting her shoulder length red hair into a pony tail she tucked it into a cap she retrieved from the back seat. The police motif did not extend to the cap it advertised Ranger Boats. A short man wearing sheriff's overalls approached her.

"Are you Sergeant Hadfield?"

"That's me," Jolene said. She saw the disappointed expression when he realized she was a woman taller than him.

"I'm Ed Landrum Investigator Baldwin County Sheriff's Department."

"Jolene Hadfield," she extended her hand prepared for a bone crushing squeeze. Landrum shook her hand limp finger style like a politician.

Landrum began describing the scene as Jolene removed a black canvas briefcase with a shoulder strap from the car and slung it over her left shoulder. The briefcase held the usual paper work note books and her Glock forty-caliber pistol.

"The property owner, a Mister Andrew Burns was fishing and he snagged the body which was still below the water surface. He pulled it in and secured it to the bank. Then he drove back to his house and called us."

"My boss told me it was a homicide. How did you determine that?"

"There is a large knife protruding from the victim's neck. Our coroner has already ruled it a homicide. He thinks the guy was dead before he was put in the water. After looking at the body I agree. Of course the autopsy will be able to confirm that."

"Any idea how he got in the water?"

"Not yet, Sergeant Hadfield. A total search of the crime scene will be conducted in the daylight tomorrow."

"I understand you have some tentative ID saying this guy is my missing person." They walked toward the water she scoped out what she could see of the flood lit scene. A black body bag on the ground about fifteen feet from the bank. It was zipped shut covering the grisly contents. A uniformed deputy stood nearby with a skinny man whose facial features resembled a rat. She figured rat face was the county coroner. Another short fat man with a pear shaped body stuffed into sheriff's coveralls was focusing a camera at some small items on top of a card table. The camera flashed as she reached the table. Before Landrum could introduce the photographer he looked up and smiled like he was about to devour a hot fudge sundae. Jolene wondered how many cases like this he got to handle.

"I'm Bob Rabun, evidence tech. I would shake hands but they've handled some pretty raunchy stuff tonight." He held up a surgical gloved hand for her to see. Rabun forged ahead obviously proud of his work.

"This is the contents of the deceased's wallet. The Mississippi Driver's License says he is your guy. Body is unrecognizable due to turtles, fish, or whatever else has been munching on it. The pathologist with Department of Forensic Science in Mobile will have to make an ID from dental records. Can you get them over here before the autopsy in the morning?" Jolene nodded, before she could say anything Rabun continued.

"General physical description and dress says he's your man, Nigel Giles Hoffman, even had some business cards from the casino in his coat pocket."

Rabun pointed to the soggy collection of cards and papers on his table. The engraved gold letters on the saturated business cards were easy to read.

Nigel G. Hoffman
Chief Executive Officer
Golden Bay Casino

Next to the driver's license Jolene saw a wet wallet size family picture Nigel Hoffman had three kids and a wife. Once they had a positive identification of the remains she would have the responsibility of notifying the family. A task she did not relish.

Hadfield looked back at Rabun and saw the hot fudge sundae look again. She couldn't resist smiling.

"Where was the body pulled out of the water?"

Rabun pointed past the body bag to the bank. A fly rod lay on the ground with line tangled around it. She noted the rod & reel were gear a coastal fly fisherman would use. And much too heavy for practical use in a farm pond. Jolene wondered how much the owner knew about fly fishing. The artificial light stopped just past the bank. She couldn't tell how much water they were dealing with.

"Got any idea how big this pond is Rabun?"

"Sergeant Hadfield don't let Andy Burns hear you call his lake a pond. I don't know how big it is but it ain't no farm pond. It was too dark when I got here to do anything other than recover the body. We're gonna keep a man out here all night guarding the scene. I'll be back in the morning to search the area. Andy will help because he is interested in how a body got in his lake."

"Wait a minute Rabun. This Andy Burns is the one who found the body right?"

"Yes ma'am and he owns the place too."

"Did it ever occur to you he might have had something to do with that body getting in his so called lake?" The hot fudge sundae expression had disappeared. Rabun clearly did not share her thinking. Jolene enjoyed working with crime scene technicians. They typically knew their stuff and were dedicated to solving the crime. And alienating the rotund deputy was not a good idea.

"Sergeant Hadfield,' Rabun answered sharply. 'Andy Burns is a retired police officer. He's a gunsmith and a custom knife maker. He put night sights on my Glock and a scope on my hunting rifle. One thing for sure is he kept this scene from getting screwed up. The new deputy that led you in was ready to jump in the water after the body if Andy hadn't said something about water moccasins. As far as him having anything to do with Mr. Hoffman's death I do not think so."

Jolene looked at Landrum, 'what are your thoughts on that Ed?"

Landrum hesitated before speaking. "Hadfield there are a lot of questions to be answered here. One is what Hoffman was doing in an Alabama farm pond a hundred miles or so from his home. I used the word pond with Burns and he smiled. He offered a look at a topo map of the property. So far I haven't gotten around to looking at that. Yes he kept the scene intact. I had no idea he'd been a cop until Rabun just said so. Burns certainly didn't volunteer that information. And that in my experience is the first thing an ex-cop does when he encounters the police is tell he has been one. That is puzzling. As far as Burns being involved in killing the guy my gut feeling says he is not. But ex-cops have killed people before and one thing is sure." Landrum paused for effect.

"They have a head start on how to cover it up and get away with it."

"I am not comfortable with him helping search his own property for evidence." Jolene responded.

"Well that is not up to me or you Sergeant Hadfield. It is up to Deputy Rabun. Our policy is crime scene searches are handle by our evidence unit. And they say how it is done and who is involved. If you don't like it, take it up with our Sheriff. He made the policy." Landrum answered.

No disrespect intended Sergeant Hadfield,' Rabun added. 'Andy found the body. If he had wanted to hide it, why would he find it? Besides, his property covers one section on a property map. That is 640 acres a square mile. He knows his land, he needs to help."

"Where is Andy Burns?" Jolene asked.

Landrum, answered. "He's at his house. Said if anybody needed to talk to him just come up and knock on the door. Follow the drive from the gate it will take you to the house. And he's got two of the ugliest damn dogs you'll ever see. They look like mad men who need a shave. Don't let em scare you when you go up there."

The arrival of the ambulance and the coroners yelling interrupted her questions.

"Hey sweetie I'm tired of standing out here with the mosquitoes. This body is going to Mobile. So if you are going to look at it get your ass moving!"

The coroner leered at Jolene as he bent down and unzipped the body bag. The flood lamp lit expression on his pale rat face made her feel like she was part of low budget horror movie. The exposure of Nigel Hoffman's skull to the light almost caused her to gasp. Rat face stood with a flourish when he completed unzipping the bag and folding open the flaps.

"There he is honey, the lake monster. Don't keep us here all night with your examination. Just believe me he met with foul play."

Jolene ignored the remarks and looked at the body lying in its black vinyl shroud. A few wet tufts of hair remained on the skull. Nigel had excellent dental work. His immaculate white teeth were exposed forever in death's rictus grin. Jolene stooped for a closer look at the knife handle protruding from under the jaw. It was a red color and the hilt appeared to be some sort of heavy metal. It was certainly not a discount store hunting knife or the usual edged weapon of choice, a chef's knife. She remembered Rabun saying Andy Burns made knives. Was there a connection between Burns and this knife that appeared to be holding up Nigel Hoffman's skull? She stood up and nodded to the coroner. The body bag was quickly zipped and loaded in the waiting ambulance.

Jolene exchanged cell phone numbers with Deputy Rabun. He assured her the scene would be protected until he had a chance to search it in the daylight. The idea of Burns helping search still bothered her. Burns could very well be a suspect. She carefully followed the trail back to the main drive and turned toward the house. As she approached motion activated lights came on illuminating the front of the house. Which looked more like a building or a fortress than a house. She parked next to a large pickup truck and saw something totally out of place... a hitching rail. Not just the standard Hollywood western hitching rail either, but one made from a telephone pole!

The house was constructed of concrete blocks. A short sidewalk led past the hitching rail to the front door. Which was a massive heavy wood thing inset into the house creating a stoop with walls on either side. Another motion detector light lit the area. Jolene felt like she was entering a medieval fortress. She looked for a door bell and heard dogs growling. Her instinctive reaction was to reach for her Glock when she heard a voice command silence the dogs. The door opened.

"Mr. Burns?" She asked. Burns nodded yes.

Jolene held up her ID "Mr. Burns I'm Sergeant Hadfield from the Biloxi Mississippi Police Department. It looks like the body you found in your lake is one my missing persons cases. I need to ask you some questions if you don't mind?"

"Come in Sergeant," Andy said with a nod toward the interior.

She saw he wasn't quite six foot tall and weighed maybe one ninety. Burns looked to be over forty how much was anybody's guess. He wore jeans and an open collar tan work shirt. His dark unkempt mane was creased in the classic hat hair fashion.

Landrum's comment came to mind as she entered the house and got a good look at the dogs. She had never seen dogs like these and pretty did not come to mind. The thick bushy fur around their noses and eyebrows gave a menacing effect. They stood about two foot at the shoulder each weighting over sixty pounds. Their whiskey color coats were shinny and glowed in the warm light. The hair was short and coarse. Their tails were neither short nor long but pointing straight up as they eyed her. Jolene hoped Burns had fed them.

She followed Burns and the dogs into the house. A small foyer opened into an immense great room finished in southwestern decor. Two large ceiling fans hung from huge wagon wheels with light bulbs. A rustic rock fireplace occupied most of the far wall. With an impressive size bearskin rug covering the floor in front of it. A Pennsylvania Rifle resided over the mantel like a silent sentinel between two brass lamps. Moose Elk and Mule Deer heads hung on the walls. Several lever action rifles and a number of swords shared their wall space. As well as the most knives Jolene had ever seen anywhere. Before she caught herself she said "Wow!"

Burns smiled slightly. The ambiance was enhanced by light reflecting off the polished blades. A reflection danced off a brilliant knife blade lying on a nearby table. It was well over a foot long and at least three inches wide. A hilt constructed from polished brass joined the blade with a highly figured piece of dark hardwood shaped like a coffin.

"That knife is awesome. What does somebody use something that big for?" She leaned forward for a closer examination.

"Anything they want but mostly to show off and brag about."

"The handle beautiful. What kind of wood is it?"

"The wood is European Black Walnut. The handle shape is why it is called a coffin handle Bowie."

Jolene noticed the words 'Burns Maker' etched on the blade parallel to the hilt. As she looked at the finely finished weapon it was apparent Burns was a skilled craftsman.

"You can pick it up if you like. Be careful the top edge is sharp." He said.

Jolene was surprised at the knife's weight. While heavy, the sixteen-inch knife balanced nicely in her hand. It felt like she was holding a short sword. Jolene extended her arm instinctively grasping the knife like she would a fishing rod.

"You've got the grip right. Are you a knife fighter as well as a detective?" Andy asked, smiling.

Jolene's flushed. Her fascination with the knife showed. "It feels like a small sword."

"For all practical purposes that's what it is. There's not that much difference between the size of that knife and a Roman short sword. Confederate cavalrymen were as likely to be armed with a Bowie knife as they were a saber. There is a lot of historical data about Jim Bowie that is probably more fiction than fact. I believe he was trained as a swordsman. It wasn't practical or comfortable to carry a sword all the time. And guns of that period only shot once. So the Bowie knife was developed out of practicality and need."

"Deputy Rabun said you made knives. What will you do with it now?"

"It is sold. A circuit court judge commissioned me make it for him."

"So you make knives to order then?"

"Most of the time and when I have the inclination I'll make one just because I want to."

Jolene motioned to the walls. "Did you make all these?" She asked.

"No that is my collection. I like Bowie knives there are so many variations."

"Was it a Bowie knife that killed Nigel Hoffman?" Jolene asked watching Burns as he answered.

"Who is Nigel Hoffman?"

"You don't know him?"

"No and I don't believe I've ever had a client by that name either. You are welcome to check my records."

Jolene thought he sounded truthful, but cops could lie with the best of them. And he had yet to tell her he was an ex-cop.

"Deputy Rabun also said you are a gunsmith. It looks like you hunt as well." Jolene said while looked around the room again.

Andy motioned her to have a seat on a tan leather couch. He sat down on another one covered in a Navaho blanket design.

"I don't hunt Sergeant Hadfield. The game heads and the bear skin rug came with the house. What else did Deputy Sundae tell you?"

"Deputy Sundae?" Jolene asked, puzzled.

"Rabun always has an expression on his face like a kid looking at a hot fudge sundae." Andy said smiling.

Jolene laughed remembering she thought the same thing.

"He said you were an ex-cop."

"I'm a retired cop. I resent being called an ex-cop. Ex-cop implies you couldn't hack the job, or got caught at something and canned."

Jolene had never heard it put that way before. While his statement wasn't correct in the case of every ex-cop. It was certainly an accurate observation about many of them.

"Where did you retire from Mr. Burns?"

"Homewood Alabama," he answered.

"Where is that," She asked while withdrawing a notebook from her briefcase.

"It is a suburb of Birmingham. That is the north central part of the state."

"How long did you work there?" She asked.

"A little over twenty two years."

"That's a long time. I sometimes wonder if I'll make that long."

"How much time have you got in now Sergeant?

"Twelve years in Biloxi four more in Jackson." She answered

"Do you know Don Smith and Mark Hildibrand?"

That question caused Jolene to smile and wonder who was interviewing who.

"Yes I know them. Mark Hildibrand was my field-training officer when I started with Biloxi. They run our SWAT team now. Where do you know them from?"

"They are customers of mine. They are due out here tomorrow afternoon with a rifle they want me a look at."

SWAT teams have weapons that most cops don't get to use. Biloxi PD's team was no exception. Burns being a gunsmith and a retired cop would make him a good source for repairing those guns, she thought. And Smith and Hildibrand would be good information sources about Burns.

"When are you going to tell me who Nigel Hoffman is?"

"It looks like Nigel Hoffman is the man whose body you found in your lake. The medical examiner will have to confirm his identity."

Burns expression was impassive.

"How did you discover the body Mr. Burns?"

"I was practicing fly casting and snagged something underwater. When I yanked on the line to free it, the body surfaced. I pulled it to the bank secured it and called the sheriff's department."

"That part of the lake seems a little out of the way from this house. Is that a good fishing spot?"

"I don't know. Owning a lake doesn't make you a fisherman. A friend of mine told me there was a bream bed around there and it would be a good place to try fly fishing."

"How big is your lake Mr. Burns?"

"A hundred and eighty acres give or take."

Rabun was right. It wasn't a farm pond. Jolene was now curious how a retired cop could afford a place like this. Smith and Hildibrand might know the answer.

"Mr. Burns I need your driver's license our report forms require that information."

He handed over his license without comment and Jolene copied the information into her notebook. She did the math and realized he didn't look his age. Hadfield returned his license.

"Are you the only one who lives here Mr. Burns?"

"Yes."

Before she could continue he stood up indicating the interview was over.

"Can I expect you tomorrow when Rabun searches the area?" he asked.

"I was planning on being here Mr. Burns, unless my lieutenant has other ideas."

"Good I'm sure you will think of more questions for me before then. Have a good evening Sergeant."

CHAPTER THREE

DRESSED in an old T-shirt and cutoff jeans Jolene pushed the fishing magazines aside on the coffee table and propped her bare feet on the wood surface. She took a long sip from a bottled beer and considered the evening's events. Burns was too quiet. His not volunteering that he was a retired cop didn't play right. Was it possible he'd accepted he is no longer an active member of the police fraternity with no business acting like he's still on the job?

Jolene sat the beer bottle on the end table next a picture. She picked up the picture and looked at the three men holding trophies. Her father was in the middle holding the first place trophy. One of his favorite sayings about police work was. *'If you don't talk you can't be caught.'* Was Burns not talking because of guilt? She looked closely at the picture again and then removed it from the frame. Written on the back of the photo was, MHP first place Homewood PD 2nd & 3rd. Homewood Police Department, the same agency Burns was retired from. It was too late to call the old man.She yawned waiting for her father to answer the phone. It was 6:00 AM and she hoped he hadn't gone fishing. She took a sip of coffee when he answered. Jolene grimaced at his abrupt impatient tone.

"Daddy how are ya?" she said as she swallowed the hot coffee.

"Sugar babe!" Jolene rolled her eyes at hearing her childhood nickname. "The trucks running in the driveway I'm on my way to the lake. What's on your mind?"

"I wish I were going with you but one of my missing persons turned up dead. The guy who found the body is a retired cop from the Homewood Police Department in Alabama. He never admitted to being a retired cop. I heard it from a deputy at the crime scene. For some reason it bothers me. I've got a picture of you at pistol match with some guys from that department. Do you remember anything about them?"

He guffawed. "Your guy's probably ashamed to admit he worked there. I sure as hell would be! That's the cheapest bunch of jerks and loud mouth drunks I ever run across. Wouldn't trade patches but they'd sell you a used one that'd been washed too many times. What's this guy's name?"

"Burns, he's forty nine worked there twenty-two, maybe twenty-three years. My notes are in the car. He supposed to be some kind of gunsmith."

"Never heard of him. I gotta pick up Roy and I'm late. Let's go fishing some time."

"Sure Dad, appreciate the help. Love you." Jolene said to an already dead phone.

Later after meeting with Lt. Alan Busby. She felt the old squad room axiom regarding a required lobotomy for promotion to police lieutenant was true. When she mentioned her suspicions about Andy Burns and his being a retired cop Busby was absolutely delighted. Jolene wondered if he had gotten a hard on. He produced roster of his classmates from the FBI National Academy and the name of a lieutenant in the Homewood Police Department. Jolene was now on the phone listening to the whining nasal twang of Lt. Michael Phillips and thinking about lobotomies.

"Sgt. Hadfield, Andrew Burns is a retired police officer from our agency. If you are inquiring about him for employment purposes the only comment we can make is that we would not re-hire him.”

“Lieutenant this is a criminal investigation. Burns found a body. The circumstances are unusual. I would like to know more about his background. I understand he is retired from your agency. I’m wondering why he wouldn’t volunteer that information.”

“That’s not surprising considering his record here. The man was a loner and a troublemaker with a very radical unhealthy interest in weapons. He was promoted to sergeant against my recommendation. He didn’t make his probation and was demoted. He covered up for the officers he supervised. And he was very cruel punishing those officers he didn’t like. He retired when the demotion order came down. It was a good thing for all concerned.”

The Homewood lieutenant’s castigation of Burns smelled. Before Jolene could respond Phillips concluded the call.

“Sergeant you are correct recognizing Burns potential as a suspect. You have a good day now. Bye.”

Jolene envisioned the Homewood lieutenant as a mousy looking police bureaucrat who, like Busby, wouldn’t be around when the trouble started.

Deputy Rabun had called earlier and asked her to meet in Mobile at the medical examiner’s office. After collecting the dental records she decided there was time to drop by SWAT headquarters and talk to Smith and Hildibrand. Don Smith was one lieutenant who she thought worthy of the job.

SWAT headquarters was in an old gymnasium near the interstate. The building was perfectly suited for the use of the muscle bound SWAT team members. All the department cops had use of the gym. The clank of free weights reminded her of an overdue work out.

“Sergeant Jo,” Mark Hildibrand said warmly when she entered the SWAT Commander’s office. The six-foot-four-inch tall bear like sergeant got up from his desk and hugged Jolene. He was the only Biloxi officer with that privilege.

Besides having been her field-training officer, Hildibrand was a mentor and close friend she liked to think of as a brother. She asked about his wife and family. Don Smith, the team commander, rose from behind his desk and extended his hand. The two men wore the black and gray camouflage military style utility uniform. Smith was buffed and muscular like his sergeant only a few inches shorter.

"What brings our ace lady detective to animal town?" Hildibrand asked.

"I understand you guys know Andy Burns."

"If you are talking about the gunsmith in Baldwin County Alabama we know him." Smith answered.

"Yea," Mark added, "we're taking a rifle over there this afternoon. And,' he paused and looked at his boss grinning, 'a so-called police sniper."

Jolene realized the part about the sniper was an inside joke between the two men. "We are talking about the same Andy Burns. He said you all were coming over today."

"How do you know Andy, Jo?" Hildibrand asked. "You get a special invitation to fish in his lake or something?"

"Burns found one of my missing persons floating in his lake. The CEO from the Golden Bay Casino, Nigel Hoffman, and a homicide victim judging from the knife sticking out of his neck. And it doesn't look like a Walmart special kitchen knife either. The autopsy is this morning in Mobile. I've got to take the dental records over for a positive ID. Then I'm going back to Burns' place with the Baldwin County evidence tech to search the area."

The two SWAT men exchanged glances and Smith spoke first. "How can we help you Jolene?"

"There will be three of us over there this afternoon, we can help search. I can probably come up with more help if need be. That is a big place." Hildibrand added.

"I may need that. I've never seen the place in the daylight. The Baldwin County guy seems real good. But he has already said Burns is going to help search. I'm not sure I like that idea. I really need background on Burns. What

I've gotten from the PD he retired from isn't encouraging. Help me out guys."

Once more the two SWAT cops exchanged glances and Smith answered "Andy Burns is a very specialized gunsmith. Rifle smith would be a better description of him. He does put a lot of night sights on the new breed of police pistols Glocks SIGS etc. etc. I think that is just beer money for him though. His real calling is building super accurate rifles. He is also licensed by the BATF to manufacture suppressors, or silencers, if you like to call them that. And he is very skilled at tuning a suppressed rifle to shoot accurately. He has built a number of rifles for SWAT teams all over this area and other parts of the country as well. And he does build hunting rifles for civilians with wallets thick enough to afford one."

"He told me he makes knives too." Jolene said.

"Don't ask the price of one either unless you are sitting down." Hildibrand said. "And when you get the knife out of your victim show it to Andy. He can tell you everything you want to know about it. He knows as much about knives and swords as he does rifles."

"What's the scoop on his police background? I understand he was busted from sergeant back to police officer." Jolene asked.

Don Smith answered with venom in his voice that surprised Hadfield. "He was busted because of politics. Politics as dirty and sorry as we have here in our own department." Smith shook his head and apparently decided not to continue.

"I got that idea when I spoke with a lieutenant from Burns' old department. I have to check everything. You know who I work for." She said rolling her eyes.

"I know where you are coming from." Smith said.

"Andy Burns is not a suspect in your case.' Hildibrand said. 'As far as him helping search the area around that lake. The Baldwin County guy is smart letting him help. You just said you haven't seen the place in the daylight. There is a six hundred-yard rifle range on the property. The area behind the impact berm is thick woods. I hate to think about what is crawling around back there. Andy knows that property better than anyone does; his neighbor's cows get out all the time and he rounds them up. He knows what's there and what shouldn't be there."

"Is Burns independently wealthy? I mean a piece of property that big seems a little beyond the means of a retired cop. The furniture is well past my paycheck. And he said something about the game mounts on the wall coming with the house. How did he buy the place?"

"Andy inherited that house and property. And the state of the art machine shop that adjoins the house." Hildibrand answered.

"He had family that owned that?" Jolene asked.

"No a friend left it to him," Mark Hildibrand answered while making his bulky frame comfortable on his desktop. Smith remained seated behind his desk. Jolene realized she had sat down in Hildibrand's chair. She didn't make an effort to move. Because she wasn't leaving without knowing everything they knew about Andrew Burns.

"What kind of friend leaves a piece of property with a hundred an eighty acre lake on it to someone who is not family?" she asked.

"A long time shooting buddy named Charlie Raifield. I think he was Andy's mentor. All I know about the guy was that he was from Mobile and well off. His wife hated that piece of property and didn't contest the will. Raifield died unexpectedly. He had just landed his floatplane at Mobile Aerospace and had a massive heart attack. Andy was living in Arizona at the time."

"What was he doing in Arizona?"

"He moved out there when he retired. Andy was in the Border Patrol after his Marine hitch. He was stationed in Arizona and he liked the place."

"Do you know where he lived in Arizona?"

"Not really, somewhere around the border I'm sure. I visited most of the Wild West towns when we went out there on vacation five years ago."

Jolene remembered Hildibrand telling how much he and his family enjoyed the two week long camping vacation west. He was fascinated with the history of the region. And often referred to himself as a closet cowboy. Hildibrand seemed to reminisce a moment as he spoke.

"Gosh I need talk to him about Arizona. I bet he's been to some of the good places."

"How long have you known Burns?"

Smith with a nod toward Mark answered the question.

"Fourteen years ago we went to an FBI police sniper school. Burns was at the school. One of the FBI instructors recognized him from the Marines. Andy was a Marine sniper in Vietnam. He was credited with," Smith hesitated looking at his sergeant again. "Quite a few confirmed kills. Do you remember Mark?"

"Over thirty"

"Anyway that turned out to be an excellent school. Burns added a lot of knowledge and experience to the week. He really helped teach. He was building rifles back then. He learned that craft in the Marines."

"I can't believe the FBI would let a small town cop help teach one of their schools."

"The FBI guys that taught that class were hardcore hostage rescue team people. Most of 'em didn't even like other FBI agents. I remember one reference to field office agents as expendable morons. Andy fit in well with them."

"I agree with Mark," Smith added. "It would surprise me if Andy Burns were involved in anything more than finding the body in his lake. Our dealings with him have been professional. He is good at what he does. When it comes to sniper rifles and shooting them his word is gospel for us."

Jolene took her leave and ten minutes later was cruising east on the interstate at eighty-five miles per hour.

It was the smell that bothered her the few times Jolene had witnessed an autopsy. The sewerage like odor validated the squad room adage used for particularly heinous passages of gas. 'It smells like something crawled up inside you and died.'

She was grateful the Medical Examiner suggested they go to his office and not the Autopsy Theater. Deputy Rabun was sitting on a leather couch diligently studying a folder of police reports. He greeted her with his best hot fudge sundae smile. The X-rays displayed on the viewing box caught her attention. Several views of the skull with the large knife protruding were hung for examination. The ME briefed her on the X-rays.

"Thanks for bringing the dental records, Sergeant. We should be able to confirm the deceased's identity shortly. As you can see death was caused by the introduction of a rather large knife below the deceased's chin. This completely severed the spinal column. Death was instantaneous. Obviously he was placed in the water after death there was no sign of water in his lungs. It appears that the perpetrator intended for the victim to stay submerged. But apparently whatever he used to weight the body came untied. We found nylon cord wrapped around the body with a loose end that appeared to have once been in a knot. The body was dragged some distance prior to having been submerged. We found grass and other organic plant life in the deceased's clothing. Most interesting was three snakebites on the corpse. I would think the possibility exists that your perpetrator was also bitten."

Her cell phone buzzed interrupting the pathologist's dissertation. She saw Lt. Busby's phone number on the screen. The ME excused himself and returned to the Autopsy Theater with the dental records.

"Hadfield,' Hoffman's Cadillac was just pulled out of the Pearl River. Some fishermen found it this morning. A state evidence team is looking around. We've sent a tow truck for the vehicle. Does that ME have a positive ID on Hoffman yet?"

"No sir, he is working on it as we speak."

"OK, they can call us when they know for sure. And I will handle the official notification."

Jolene wonder what Busby was up to. Taking a distasteful task like a death notification was not something one volunteered for. Maybe Captain Thigman had ordered him to do it. The medical examiner returned to the office and handed her a note.

"The ME has positively identified the remains as those of Nigel Hoffman."

"OK Hadfield I'm sending Griffin and his partner to the Pearl River scene. You go back to the Alabama scene and search with those sheriff's people. We need something to connect this Burns guy to Hoffman." He hung up abruptly.

Rabun had not moved from the ME's office. Jolene watched the hot fudge sundae expression appear when she told him the news.

"Hoffman's car just turned up in the Pearl River about fifty miles from Biloxi. Somebody went to a lot of work to put him in a lake in Baldwin County."

The deputy asked if they had a workable crime scene at Pearl River. The evidence geek was just like a bird dog, she thought, always looking for the scent. And for no reason she wondered about Burns' dogs. What kind of dogs were they?

"Sounds like a jurisdictional nightmare," the Medical Examiner said causing Jolene to come back to the moment.

"You got that right, Doc."

"One thing is for sure, Sergeant. Mr. Hoffman was killed with the fanciest shiv I've ever seen in a homicide. This is the first custom made Bowie knife I've had the occasion to remove from a body. It is almost like it was left there on purpose."

He handed her a clear plastic evidence bag containing the knife. The knife was smaller and lighter than the one she had handled at Burns' house. The blade wasn't as polished either. The red handle was straight and rounded at the end. And the hilt was stained green. Curiously the only markings on the blade were in the same place Burns had inscribed his the knife. The mark: THEO-98

The Medical Examiner excused himself with the offer for her and Rabun to remain in his office as long as needed. Jolene looked at Rabun.

"Are you ready to search a crime scene?"

A huge grin appeared, maybe it was one reserved for looking at a banana split. Deputy Sundae practically ran out the door.

CHAPTER FOUR

"RABUN why don't you head on to Burns place. I've got to change clothes for the search. I can find that country store wait for me there I can follow you."

"Yes ma'am. I've got a couple of deputies on standby to help us. They can meet us there too."

"Rabun you can drop the ma'am business anytime. My first name or last name works just fine."

"Yes ma'am."

Jolene quickly changed into jeans hiking boots and a long sleeved shirt before leaving the ME's office. With her lead foot driving she'd caught Rabun as he exited the interstate. He drove the Sheriff's van exactly at the speed limit. The spring sunshine was a pleasant distraction from the annoying pace. When they passed the country store she barely noticed to the other deputies' fall into their caravan. The nice weather and the rural surroundings lulled her senses. She was enjoying the day and visualizing what Burns place would be like in daylight. Her day dreaming caused her to brake abruptly avoiding a collision with the sheriff's van. Jolene realized she hadn't seen the turn signal flashing.

The dirt road wove through the woods for over a quarter mile before they entered a clearing. She slowed up and took a closer look seeing what she couldn't see the night before. The heavy steel gate was open support beams extending several feet to either side kept anyone from driving around it. Thick weeds and foliage offered an effective deterrent for those choosing to avoid the gate and climb the barbwire fence that snaked into the tree line on both sides of the road. The weeds effectively hid coils of razor wire lying on the ground to foil trespassers.

Inside the gate was something else she hadn't seen in the dark. Two windowless concrete block buildings with metal garage doors sat like sentinels facing the gate from either side of the driveway. When the house came into view she noticed a wood barn with a paddock and tractor shed fifty yards further down the drive.

Whoever built the house was in love with concrete block construction. A single story structure generous overhanging eaves shading all sides. The windows were protected by burglar bars and functional heavy wooden storm shutters. It was as much a fortress as a house. The absence of power and phones lines meant the utility service was underground. A propane tank could be seen in a nearby block enclosure with a chain length gate and that adjoined another block building that was obviously an equipment room of sorts. Jolene suspected it held a large generator. The place looked like it could withstand the strongest hurricane making landfall from the Gulf of Mexico twenty miles or so south. A saddled buckskin color horse was tied to another heavy duty hitching rail near the closest rear corner of the house.

The convoy of police vehicles parked near the house. One of the sheriff's units was an SUV pulling a trailer loaded with a pair of ATV's. The two deputies began unloading them. Rabun loaded his equipment in ATV. Jolene saw the bed already held barb wire and an assortment of tools. Rabun got the evidence bag containing the bowie knife from his van.

Andy came from the rear of the house. He patted the horse on its rump as he watched Jolene and Rabun approach. The big gelding was perfectly marked with a long black mane and tail complete with black stockings on each leg. The horse turned his head and looked the visitors over. He went back to grazing the grass he could reach from his tether.

Burns looked like he belonged with the horse. He wore a dirty white straw Stetson and a faded blue long sleeve western shirt with fake pearl snaps instead of buttons. His equally faded jeans were held up by a heavy leather belt sans the usual large silver buckle. Scuffed cowboy boots complete with spurs enhanced the cowboy image. Rabun handed him the plastic evidence bag containing the knife.

"What can you tell me about this Andy?"

Burns looked at the knife through the plastic for a moment. He turned and motioned them to follow. They crossed a covered concrete patio and entered via another sturdy wood door. Jolene surmised this was the state-of-the-art machine shop Hildibrand had mentioned. The shop and machinery looked too clean for a workshop. There was another room off to the side. Its entry way was blocked by the dogs lying on the concrete floor quietly watching her and Rabun.

Burns sat on a stool next his bench and put on a pair of white cotton gloves. He removed the knife from the evidence bag. After a careful inspection he laid it on the bench.

"It is what I suspected. But not what I wanted to see.

"This knife is made from a kit. They are sold through catalogs to anyone who wants to make their own knife. The blades are all the same. Each one is machined stainless steel stock. The bowie knife is one of several different kits available. It takes some skill to assemble them. And you don't need a lot of special tools. With a little attention to detail when fitting them together you can make a nice knife. The finish and polish is what makes this knife above average for a kit build. But then it should be because I taught the man who made it how to do it."

Rabun looked up from the notes he had been scribbling. He looked like the cherry just fell off his sundae.

"Who?" Jolene and Rabun asked at the same time.

"Theodis Cleckler, he etches his knives with Theo and the year. He made three here in my shop. Then he bought his own tools and set up shop in a shed behind his house. Now he is building several different styles besides Bowies. He sells them at gun shows in Gulf Port and Hattiesburg."

"You're telling us that Theodis Cleckler the black preacher who leads demonstrations at every new casino made this knife. And you taught him how to make it?" Jolene said pointing at the knife with a skeptical expression on her face.

"Yes Sergeant that is what I'm telling you." Andy answered looking her directly in the eye. He placed the knife back in the evidence bag.

"Do you need to know anything else about this knife Rabun?"

"Not at this time, I'm going to write up what you told us. If you have contact information on this Cleckler person I need it. Sergeant Hadfield got word this morning that Hoffman's car was pulled out to the Pearl River in Mississippi. My guess is the killing happened someplace else. Oh yeah the ME gave us positive ID on the body."

Hadfield shot Rabun an annoyed look. Something that did not go unnoticed by Burns. He produced an address book from a drawer and gave Rabun the information he needed. Burns handed the evidence bagged knife back to Rabun and unrolled a topographical map out on the bench. The other two deputies were now standing in the open door way. Andy motioned them to come inside.

"Rabun I understand you these gentlemen and Hadfield are conducting a crime scene search this morning. I made sure your deputy guarding the scene had coffee and chow this morning." That comment got a smile from the men. Jolene remained impassive.

"As you told me when you left last night Hadfield does not want me helping. Is that right Sergeant?"

"Yes Mr. Burns until proven different you are a person of interest."

"That is what I figured and exactly what my lawyer said. And he is prepared to call the Sheriff and insure that you can only search an area fifty feet to either side of where the body came out of the lake and fifty feet from the bank. Any larger area than stipulated you will need a search warrant."

From the expression on Rabun's face the sundae had just melted. His cell phone rang at that moment. He excused himself and went outside to answer it.

"Does this mean you are not going to cooperate Mr. Burns?"

Rabun came back inside before Burns could answer. "The Sheriff just ordered me to only search a fifty square foot area where the body came out of the lake. Unless Andy agrees to let us search a larger area. The Sheriff called the District Attorney and the DA doesn't think we can justify a warrant for a larger search area."

"Let's go back to square one for a moment. I found a body in my lake. That pisses me off. Someone other than me put it there. A close friend made the knife that apparently killed this person. That does not set well either. I understand my being a person of interest. I was a cop for twenty three years and a Border Patrol Agent for four years prior to that.

"This property is exactly one square mile. That is 640 acres. The lake counts for almost a third of that. And two hundred acres on the southwest side is pasture leased to my neighbor to run cattle on. All of the property is fenced and the pasture area is cross fenced. There is a rifle range on the property. My friend who passed away and left me this place took security very seriously. He had a strong dislike for poachers and trespassing hunters. He had some other quirks about jack booted government thugs coming to take way his guns. The fences are four foot higher than normal with a lot more barbed wire. The range impact area is cross fenced with ten foot high chain link fencing topped with razor wire.

"The area around the house gate and driveway has video surveillance. There are motion detectors inside the fence along the paved road that activate cameras in case of intruders. Poachers and night hunters like to come in the northeast corner off a road that is more of a path. Motion activated cameras cover that and the northern edge of the impact area. The only gap in camera coverage is along the north fence line."

One of the deputies said. "This is the place the game wardens talk about with all the cameras warning signs and booby traps. They say some super rich guy owned it. He died and willed it you? How do you get friends like that? I need one."

"You stay friends with them for over twenty years. Have common interests and never discuss their wealth. Then when they leave you a place that is overrun with cops after a body turns up. You wanna say thanks pal."

Everyone but Hadfield laughed at Burns' remark. She did smile slightly.

"I ride the pasture fence line every morning. There are no breaks in that fence. A firebreak is cut inside the fences around the whole property. You can ride the firebreak and check the fence. I expect you will find it cut somewhere. The grass is high enough that you can probably find a trail leading to lake from where the fence is cut. I rode the entire firebreak three days ago and there were no cuts in the fence.

"I'm going to allow you to search the property. My lawyer has faxed me a consent form that also addresses the liability issues of your being on my property. Everyone gets to sign it or there will be no searching. And....' Burns paused and looked at each cop. 'Be extremely careful where you step and where you put your hands. I've lived on this place for almost two years and I have killed eighteen poisonous snakes. There are snake proof chaps in the equipment shed. I urge you to wear them. Now gather around and look at this map."

When the group was ready to leave Rabun spoke up. "Andy is there any chance you have surveillance tapes we can look at?"

"Sure they are time lapse and record over after seven days. You and Hadfield are welcome to look at them.

"One other thing. If you find a hole in the fence and can't find a trail. Call me. If Sergeant Hadfield will let you. I can cut sign."

"Cut sign?" Jolene asked.

"Find tracks and follow them. It's a Border Patrol thing."

Hadfield and the deputies returned to the ATV's. She paused and looked over Burns horse. The buckskin turned his head in her direction. After a few seconds of inspection and he extended his nose. Jolene tentatively reached toward him when Rabun called out. "You're riding with me Sarge." He cranked the ATV. Startled she jerked her hand back from the horse. He whinnied causing her to stumble backwards. She recovered to see Burns standing next to his shop door smiling.

Jolene joined Rabun in the small cab of the ATV. He explained the deputies would ride the fire break on their ATV's from opposite directions and call if they found a cut fence. They would start searching where the body was found and work their way around the lake hoping to find evidence of where the body was put in the lake.

"Rabun how are you justifying the time and personnel for this search?"

"Sarge we believe Hoffman was killed elsewhere. So we are looking for something that may lead some agency to the killer. Just taking a few pictures and writing a report would be poor police work. Our Sheriff campaigned on bringing the Department up to date with equipment and skill. He likes to say we leave no stone unturned in an investigation."

The hot fudge sundae expression appeared as he looked at Hadfield. "It also helps that he is my uncle."

Two hours had passed since they started search. They found a couple of concrete blocks and some nylon rope on the bank two hundred yards from where the body was recovered. Rabun's attention to detail amazed Hadfield. He used a compass to fix headings on the recovery point and where they'd found the blocks. Now they were with the deputies who rode the firebreak. They'd found a hole in the fence. Eight strands of barbed wire had been cut almost midway between the fence posts leaving a ten foot gap. There were tire tracks on the opposite side of the fence in what appeared to be a road. Mashed down grass was evident in the fire break and the wooded area across from the gap. Rabun found shoe prints near the tire tracks. There was enough detail to make plaster casts. A piece of cloth hung in the cut barbed wire. He photographed everything.

"It looks like a trail to me. We need to call Andy." And he began dialing Burns number.

Andy arrived on his horse with the dogs following him. The plaster casts were drying and Rabun was putting the last bit of dental molding material on the wire cuts.

"You can't glue that wire together Rabun." Burns quipped as he dismounted.

"Making impressions for a tool mark exam. If somebody finds a suspect with wire cutters that match these cuts. Too bad for him. Do you mind looking around and doing your sign cutting thing?"

Burns handed the horse's reins to Jolene. "His name is Major and he doesn't bite."

Before she could respond the horse nuzzled her neck. She felt her face heat up as the deputies laughed. She fought the urge to tell Burns to hold his own horse. The equine was calm after he'd put the move on her. She didn't think Burns was having a joke at her expense. Andy joined Rabun at the fence and squatted down looking at the tire tracks. He moved a few times over the next several minutes studying the ground. Jolene watched with interest. If he were acting the performance was worthy of an Academy Award.

Burns stood and gestured toward the other side of the fence. "That is the dirt road I showed you on the map. It terminates about a hundred yards west and about a half mile east at the paved road. It was used when the lake was built."

"That is a man-made lake?" One of the deputies asked.

"Yes it started out as a pond fed from an underground stream. The guy that founded Bassmasters designed it. They used the dirt to build the impact berm for the rifle range."

"I'll fix your fence if you'll let me bring my boat and fish it! I grew up fixing barbed wire fences. Never seen eight strands of wire before on one fence but I can fix it." The deputy answered.

"You got a deal. Fix it today and fish next time you're off."

Hadfield kept her mouth shut before she offered a fish dinner to Burns for a chance at the lake. Burns continued his dissertation about the tracks.

"It looks like someone came in from the east one four wheel drive vehicle. That is the only thing you can get down that road with. They stopped turned around and backed up to the fence. There are two different shoe types and it appears they carried something heavy from the vehicle across the firebreak and sat it down when they got to the weeds."

"How do you know that?" Hadfield asked.

"The foot prints are deeper and you can see where weeds are flat. There is also indication that the person with smaller feet came back from the weeds running toward the fence. That is probably where the torn cloth comes from."

Andy pointed at the tracks. "You can tell that by the length of the stride and how the shoe impacts the dirt. Something happened to cause this guy to run like that."

"A snake would make me run like that." A deputy added.

"That would be a likely scenario." Burns responded.

"If you follow the drag marks and foot prints you will wind up at the lake. It is about a quarter mile from here. From what I see the trail is obvious enough for a city cop like Hadfield to follow."

Rabun was holding his compass and pointing into the woods. "This is right on the heading where we found the concrete blocks."

"You found blocks?"

"Yes sir and some nylon rope that looks like what was on the body. The crime lab in Mobile can tell for sure."

"Looks like y'all are doing a good job Rabun. Follow that trail back to the lake and you might find something else. It is an easy trail to follow. These people were dragging a body. No pun intended but that is dead weight. You are looking for at least one extremely strong and very fit person. Did you see any tracks where you found the blocks?"

"Yeah but looked there was only one set and they were big shoes. About the size of the large prints here. Not enough detail to make casts."

"OK y'all would do best by one person walking ahead of the ATV's following the tracks. It is thick back in there but you can make it. Just watch where the hell you step. Rattlesnakes and water moccasins don't like being stepped on. And they bite."

Burns paused and took a breath. He looked at Hadfield for a moment before he spoke. "One other thing Rabun. Before you leave today you make casts of the tires on my truck.' Rabun started to protest. Burns held up a hand to silence him. 'You will also take tool mark impressions of every set of wire cutters I own. You can start with the two pair in the back of the ATV you're driving. They are with the fence tools. There are some more in the tool shed. And there is one pair in my workshop heavy enough to cut fence."

He stepped to Hadfield and took the reins from her. "Thank you for holding my horse Sergeant." Burns swing into the saddle. He looked at the deputy who offered to fix the fence.

"Deputy if you are serious about fixing my fence everything you need is in the ATV. Fix it and you can fish my lake anytime you like. The only rules are no guests except your immediate family. Let me know when you want to come fish. And above all don't wear out your welcome."

With that Burns turned Major and spurred him into a lope. The dogs ran after them.

A large computer monitor dominated space between the cabinets above Burns work bench. He was entering the machining perimeters for a barrel blank mounted in the CNC lathe when a klaxon blared and the screen changed to a split image view from all the cameras near the house. One of the images was blinking. Burns saw a person on a four wheeler approaching from the east. He clicked a mouse and zoomed in on the ATV. Jolene Hadfield was riding it. Another click turned on a screen saver. He walked outside. Hadfield expertly parked the four wheeler near the hitching rail. Major snorted as she walked past him. Jolene paused and patted his neck. She was rewarded with whinny. The horse turned its head and she stroked his nose and smiled.

"You get tired of Rabun?"

"A little his enthusiasm can be a bit much at times. I borrowed the ATV from the deputy fixing your fence. He will ride back with Rabun. By the way that was a very kind gesture you letting him fish. He was over half finished with the fence when I left. He can't wait for his next off day. Makes me wish I knew how to fix fences."

"You fish Sergeant?"

"Yeah. I have my own bass boat."

"You may not fix fences but you can mend one. When you decide I'm no longer a person of interest you can come fish."

"That sounds like a bribe."

"A good one too. Theodis caught a nine pound bass last time he was here."

"The same Theodis who made the murder weapon?"

"One and the same."

"My lieutenant really likes you as person of interest. When he learns about Cleckler and the knife and your connection he will be trying to get warrants. There is a big political payoff for him somewhere if he solves this case."

"Even if you solve it for him. That sounds like the FBI. Somebody else does the work they grab the credit."

"You're right he's a national academy graduate. He's bucking for captain at the end of the year and he has powerful friends. Burns forgive my talking out of school, but Busby is a prick and he is dead serious. You will be a person of interest until he says so. And with the way this case is shaping up it is not likely to be anytime soon."

"I understand."

"I hope you do. Rabun is convinced you're not involved. But his evidence hunt could work against you. It just brings more questions. He has decided to let me view your video tapes. And I wanted to be up here when Don and Mark get here."

"Your timing is good. There is a Biloxi cruiser coming up the drive. When I'm done with them you can look at the tapes."

"Thanks and I would like to ask more questions."

"No problem."

Lt. Don Smith and Sgt. Mark Hildibrand greeted Jolene. "How'd the search go? Anything interesting?" Hildibrand asked.

"Plenty I'll fill you in when we have a few minutes."

Hildibrand raised his eyebrows and nodded yes. The third SWAT officer removed a long rectangular aluminum gun case from their car trunk. He joined them on the concrete deck by the shop door. When she recognized the sullen young cop, the word exchange between the SWAT Team leaders that morning made sense.

"Officer Peterson, how are you?" Jolene asked.

"Not worth a shit ma'am because I don't know what the hell this is gonna prove. I already said that piece of shit rifle won't shoot. It needs a new barrel. We're wasting time out here this gun needs to be sent to...."

A growl from Hildibrand shut the small-statured officer up. "PUT A LID ON IT PETERSON!"

"I'm sorry Andy,' Smith said. 'This was apparently a mistake."

"You sure as shit got that right!" Peterson snarled.

"Can the insubordination Peterson or have a seat in the car." Smith ordered.

Peterson glared at Lt. Smith. The standoff was interrupted by the arrival of Rabun and the two deputies. They parked the ATVs and joined the group. All three politely greeting their follows from out of state. The fence fixer, a raw boned looking solid late twenties something man spoke.

"Got the fence fixed Mr. Burns."

"Great,' Andy answered. He turned to Peterson. 'Unpack the rifle. Make sure it is unloaded and bring it in the shop."

Peterson slammed the case on the concrete. He bent down opened the case and removed the gun. It was a heavy scope equipped sinister looking weapon. As he stood he pointed the muzzle at Jolene.

"Watch where you point that thing!" Jolene admonished. She saw the contemptuous look in his eyes as he mouthed the word bitch and continued to swing the rifle muzzle across the group of lawmen stopping with it pointed at Burns.

"You dumb son of a bitch!" The fence fixing deputy said causing Peterson to turn his head. This gave Andy the chance to defect the barrel and wrench the rifle from the cop's grasp. Before Peterson could react Burns opened the rifle's bolt ejecting a live cartridge from the chamber.

The punk cop's demeanor changed abruptly. Burns fingered the safety and looked at Smith.

"Live round in the chamber and safety not engaged. Don disarm this little jackass and take him out to the paved road. He will not remain on my property and if he comes back I will have him arrested for trespassing. You can handcuff him to a tree if you like.

The wide eyed frightened Peterson grasped his holstered pistol and was promptly knocked on his ass by Hildibrand. When the cop was disarmed. The two deputies stepped forward and took custody of Peterson. The fence fixer looked at Hildibrand. "We'll handle this Sergeant. It's our jurisdiction."

Everyone watched as Peterson walked between the two ATV's. The deputies escorted him off the property.

Smith Hadfield and Hildibrand joined Burns in his shop while he examined the rifle.

"My chamber gauge shows this rifle has at least 97 percent barrel life left. Everything else checks out. This gun should shoot a minute or better. I think the problem is your shooter not your rifle. I will be happy to test fire it but I don't think it is necessary."

"I would appreciate your shooting it. I am going to need all the evidence I can get to win this fight."

"Big Dago ain't gonna let us win it Don. We'll be working third shift when he finds out what happened today." Hildibrand said remorsefully.

"Mark if you would take a fresh target down to the two hundred I would appreciate it." Burns said as he hefted the rifle.

Jolene followed Hildibrand outside where he picked up a target frame with an unused target attached and began the two hundred yard trek down range. She tagged along.

"What does shoot a minute mean Mark?"

"It means a minute of angle. Which is one inch at hundred yards. A minute at one thousand yards is ten inches. What Andy says is our rifle should shoot at least a one inch group at 100 yards or two inches at 200 the range he is going to shoot. I could shoot it that well. But it is better he do it. Not that it will mean anything. Don can't get us out of this one. The Big Dago has too much clout."

"I know I'll be joining you on night shift when Busby gets his way."

"Not if you make him look good with this case. What did y'all find?"

"It looks like Burns is in the clear unless he is sitting us up. Theodis Cleckler made the murder weapon and Burns taught him how to make it."

"No shit?"

"No shit. And that fat deputy is trying his damnest to prove Burns isn't involved. He could be right too. But everything he finds can also point to Andy and Cleckler being in cahoots on killing Hoffman. Cleckler has the motive. Burns is Cleckler's old buddy. Which is strange in its self, Burns being white and Cleckler black."

"The fat deputy...he the one smiling like a kid in an ice cream parlor?"

"That's him. He is the local sheriff's nephew and he thinks Burns hung the moon."

Hildibrand set the target frame in holders at the two hundred yard marker. They began the walk back.

"Jo I'm a member of the Andy Burns hung the moon club too. He and Rev. Cleckler were in the Marines together and in Vietnam at the same time."

"You're not going to tell me Cleckler was a sniper."

"No he was some kind of a clerk and a chaplain's assistant."

"I'm glad that would have been a little too much."

"Jo, listen to me here. Your imagination is what makes you the best detective on the Gulf Coast. But in only in your wildest dreams are Andy Burns and Theodis Cleckler murderers."

"Thanks for the compliment."

They returned to the firing line and watched Burns put five large rifle cartridges in the watch pocket of his jeans. He turned sideways to the target and held the rifle loosely with both hands. His arms hanging down to past his waist. He looked at the target and shouldered the rifle a way Jolene had never seen. Instead of his left arm extended toward the muzzle with hand gripping the stock. He moved his left hand rearward and held his left arm against his torso. The rifle balanced while he aimed. Andy moved his right foot slightly and aimed again. Satisfied he lowered the rifle and loaded a bullet.

"You shooting off hand instead of using the bench?" Hildibrand asked incredulously.

"Why not?"

"Show off."

Burns became serious and took a deep breath as he gazed at the target. With no wasted motion he shouldered the rifle aimed and fired in less than five seconds. His movements were like a machine with no wasted motion as he repeated the process four more times without taking his eyes off the target. With the bolt open Andy laid the rifle on a bench. And asked who wanted to fetch the target. Hildibrand jogged down range. Jolene didn't follow.

Mark jogged back carrying the target frame. "I don't even believe this and I watched it happen, a fucking jarhead showing off."

Burns looked at the target. There were five holes in a horizontal line across the center. Andy pulled a short metal ruler from his shirt pocket and lay it under holes. From edge to edge on the outside holes the line measured one inch.

"The gun shoots half minute groups. Don spend your money on ammo and training another officer to shoot it. It doesn't need a new barrel." Burns replaced the rifle in the case.

Don Smith smiled and shook Burns hand. "I appreciate you taking time to do this for us. I've never thought we needed to do it. But I'm caught between the rock and the hard place. What do we owe you?"

Burns shook his head. "Nothing from what you told me I expect you have enough problems. But I would appreciate your putting a word in with your lady detective. I thinks she wants to put me in jail."

"Consider that done. Once more please accept my apologies for Peterson's behavior."

"Accepted."

Jolene followed Smith and Hildibrand to their car. She watched Mark put the gun case in the trunk. "If you have time come by and see us tomorrow. We'll be there till quitting time. I wouldn't put any bets on the next day." He said.

"If you know anybody at the Border Patrol I would like some more background on Burns. I'm not sure about what I saw today with all that sign cutting business."

"The local supervisor shoots with us. I'll call him in the morning."

She stopped to pet Major's muzzle on the way back to the shop. Rabun had returned from whatever he had been doing. He was looking at the target. His appreciation showing with the hot fudge sundae grin. "That Andy sure can shoot."

Burns directed her to his office and showed her how to watch the surveillance tapes. It took over an hour to complete the task. She found nothing to indicate anyone other than Andy clients and sheriff's personnel had entered the property in the past seven days. His appointment book verified every non law enforcement person. She copied the tapes with his blessing. He was cooperating. But was he hiding anything? That bothered her as walked into Burns' shop. He was watching through the observation window of the lathe automatically turning a rifle barrel. Satisfied with the process he looked up and spoke.

"Find what you need on the tapes Sergeant?"

"No, it appears you are telling the truth about who has been here. I'm willing to accept no one came in the front gate and dumped the body. I didn't find anything showing who ever cut your fence."

"You won't. There is no camera coverage for almost a half mile along that fence. I've never understood why Charlie didn't install them."

Hadfield decided on a different line of questions. "Do you get your knife kits from the same place Cleckler does."

"Damn it Hadfield! Follow me!" He aggressively walked into the next room. The dogs scattered. Burns flicked a light switch and gestured around the room. It was not as clean as the machine room. The shelves held wood and metal pieces. The benches were affixed with motors holding grinding and buffing wheels. An acetylene torch and tanks resided in a corner. The middle held something Jolene had only seen in westerns. An anvil mounted on a large block of wood. Nearby was something resembling a round barbeque grill without the grill. A propane tank was attached to it.

Burns raised his voice past normal conversation level.

"Look at the shelves Hadfield...what you see are steel brass and wood blanks.' He picked up a plate of steel that had the shape of a knife drawn on it in chalk. 'I start with a piece of steel like this and I use a torch to cutout the basic blade shape. Then I heat it on the forge grab a small sledge hammer and beat out the blade shape some more. Then I quench it till it cools and start the grinding process. After that I fit the hilt and handle. Then it is back to the grinding belts and then the polishing wheels. When that is done I sharpen it. Then I make a leather sheath for it. I've been making knives for over twenty years. I don't use kits. I use raw materials.

"I was really blessed when Charlie Raifield left me this place with all the CNC equipment. I had to take classes to learn to work it. I'd put my old stuff in storage when I retired. I didn't make a knife or build a rifle for over two years. I played cowboy and got drunk. A woman broke my heart and Charlie Raifield's dying gave me my life back.

"Major needs tending to. This conversation is over!" He stormed out the room and went outside. The dogs followed. Jolene thought it best to wait a few minutes before she joined him. When she followed she found him throwing sticks for the dogs to retrieve.

"Sorry for the outburst Hadfield. It takes me twenty hours or more to build a knife. Theo slaps one of his kits together in a couple of hours. Major needs to go to the barn. You can walk with me or you can ride him."

"Burns I haven't rode a horse since summer camp as a teenager."

"Nothing has changed about it. You put one leg on one side and one on the other. He won't hurt you." Her protests fell on deaf ears as she watched him adjust the stirrup length. He untied the horse and coiled the lead rope around the saddle horn.

"Put your left foot in the stirrup step up and swing your right leg across."

It was easier for him to say it than it was for her to do. He grabbed her left foot giving her a boost up. Jolene felt her heart beat faster when he handed her the reins.

"Just squeeze him with your legs. He will move. The harder you squeeze the faster he goes. Major take Hadfield for a ride. Make her think she is in charge. She likes that."

Burns walked toward the barn. He was out of sight before she worked up enough nerve to squeeze Major. When she did he ambled along at a slow walk. The dogs followed. Daylight savings time made the late afternoon longer. It was cool and peaceful. The shade from the thick trees and the hoofs steadily thumping against the hard packed driveway gave her a sense of well being she seldom felt.

"Almost went to sleep waiting on you Hadfield. Major can go faster."

Burns took the reins from her and the horse stood still as she tried to gracefully dismount. It didn't work. She would have been flat on her ass had she not grabbed Burns' shoulder to keep her balance. Embarrassed she stepped away quickly hoping he wouldn't notice her face flushing.

"Most people do the same thing if they haven't ridden for a while. Don't worry about it. Andy removed a rifle from the saddle scabbard. He propped it against a fence post. With her apprehension she'd failed to notice the gun and scabbard.

"You always ride with a rifle Burns?"

"Yes"

She listened to him speaking softly to Major while he removed the saddle. The buckskin craned his neck toward her. She stroked his velvet soft nose and perfect face.

"He is beautiful. What kind is he?"

"He's a quarter horse."

She stopped petting and Major nudged her with his nose until she resumed.

"Burns do you ever pet him or the dogs?"

Andy finished putting up the saddle and he poured feed in a bucket. This got Major's attention. Burns started brushing him as he ate.

"Yes Hadfield I pet them. They are working animals first pets second."

The dogs sat by Jolene their tails thumped the ground anticipating affection.

"Are these dogs a special breed or just ugly mutts? I've never seen anything like them before."

"Hadfield, first you insult my knives then you call my dogs mutts." Andy smiled while he continued brushing.

"They are Pudelpointers."

"Poodle Pointers as in French Poodle?"

"No, P–U–D–E–L-pointer. It is German. The breed is a cross between a Wasser Poodle and a German Shorthair Pointer. They have been breeding them a hundred and twenty years or so. They are rare in this country. There are only two breeders in North America."

"I gather they are hunting dogs."

"Yes they retrieve point and track wounded game. Besides being great pets and good company they are smarter than the average cop particularly one this afternoon. And they aren't half bad herding dogs when the neighbor's cattle gets out."

Burns finished grooming Major and turned let him out in the paddock. He picked up his rifle holding it by his side. Jolene wasn't uncomfortable with him holding the gun. He wasn't a threat. She opted for a leading question looking for a guilty answer.

"How you know where to send us searching today."

"Hadfield I'm tired of that bullshit. I know what you're doing. I was a cop once, remember? I know my property all it took was common sense. You should try using some.

Question time is over. You're annoying me. Pick up some sticks and throw them toward the house. The dogs need to play while we walk."

Major let out a pitiful whinny when they left. She threw sticks and the dogs fetched until they reached her car. Hadfield thanked Burns for his time and left. Stopping at the paved road she jotted down the Arizona license plate from Burns' horse trailer she'd memorized it while they were at the barn. It would be dark before she reached Biloxi. A long day. Burns opened up more than usual during his lecture about knife making. And she felt he was being truthful. Something still bothered her. There was an attractive side to Burns. Hadfield was not happy with the attraction.

CHAPTER FIVE

HADFIELD'S morning was not pleasant. Busby mentioned a meeting scheduled with Captain DePiano after lunch. Bernard DePiano being involved in an investigation did not bode well. She thought about the incident at Burns place the day before. Maybe the hatchet wouldn't drop on Smith and Hildibrand so soon if the Big Dago was distracted. Busby interrupted her thinking.

"Hadfield can't you see this guy Burns led you and those sheriff hicks around by the nose. He knew there wasn't any camera coverage where he and Preacher Cleckler cut the fence. Burns is playing you for a fool. He might not have killed Hoffman but Preacher Cleckler sure as hell did. You need to talk to Cleckler today. He will be the weak link, Burns was a cop he will be harder to crack. Go see Cleckler and start working on him. Bring him in and get him into interrogation ASAP. Then we can beat a confession out of him."

Busby smiled at his last remark. "Pun intended Hadfield—pun intended. And you need go see this Burns guy as many times as it takes. Now get out of here."

On her way out of the office Jolene passed Captain Lyle Thigman. He motioned her into his office. "I've read your reports on the Hoffman case. Busby about had an orgasm when he learned Preacher Cleckler made that knife. He has got Burns and Cleckler convicted already. Busby will try to railroad them Your job is make sure that doesn't happen unless a good case can made. Right now I don't see a case against either one. Watch your back with Busby. He's out to get you and I won't be here much longer."

Her trip to Cleckler's church produced nothing. His secretary said he was out visiting with bereaved church members and would be conducting funeral services later in the morning. Rev. Cleckler would not be in his office until after lunch. Jolene was impressed at how clean and neat the old church was. The red brick building with a steeple sat across a wide street from the projects. The epicenter for Biloxi's gang activity. She thought Cleckler must be a really inspired preacher to keep a church going as long as he had in this neighborhood.

A few minutes later Jolene picked up Mark Hildibrand at SWAT headquarters and they drove to a nearby restaurant. "You said yesterday Burns was a Marine sniper," she said after they ordered coffee.

"Yeah Andy did a sniper tour Vietnam. He volunteered to extend. But the Marines sent him back to Quantico to the RTE shop where he worked as a gunsmith."

"What's the RTE shop?"

"Rifle Team Equipment, Andy was trained as a gunsmith. He primarily worked on developing better sniper rifles. The Marines are big on competitive shooting and he competed. I wish I could shoot half as well. That was the damnedest display of rifle shooting yesterday I've ever seen. These kids going to police sniper school now days can barely hit the target when they shoot standing up."

"You were green when you saw that group." Jolene taunted.

"When I think I can keep up with him. He puts me back in my place with shooting like that."

"I don't understand why y'all were out there to begin with. What was going on? If you don't mind my asking."

"That little asshole Peterson is Maureen Peterson's little brother."

"Our communications supervisor?"

"And DePiano's girlfriend. How you think Peterson got hired in the first place?"

"That explains the rumor that somebody fixed his not passing the police academy."

"The fixer himself. Bernard DePiano aka Big Dago. That's why we have him in SWAT. Fortunately he's not on the full time crew, yet."

"So what is so important with the rifle?"

"We were ordered to send him to sniper school. He was kicked out the second day. We were told he was unsuitable. DePiano couldn't fix that. Peterson blamed the rifle. He wants us to send it to some big name gunsmith out west for a new barrel and scope package costing five grand. He read about the guy in some police gun magazine. Police gun writers can say camel shit in a black nylon bag with Velcro improves your sex life and idiots like Peterson would buy it.

"Don believes it's a waste of city money and DePiano says send the gun off or we're history with the SWAT team."

"I hate to hear that Mark. Did you talk to your Border Patrol buddy?"

"Yeah, he checked Andy's service record. Back when he was hired the Border Patrol Academy was in Texas and had some had real serious trackers teaching sign cutting. His record indicates he was an exceptional student."

"It looked like he knew what he was doing yesterday. I'm beginning to believe he is not involved in Hoffman's death. But I'm getting pressured to find otherwise. If Burns is such a great gunsmith why isn't he in the police magazines?"

"His reputation is word of mouth he doesn't advertise. Gun writers don't know he exists and for good reason. He has a top secret security clearance. He builds guns for government agencies. He didn't build a gun or work on one for two years. And he was still in demand when he decided to work again. I wouldn't be surprised if you push too much on Burns. Somebody higher up the food chain than Busby and Thigman will get a phone call warning them. And you will be the scapegoat."

"That's a little,' she hesitated, 'farfetched Mark. But Busby would like the scapegoat part."

Her cell phone began to buzz. Busby's number shown on the caller ID screen. Before she answered Hildebrand's radio sounded an alert tone. He practically leaped out the booth.

"I've got to get back to the office. Now!" He said throwing a few bills on the table. Jolene chased him to the car. She drove like hell back to the SWAT office. Hildebrand acted like the SWAT Team was being called out. Unfortunately, that was not the reason.

When they entered the SWAT office Captain Bernard DePiano was beating his fist on Don Smith's desk and cursing him. Smith sat calmly in his chair. Peterson wearing a smug look leaned against a wall. DePiano turned his venom on Hildibrand

"It's about time you got your ass in here! You been having a quickie with Hadfield. Maybe you don't mind she spent all yesterday screwing a murderer!"

"That's enough, DePiano!" Hildibrand snarled.

"That mouth just bought you a thirty day suspension without pay for insubordination asshole!" DePiano shot back.

"YOU ARE OUT OF LINE CAPTAIN!" Jolene shouted.

"Out of line Missy Sergeant!" DePiano shouted sarcastically using his size advantage to back her against a wall. Jolene's cheeks burned as her anger increased. She smelled the Big Dago's foul breath.

"Who you gonna report me outta line to Missy Sergeant? Your captain? That gray haired old fart is retiring! He can't save your broad ass forever! You can kiss your gold sergeant's badge goodbye! Missy if you're lucky you can join your two buddies here on night shift! Cause that's where they are going starting tonight! Maybe if you give them a sympathy blow job they'll give you good off days when you get out there..."

Jolene kneed DePiano squarely in the crotch before she had time to wonder if the Baldwin County Sheriff's department had any openings. Mark Hildibrand followed up with a kick in balls that laid DePiano on the floor puking. The Big Dago would forever have a second moniker, Cantaloupe Cods. Mark spun around and landed another kick. Peterson got an alias. Little Big Balls wasn't quite the macho sobriquet he would have preferred.

Jolene saw Don Smith look at her and jerk his thumb toward the door as he said. "You weren't here." She didn't have to be told twice.

Smith leaned over the prostrate DePiano and shoved a pocket tape recorder in his face and hissed. "Listen close asshole! If anything happens to Jolene Hadfield this will go public."

After driving a few blocks Hadfield parked. She sat still willing herself to calm down. The women's pro bass fishing tour looked good maybe she could qualify and make enough money shooting craps to get by. Her cell phone display indicated there several 911 marked messages from the impatient Busby. She pushed the redial button.

"Where in hell are you, Hadfield? Have you talked to Cleckler yet?"

"No he was busy this morning. I will talk to him after lunch?"

"Since when are nigger preachers too busy to talk to the police Hadfield? Go drag his ass out of what he's doing and talk to him!"

"That's a great idea Lieutenant. Why don't you drag him out of the funeral service he's preaching. I'm sure the NAACP would love that."

There was a pause while Busby talked to someone in his office. "Hadfield Bernard has been injured in a training accident. Find probable cause to bring Burns and Cleckler in for interrogation. Good bye."

Jolene's phone rang before she could put it down. The caller ID showed the communications center number. She answered and heard Maureen Peterson's syrupy accent.

"Sergeant Hadfield we've got that information you wanted on that Arizona license plate. Can you copy?"

"Give it to me," Jolene answered.

"It's a permanent horse trailer registration to Andrew Jackson Burns at a P.O. Box in Tombstone Arizona. I always thought Tombstone was some make believe place they made up for the movies."

"You're not the only one," Jolene said, momentarily trying to visualize a real Tombstone Arizona.

"Anyway the registration is for a 1989 Turnbow horse trailer. It doesn't say anything else about it. I took the name and sent an administrative message to Arizona DPS and they checked for local warrants. This Burns has three outstanding warrants in Tombstone, Arizona."

"What are the warrants for?"

"Drunk and Disorderly, Reckless Endangerment, and Alluding. They are all misdemeanors and there is a notation that the Tombstone Marshal's office will not extradite..... Oh my god! *What!* How bad! Oh my god! Sergeant Hadfield my little brother has been injured in a training accident—I gotta go bye!"

Reverend Theodis Cleckler was not what Jolene expected. He stood and greeted her when she entered his office. The deep baritone voice did not fit the five foot eight inch tall man dressed in a conservative dark suit with a white shirt and subdued tie. His round dark gentle face conveyed such peace and serenity. That Hadfield knew a jury wouldn't convict him of jay walking much less murder.

As he joined her in the sitting area of his office he offered fresh coffee. She accepted and he served it from a nearby container.

"Sergeant, Andy Burns called me last night and told me to expect you. I was very disturbed to learn one of my knives had been used in Mr. Hoffman's murder. The Lord will forgive me for saying this. But, I can't believe that it is His will for a life to be taken from us by such an incomprehensible act. I called Mrs. Hoffman this morning and expressed my condolences. I disagreed with Mr. Hoffman's occupation even though the law allows it. I think it is a sin. Nigel Hoffman was a gentleman he respected my feelings and was always fair in his dealings with me and my church members.

"Before his casino opened he actually came here and sat down with me in this very office. He told me he knew I was going to lead a demonstration when he opened and that he wouldn't be able to talk me out of it. He assured me there would not be any problems. And there weren't any. He made sure our people had water and soft drinks and a place out of the sun to rest. All his employees where kind to us. And you know Sergeant Hadfield we didn't stay there near as long as we did for the others.

She watched him smile and blink away a tear. "I think we were conned. Nigel Hoffman won that day with a smile and a hand shake. He was a good man. I don't know where he stood with the Lord. But I have prayed for the Lord to look kindly on him. You didn't come here to listen to me speak. I'm sure you have questions."

"Reverend Cleckler you are a person of interest in our investigation. So is Mister Burns. I need to know your whereabouts for the past seven days and the names of those who can verify the information you give me."

"Andy said you would ask that. I have taken liberty to have my secretary copy my schedule and list all my appointments and visits as well as my time at home. Names and phone numbers are provided. Like Andy I intend to cooperate and assist you anyway I can. However, I will follow Andy's advice and call a lawyer if you decide I have to come into the station."

"How long have you known Andrew Burns Reverend?"

"Since 1965, we were in Marine boot camp together."

"That is a long time. How have you managed to stay in touch?"

"Sergeant Hadfield. Our staying in touch is God's will. When I joined the Marines I was a black kid from

Poplarville, Mississippi. A town where black folks knew their place so to speak. There were few blacks in the Marines then. Recruiters didn't encourage us to apply. I was lucky my recruiter was behind in his quota and mad at his superiors. He signed me up. At boot camp hell-on-earth commenced. Andy Burns had the bunk above mine. He saved my life twice in boot camp. Once in the swimming pool. And another time when several rednecks decided I was going for a swamp march. I'm convinced he became my guardian angel. Our paths crossed in Vietnam and again at Quantico.

"When he was in the Border Patrol we corresponded with holiday greetings. Andy returned to Alabama and when he came to the coast for rifle matches, he would stop by for a visit. What I'm about to tell you is confidential. It was through Andy's friendship with Mister Raifield that we were able to save this church from foreclosure. A very wealthy local family controlled the bank and they wanted this property. Charlie Raifield purchased it and deeded it to our congregation. Through his benevolence we do not have a mortgage. Now I hope you can understand Sergeant Hadfield, why I believe our friendship is God's will."

"What made you want to make knives?"

"When Andy moved to Baldwin County after Charlie Raifield blessed him with such an inheritance. Andy invited me and my boys over to fish. It was during one of those visits I watched him finishing a knife and realized what a skilled craftsman he is. I told him I wished I had that talent. On our next visit he had a Bowie knife kit. He said the big knife was easier to start on. Andy was a hard task master. But I was a willing apprentice. I wound up making three Bowie knives in his shop. I sold one of them to a member of my congregation and the other two to collectors I know from the gun shows. Those first three were the best ones. I bought my own tools. Nothing like Andy has, but enough to get the job done. I made three Bowies in my own shop. They weren't as nice as the ones I made at Andy's. I've only built six because those kits cost more. And I like making smaller knives better. For me they are easier to finish."

"Do you have any left?"

"No Bowies. I've got some hunting and skinning knives and a real nice fisherman's filet knife."

"Do you remember who bought those last Bowies?"

"No my boys actually sold them. They tell me the same man bought all three of them. I find that hard to believe because we sold one each at two different Gulf Port shows and one at a Hattiesburg show."

"How old are your boys?"

"One is fourteen, the other is twelve. They are my only two children. All the others I have are God's children. They are the hungry ones from the projects. Mrs. Cleckler and myself we feed all we can. There are always children around our table, Sergeant Hadfield. Andy lets me bring them out to his lake and fish. He bought twenty rods and reels just so the children can have something to fish with. We always catch enough to have a fish fry. The project children don't know what it is like to enjoy fishing and things outdoors. Andy is not much of a fisherman but he was blessed with that fine lake. And he uses that blessing well."

Theodis Cleckler gave her the knife purchaser's names. She picked up a very detailed list from his secretary. Burns coached his friend well. Busby wouldn't like it if all the information provided checked out. Her cell phone buzzed.

"Hadfield."

"Tucker Lee Harrellson left a number for you."

Jolene copied Harrellson's phone number. She asked the dispatcher to find her a contact number for the Tombstone Arizona Marshal's office. The woman said she would call her back.

Hadfield belonged to a private gym. The cost was worth the nicer surroundings and lack of ogling cops. Tucker Lee Harrellson was a serious body builder she met at the gym. Other women members thought he was a hunk. When he wasn't pumping iron he was a construction engineer with

Gulf Power & Light. His family was wealthy enough that he probably didn't have to work. And he dressed like a model for an Orvis outdoor clothing catalog. Harrellson had a keen interest in the environment and loved fishing. When he learned Jolene fished he had asked her out for dinner several times. So far she had not agreed. She parked in the same shopping center lot and considered returning Harrellson's call. It was time to take him up on his offer. The dispatcher called back with the Tombstone number.

Jolene dialed the number. She identified herself, said what she wanted and was politely placed on hold. After several minutes the Marshal himself came on the line and thanked her for waiting. He asked for a moment to review the information. After a few minutes he laughed.

"Sergeant Hadfield this could only happen in Tombstone. I wasn't working here at the time. Andrew Burns in a state of intoxication rode his horse into the Crystal Palace Saloon."

Jolene suppressed a giggle. The Marshal continued. "He escaped from our deputy who apparently attempted to chase him."

She imagined Burns riding Major being pursued by a police car down the dirt streets of a western town. It was harder to control the giggle reflex.

"Burns' accomplice roped the deputy before he could get back to his car. The accomplice was arrested. When he appeared in court prosecution was declined and the charges dismissed. The charges against Burns will be handled the same way. The deputy no longer works here. He was a young guy and he got a job in a larger department."

Jolene had a pleasant thought of DePiano and Busby being roped. "Is it normal to dispose of cases like that?"

"No, there were extenuating circumstances. Burns' accomplice was the father of his girlfriend. This was the night after her funeral. She was a victim in a double homicide and suicide."

"Can you give me the details on those cases?"

"No. There is still a lot of speculation and rumor about them. I really can't say anymore. You need to talk with Buddy Russell. He is an investigator with the Cochise County Sheriff's Department."

The Marshal provided Russell's phone number. Jolene thanked him and tried to call Russell. She got his voice mail. Hadfield left her name number and the information she wanted.

Before she left for the day she learned Smith and Hildibrand had been transferred to the third shift. The entire SWAT team resigned.

CHAPTER SIX

JOLENE awakened to her cell phone ringing. She threw off the bed sheet and rolled out of bed. The quest to find the phone began. Standing in her living room bare foot wearing a T-shirt and panties, she snatched the cellular from her shoulder bag. Fumbling to find the talk button she saw her profile in a nearby mirror.

"Oh hell my butts too big!" she groaned.

"Hello, uh Hadfield." Jolene tugged at the elastic in her underwear trying to cover an exposed ass cheek when she heard a male voice chuckling.

"Sergeant Hadfield." The man said.

"Oh, shit."

"Buddy Russell, Cochise County Sheriff's Department, returning your call."

"I'm sorry Mister Russell, I'm Jolene Hadfield, thanks for calling me back." She said heading for the kitchen looking for a shot of caffeine. A half-bottle of Mountain Dew from the fridge would do until the coffee was ready.

"Drop the mister I'm Buddy. Your message said you are interested in Andy Burns and the Emmonds' case."

She took a long pull off the Mountain Dew and blinked her eyes. It was Saturday.

"Buddy how did you get screwed, er stuck with working on Saturday?" Jolene stalled until she was fully awake.

"I was called out on a homicide last night. I'm just now getting back to the office. Andy Burns ride his horse into a casino or something?"

Either the question or the Mountain Dew jolted her brain into full operation. "I wish it was that simple. Burns found a body in his lake. I'm looking into his background, either to eliminate him as a suspect or make him a better one."

"How did your victim die?"

"Large Bowie knife in the throat. And apparently he was dumped in Burns' lake after the main event. After the search team found a cut in the property fence. Burns was quick to point us to a trail leading back to the lake. I'm having trouble with this sign cutting and tracking business. He identified the knife, told us who made it and claimed to have taught that person how to make knives."

"Don't waste your time worrying about Andy following a trail. I'm fifty percent Apache. My daddy is the only white man in my family tree. Andy is better than any of the old trackers on the reservation. He's the best I've ever seen. Apparently your do'er left the knife, or you wouldn't know it was a Bowie. Andy wouldn't leave his knife and he wouldn't use one for killing unless he had to. You would never find the body either. I would look for another suspect. What is this business about his lake?"

"Burns inherited a large piece of property with a lake on it. This happened about the time he left out there. You seem to know a lot about him?"

"Yeah I heard about his inheriting something after he left. I met Andrew Burns when he was with the Border Patrol. He was assigned to the horse unit at Naco. I'd just started with the sheriff's department. I probably knew him better than most folks except maybe his wife. She wasn't happy out here and he quit and moved back to Alabama. I wasn't surprised they divorced. He can connect with horses in a way most people can't. Do you know if he still has that buckskin?"

"I'm not much on horses, but the one he has is beautiful."

"Yeah that horse has perfect markings. It is a good horse too. Andy has a lot in him and I don't mean cash either."

"What do you mean?"

"Emotionally. When he came back here after retiring from that PD. He was devastated. He sure as hell didn't know what he was looking for out here. But he figured he would find it with a horse. So he went shopping for one. That is when he met Roxana Emmonds. The prettiest Mexican girl you ever laid eyes on."

"Emmonds doesn't sound very Mexican." Jolene said intrigued by Russell's story.

"It's not. Collazo was her maiden name. Roxie married a gringo named Fred Emmonds, one of the sorriest humans to ever set foot in this county. She divorced Fred and took up with another loser named Wilbur Jackson. Andy came along looking for a horse right after Roxie dumped Wilbur.

Roxie ran the family feed store in Tombstone. Fred walked in with a shotgun one morning just after she opened. He put two rounds of twelve gauge buckshot in her face. "Then he drove out Gleeson Road to Wilbur's place. Wilbur was feeding his goats. Fred gut shot him first then fired the second barrel in his face. He drove his truck halfway to Gleeson and pulled over. We found him in the truck bed. He'd taken his boots and socks off so he could work the triggers on that double barrel with his toes. Fred stuck both barrels in his mouth and double bang."

"Where does Andy Burns fit into this horse opera Buddy?"

"Wilbur had been making Roxie's life hell since she dumped him. Fred had never stopped making her miserable. When Andy came into the picture those assholes intensified their efforts. Fred and Wilbur were trying to grow the cajones to take on Andy when Manny Collazo reminded them of the legend."

"Hold on a minute Buddy," Jolene said pouring a fresh cup of coffee. "I haven't had enough caffeine to keep up with all the players. Who is Manny?"

"Manuel Collazo, Roxie's father. The Collazo's are as native to Cochise County as my ancestors are. They were here before Arizona was a territory." Russell answered.

"Now what's this about a legend?"

"La migra con el rifle disparandole a narco traficantes," Russell said in Spanish. He switched back to English. "The Border Patrolman with a rifle shooting drug smugglers.

"During the time Andy worked the border, drug smuggling was beginning to be a problem. And the Mexican authorities were finding drug smugglers bodies on their side of the fence. Everyone was killed with a single rifle shot. Rumor was a gringo border patrolman with a rifle was shooting them at long range from this side of the border. Andy always had a scoped rifle in a scabbard on his saddle. The killings stopped when he resigned and went back east. The rumor became a legend. It is still told almost thirty years later."

"Didn't anyone question him about that?"

"Sure, they checked his rifle against some bullet fragments the Mexicans came up with. Nothing conclusive was proved. But the traficantes started crossing at different parts of the border. The legend is, well.' Russell hesitated. A legend with some truth to it. The bodies were real. Andy Burns worked that part of the border. And he's the best damn shot I've ever seen."

"But it wasn't enough to scare off Fred and what's his name?"

"It worked. Fred and Wilber laid low and stuck to harassing phone calls. Andy had to go back to Alabama for a court case. The killings happened while he was gone. He got back the day after the funeral. That night Manny Collazo and Andy got drunk and made a fool out of a young deputy in Tombstone. Andy left town the next day. This is the first I've heard of him since."

"The marshal said there are some rumors about the case anything substantial?"

"Rumor is the town sport of Tombstone. The locals walk down Allen Street and if they haven't heard a rumor in two minutes they start one. And they are all ludicrous."

"And you haven't had any contact with Andy Burns since?"

"No."

"Anything else you can tell me about Andy Burns?" Hadfield asked.

"I don't think I've ever seen anybody as in love with a woman as he was with Roxie. And I can't say as I blame him either. She was absolutely beautiful with the brains and personality to match. Her only problem was the men she picked. I don't think Roxie realized what kind of man she had in Andy Burns. I don't think she could get used to a man being good to her."

Jolene took a deep breath and thanked Buddy Russell for the information. She finished her coffee thinking about Andrew Burns.

Jolene parked next to Harrellson's dark green Land Rover. They were meeting for lunch at the Fish Shack a decrepit looking place. The old wooden structure complete with peeling paint was off the tourist path. Frequented by locals the seafood fare was delicious. She spotted him waving from a corner table.

The genteel prince of the Mississippi Gulf Coast had an arrogant aura about him. A prosecutor who worked out at the same gym was more pointed in his description. Asshole was the word used. A wooden cane lay against the table next to Harrellson.

"What's with the cane, Harrellson?" She asked as she sat down.

"I got bit by a water moccasin at the job site near Pass Christian. I was angry about some proposed changes in my design. And I wasn't paying attention to where I stepped.

The damn thing got me just above my right boot. I'm thanking my lucky stars for heavy Levi's and thick boot socks."

Jolene shuddered at the thought. "Let's talk about something else I've heard enough about snakes this week."

The waiter brought their food. They ate silently with occasional comments about food quality. Jolene was hungry, she tried to eat like a lady. Not like a cop at a free buffet.

"The gumbo here is always great. I've had gumbo in some places that doesn't compare." She said between mouthfuls.

"Some of the stuff they serve in the casinos might as well be called fish soup. It is not gulf coast gumbo." Harrellson answered.

"Now there are some good eating places in the casinos the Golden Bay Casino has an excellent restaurant. And I understand the Caesar's Grill in the Gulf Palace has a five-star rating."

"I don't frequent those places so I wouldn't know."

Finishing her meal Jolene watched quietly as Harrellson summoned the waitress for more iced tea. He was polite and friendly with the homely middle aged woman who had provided them with excellent service. Was Harrellson as bad as Jolene thought him to be? Or was she just jealous of his affluence?

"I'm surprised you don't visit the casinos."

"I don't have anything against casinos. I don't like what they are doing to the environment here. Most people think they are good for the economy. At the rate they are building Biloxi and the gulf coast will be the big losers. This restaurant won't be here in five years. Some big gambling outfit will buy the land making the owner rich and destroying the simple sleepy lifestyle.

"You have probably seen an increase in crime since the casinos took over. I don't mean gangsters shooting one another unless you mean those little nigger dope dealers. I mean prostitution, loan sharking, bogus checks.

"There is nothing wrong with legal casinos in their proper place. There have been illegal ones here for years. Las Vegas was unheard of until the casinos came. There may be more harm to the ecology out there in the desert than here. There is enough moisture from pools and fountains added to that ecosystem to possibly cause harm. Who is to say this is not a better place to build a gambling Mecca? Who is to say we don't need the jobs? And there have been whores here as long as the air base and shipyard have been around.

"My point is I don't like what they have done to my hometown. I don't like the people the casinos bring in to run the place. Sure the locals get a few jobs. But the big salaries go to outsiders. I don't like the traffic and the tourists. Yes we've always had summer tourists. Now they're year round. The first few riverboat casinos permanently attached to piers weren't much of a problem. But as soon as the politicians opened the gate more and bigger casinos are being built.

"I can't raise hell and preach damnation from a sidewalk soapbox like Preacher Cleckler can. I have to be the gentleman devil's advocate in engineering meetings and politely disagree. After all I'm an employee of a public utility that enjoys increased revenue from power consumption. And customers aren't paying any less for their power. Little laid back corrupt Biloxi Mississippi with booze and card games certainly has lights now. It is the price we are paying for Biloxi's lights that worries me."

He sipped his iced tea quietly after his impromptu dissertation. She wanted to ask him why he worked at all. His family owned a local bank for years that had recently sold to a large regional bank. They were well known for their land holdings businesses and investments.

"I would like to continue this conversation the rest of the afternoon. But I've got a two o'clock tee time at the country club. So I guess you've got to do whatever it is you do when you are on call for the city. Do you play golf?"

"I'm not a golfer. Can you play while walking with a cane?"

"Have you ever heard of golf carts?"

"Yes I have. I wasn't thinking."

"Now that you've had lunch with me and checked out my manners. How about the deep sea fishing trip I've been trying to get you to go on since I met you?"

"I'm not on call next weekend."

"Good, weather permitting we'll fish next Saturday. I'll call you with the details next week. And you can drop the cop stuff when you get on the boat and call me Tucker."

Driving along US 90 Jolene was enjoying the day the saltwater smell the sun and even the traffic. She gazed at the marinas and the boats bobbing near the piers. She wondered if Harrellson kept his boat at one these places. The convention center marquee sign caught her eye. GUN SHOW.

Jolene abruptly cut into the right lane and turned into the parking lot. The maneuver earned her a single finger wave from another motorist. The show hall was crowded. Peopled milled about the tables and displays. She hadn't attended a gun show in years. There were few of the blued steel and nickel plated guns she'd grown up with. Now most of the guns were ugly black ominous looking things. Guns that made her father long for the days of blue steel revolvers leather holsters and western six shooters. The tables displaying ammunition magazines and assault rifles had customers waiting to purchase. A barker on a platform cajoling the crowd to step right up would be right at home.

All the knife tables were grouped together. She found Theodis Cleckler's table. Two clean cut neatly dressed young men vied to sell her the fillet knife she looked at. Theodis greeted her warmly. Andy Burns and another man were seated behind the table. That man stood and handed her a card as he introduced himself. The card said he was a lawyer.

"Sergeant Hadfield I am B. Johnson Hassinger, Reverend Cleckler's attorney. He has indicated his willingness to cooperate in your investigation. And he has provided you all the information I feel like you need. Call me if you wish to speak with him again. I also represent Mister Burns' interests while he is in our state."

Before Jolene could reply Theodis' youngest son spoke you. "The same man brought all three of the last Bowies Daddy made."

The oldest son couldn't stay out of the act. "Yeah he was a roided up white dude."

"Theodis Junior if you use the word dude one more time you are grounded for a week. That word is disrespectful and you will not use it again in my presence. Furthermore I would like to know what roided up means? And Jerry, son you don't know for sure the same man purchased all three of those knives."

"I do Daddy." The youngster protested.

"He's right.' Theo Junior added. 'We know what we saw and you weren't at the table when we sold them. And it means uses steroids." The teenager added.

Burns spoke before the exchange between Cleckler and sons got out of hand.

"Hadfield if you promise B.J. you will come get him before you take me to jail I'll buy you a cup of coffee."

That provided her a graceful exit and she accepted with the provision for separate checks.

They took seats at a table near the food court. "Thanks for getting me out of that situation. I would have liked to hear what Reverend Cleckler's boys had to say. But I don't think that lawyer would have allowed it. And one other thing Mister Burns you did an excellent job of coaching your friend. My boss is ready to bring both of you in for questioning."

"Hadfield I can deal with you and your boss in the interrogation room. Theo cannot. You don't have and won't have any legitimate cause to bring either one of us in. I didn't kill Hoffman. Theodis didn't kill Hoffman. I think you are too smart to be influenced by a boss wanting to make a name for himself. I want to know who put Hoffman in my lake as much as you do. So go find them."

"How do you suggest I start?"

"I would get Theodis' boys with a sketch artist or Identikit operator and have a composite picture made of this guy who purchased the three knives."

"Is it normal for someone to purchase three of a certain knife?"

"Yes and no. All the knives hanging on my wall are Bowies. But they are all variations of the design. Some people collect knives by certain makers. B.J. Hassinger is a knife collector. He owns two I made and he bought Theo's second Bowie. I find it unusual that one person would buy three kit knives made by the same person. Gun shows around here happen every ninety days. The one in Hattiesburg was the last one before this one. I don't think there is a coincidence here. Either it was planned this way or the buyer is one peculiar knife nut."

"Do you go to all the gun shows?"

"This second one I've been to since I moved back to Alabama. The only reason I'm here today is make sure Theo and lawyer Hassinger got together."

"Why are you so interested in Reverend Cleckler having a lawyer?"

"Because I know cops will brow beat a confession out of someone because it's easier than finding the real culprit. You strike me as a diligent cop trying to do the right thing. But you have a boss on your ass to produce results. And a black preacher with an agenda against what the victim represents is a tempting target. Particularly for a credit grabbing lieutenant."

"I agree with you, but I still have a job to do. Do you think I can get around the lawyer and get the boys to do a composite?"

"I'll make sure you can."

Jolene considered this for a few minutes. It was not likely the micromanaging Busby would go along it without

Thigman getting involved. She still had questions for Burns.

"How often does Reverend Cleckler bring his kids out to fish?"

"He comes as often as he can. Once or twice a month. He brings the project kids as often he and his boys come over. He is planning on bring a group out next Friday."

"Tell me about the Border Patrolman with the rifle shooting narcotics smugglers."

"La migra con el rifle disparandole a narco traficantes.' Burns replied. 'You've been talking to that crazy half breed Apache Buddy Russell. What did he tell you?"

"That there was some truth to the story."

"Some truth is correct. I spotted four of the bodies myself from our side of the border. I was suspected of doing the shooting. They had my rifle for three months checking the ballistics. It was bullshit they didn't have anything to compare with. The bodies were always in Mexico and our people couldn't go over there and look for evidence. And the Federales couldn't find anybody so a La Migra with a long range rifle was a good a scapegoat as any. It was the proverbial straw that broke the camel's back for me."

"La Migra?"

"Slang Spanish for Border Patrol. Don't yell it in a Mexican restaurant if you want service."

Jolene smiled. "You want to tell me about Tombstone and the warrants?"

She watched Burns expression change. There was a faraway look in his eyes. He didn't respond for several seconds.

"No. Let's go back to Theo's table. I'll suggest that he let the boys help make composite drawings."

CHAPTER SEVEN

THE Monday morning detective division meeting was conducted by Captain Thigman. Busby was a last minute substitute for DePiano at a police management conference in Jackson Mississippi. Thigman was tasked with running his division and DePiano's. The Big Dago's swollen balls would delay Thigman starting a month long vacation for two weeks. He was not happy. Hadfield was promptly placed in charge of the detectives during Busby's five day absence. The meeting was over in twenty minutes.

An impatient Identikit technician attempted to produce a composite drawing of the knife purchaser. In attendance were Theodis Cleckler, his two boys, and an associate from B. Johnson Hassinger's firm. Jolene could only watch the session deteriorate as the boys argued over who was right. Her suggestion that the technician work with them individually was stonewalled. Cleckler wasn't any help because he refused to believe one man bought all three knives. A good idea that might have prevented future deaths turned into a monumental waste of time. Which the tech would duly report to Lt. Busby on his return.

Jolene followed up on Cleckler's alibi appointments and found each of these witnesses to be as truthful as the Reverend himself. An interview with the head of security at the Golden Bay Casino verified the amicable agree to disagree relationship between Cleckler and Hoffman. The security boss was a retired detective from Las Vegas PD. He was surprised to learn about Theodis' knife making sideline. According to him it wasn't a hobby one would associate with a preacher. He'd witnessed the interaction between Cleckler and Hoffman during the opening protests. He found it a real stretch that Cleckler was Hoffman's killer. After hearing the details of Hoffman's death. He old detective said he didn't believe Cleckler capable of killing a man with a single thrust of a knife.

Jolene received a computer message from Nevada regarding a mother and daughter missing person case she had entered in the National Crime Information Center data base. A routine background check for warrants produced a hit on the duo. They had applied for work permits in order to join the oldest profession at a legal brothel. The pair hadn't been heard from in over a month and the alcohol impaired husband told Jolene he suspected alien abduction. Both mom and offspring were of legal age and the glamor shot photos accompanying the reports indicated they might be successful in their new endeavor. Hadfield wondered if she could get away with telling the husband that his suspicions were correct.

The week passed quickly. With their condescending micro manager out of the way, the detectives were productive solving cases and making arrests. The onset of a stormy weekend did not mar the vacation like atmosphere in the detective division. Monday morning was a different story.

"Hadfield!' Busby was livid. 'You are a perfect example of why diversity quota hiring and promotions are a mistake! However promoted you to sergeant and made you a detective must have been temporarily insane! This is poorest example of investigating I've ever seen and it is directly opposite of what I ordered you to do!"

The other detectives at the meeting twisted uncomfortably in their chairs. They all at one time or another had suffered the wrath of Busby. Only one of them, however, would stand up for their fellow detective. A young black man named Desmond Taylor got out of his chair and instantly drew abuse from Busby.

"Where in hell you think you going Taylor this meeting is not over!"

"Lieutenant I am not going to sit in this room and listen to you disrespect Sergeant Hadfield. I am going to the Captain and report this incident. And furthermore I am going to transfer back to patrol."

"YOU'RE NOT GOING ANYWHERE YOU BLACK SON OF A BITCH!!" Spittle from Busby's mouth struck Taylor in the face.

An older detective, Web Griffin, grabbed Taylor by his arm. "Sit down Des and keep your mouth shut." The other men in the room nodded at the young man indicating that he sit down. Reluctantly he sank back into his chair.

"Taylor you do not have permission to go to the Captain about any matter! Do you understand what I'm telling you?"

"Yes Lieutenant."

"YES LIEUTENANT WHAT?" Busby yelled his face red as a ripe tomato.

"Don't push it boss you might have a stroke. Whatcha want us to do. We'll handle it." Griffin said trying to defuse the situation.

Busby took several deep breaths and then grabbed Hadfield's reports off his desk and threw them at Griffin.

"Pass those out and you people drag all these church niggers in here and break Cleckler's alibi. They are all lying for him. I will be in New Orleans for an Academy Associates luncheon today. When I get back this afternoon I want to see paper work ready for the DA to arrest Cleckler and search his house and church. Hadfield you will remain in the office and handle the walk in's. Taylor you will go through all the files and make sure each case is showing the correct disposition. Griffin your request for vacation next week is denied."

Busby picked up his briefcase and stalked out of the office like a man possessed. After giving him a few minutes to clear the building the detectives went to their desks. A few murmured their regrets to Jolene and Taylor. Back at her desk Hadfield gave some serious thought to filing a harassment complaint against Busby. She realized the only person who would back up her story would be Taylor. And whether he would actually do it was another matter. Taylor went to his desk and called the ACLU.

Andrew Burns sat at his workbench inspecting a rifle under the watchful eyes of two FBI agents. They were members of the Mobile office SWAT team and competent marksmen. Or at least one was, he'd only met the second one twenty minutes ago. Double H or Special Agent Havelee Harris had her dumb blond routine down pat. She also knew how to describe the problems that got the gun on his bench. That scored her high with Burns. He looked at the agents.

"Whatdaya think Gun Doc?" The thirtyish athletically thin Harris asked her eyes twinkling.

"Tell her there's nothing wrong with it. She just needs to practice." Special Agent "Jack" Jackson quipped.

The H.H. playfully punched him on the shoulder. "You won one lunch bet it's not happening again. I cleaned your clock with pistols and sub guns. You set me up with the rifle." She looked back at Andy and raised her eyebrows as if to say, well.

"I think Jack gave the new girl the worst rifle in the armory so the good old boys wouldn't have to brown bag lunch." She giggled and hugged Burns.

"This is an old rifle with a lot of rounds through it. It is a good candidate for a total rebuild saving only the receiver bolt and serial number. Or just doing a minimum overhaul. What's done depends on your budget. You might want to send this one back to Quantico."

"No we've got a local repair or rebuild authorization from a qualified outside contractor." Jackson answered.

"Which you are.' Harris interjected. 'So how long will it take? Can we fish while we wait? Can I ride your horse? Can I shoot the rifle in the saddle scabbard?"

"Yes you can ride my horse. Yes you can fish. This is not a while-you-wait repair shop. Shooting my rifle is under consideration. To be decided after y'all tell what we're doing with your rifle. I can just fix it or I can make one HRT would take away from you. It depends on how thick your wallet is."

"Can I really ride your horse?"

"Yeah, tighten the cinch before you get on him."

"You going to check my ass on camera while I do it?" Havelee asked nodding to the screen above bench.

"Already have and used the zoom too. You went straight for Major leaving your partner to haul your rifle in here." Burns dead panned.

His cellphone rang. Theodis Cleckler's name was on the caller ID.

"Excuse me.' Burns asked the agents. 'What's up Theo?" Andy listened to his friend.

"If Hadfield said it was out of her control I believe her. Call B.J. Hassinger and have him get his people over there and stop those interviews. That dickhead lieutenant has stepped in it this time. And tell B.J. to arrange a polygraph for you, but not at Biloxi PD.' Burns paused for a few seconds then interrupted. 'That is not your worry Theodis. Listen you might want to consider filing a civil rights complaint with the FBI if this harassment continues. Keep me posted."

Andy laid his cell phone on the bench and looked at the two FBI agents.

"We don't want to butt into your business.' Jackson said. 'We heard your side of that conversation. Our agency, the most prominent defense lawyer on the Mississippi coast and Biloxi PD were all mentioned. Do you mind telling us what's going on?"

Burns recounted the story to the agents. H.H. spoke first.

"We were briefed on the Hoffman case. We wouldn't be here if we thought you had anything to do with it. I believe Sergeant Hadfield is trying to do right by you and Reverend Cleckler."

"I agree with H.H. And I know Hadfield. Her lieutenant is an asshole first class. He gives the good cops who get into the national academy a bad name. And his boss Captain Lyle Thigman is no fan of the FBI either. I suspect he was the target of a civil rights complaint long before our time. I'm surprised he hasn't retired yet. He's got be pushing seventy. While H.H. plays cowgirl I'll make a few phone calls and see if we can't prevent a complaint from happening."

Jackson and Burns watched H.H. on the camera monitor screen. She expertly adjusted the stirrup length and tightened the cinch. As she mounted Major, Jackson strolled outside. "Hey Helium Head, if you bust your ass I'm not covering you with the SAC!"

H.H. grinned and flipped her partner the finger. She gave Major a firm nudge with her heels and the buckskin responded. Burns watched the as she urged Major into a lope. "A horsewoman that shoots. They don't get much better than that." He said as Jackson walked back inside.

"Yeah and she don't hurt your eyes to look at either." The FBI man responded.

"Hadfield and Thigman are some of the good guys over there. Your friend Cleckler will have to weather the storm for a while. Anything else is need to know. Harris is not read in on the operation. A total rebuild including a can and a new scope are authorized on that rifle. If you will give me a written estimate, you can start on it. And don't do such a good job on her rifle. I can't afford to feed her every time we go to the range."

"You keep calling her Helium Head and I'll build her one that will sit records."

"You'll do that anyway. With her the air head stuff is just an act. Gun Doc."

"I've already figured that out." Burns said smiling.

Lyle Thigman had passed the not happy state and was just plain mad. He had had a cop to cop meeting with Lt. Don Smith earlier in the afternoon and learned the real reason for the Big Dago's swollen nuts. If he could have gotten to DePiano then he would have personally castrated the jerk. And his protégé Busby had informed communications that he would not return to office this afternoon. He would be in tomorrow morning. The privilege of telling communications you would not return to office after a day trip to the Big Easy was not extended to lieutenants. But it was the wail of a black woman in an interrogation room that pushed Thigman over the top.

"I been telling you da truth! And you be telling me ta lie! It ain't right!"

Captain Thigman recognized the woman. She was a local seamstress who had raised four boys and buried two husbands. She had hemmed Thigman's trousers for at least thirty years. He opened the interrogation room door and slammed it against the wall. "What the hell is going on in here?"

"Mister Thigman please help me. Dey brung me in here in handcuffs. Dey told me I would be in jail if I didn't lie on Reverend Cleckler! Please help me Mister Thigman please!"

The woman was in tears. And it took about a tenth of a millisecond for Thigman to figure out what was happening. He had read all of Hadfield's reports and approved them. Detective Desmond Taylor was just down the hall. He responded promptly when Thigman shouted his name.

"Yes Sir Captain."

"Detective take this lady home. If she needs to stop on the way for anything you do it. If she doesn't have the money for what she needs you pay the bill and I will reimburse you. Close the door on your way out."

The two men in the room with Thigman waited quietly for the axe to fall. Their wait was short. The gray haired captain picked up a chair and slammed it against the wall.

He leaned across the table and glared at the two men. "You two assholes speak now!"

After hearing the complete story from both men, Thigman asked one question. "Did it occur to either one of you that what you were doing was wrong?"

"Captain, Lieutenant Busby ordered us to do it."

"Hitler's generals used the same line. And a lot of them were hung. Both of you are relieved of duty pending disciplinary action. Give me your badges."

If that wasn't bad enough Thigman went hyper ballistic when he found out what the FBI agent sitting in his office wanted.

The detectives hardly acknowledged each other the next morning. Hadfield was busy at her desk and Taylor just sat with a sullen expression on his face. Web Griffin wondered why two of their colleagues were missing. Busby walked in looked around at the group and inquired about the absent duo.

"Where are Cole and Haley?"

A bellow from Captain Lyle Thigman prevented any reply.

"BUSBY MY OFFICE NOW!"

"Captain were are about to convene a progress report meeting..."

"WHAT PART OF *NOW* DO YOU NOT UNDERSTAND JACKASS!"

Busby angrily walked down the hall to Thigman's office and was motioned inside. Those lurking the hallway in search of a good rumor promptly found somewhere else to be.

"Captain I don't appreciate your yelling at me and using derogatory slang. That was unprofessional to say the...."

"Shut up you cock sucking son of a bitch!"

Busby's eyes widened. Lyle Thigman's nick name was Blackjack Thigman. And he was seated behind his desk tapping one against the desktop.

"I've been here thirty eight years and I've never seen anyone as stupid as you get to where you are in this department. You must give one hell of a blow job. Because you sure as hell aren't smart enough to have anything on anybody."

"Captain you can't talk to me that way!"

"I can talk to you anyway I want asshole. Because I'm white and you're white. And we are behind closed doors. Professional! Why the hell should I be professional with a lying back-sticking son of a bitch like you. That uses his rank to destroy good cop's careers. Does DePiano give it to you in the ass?"

"Captain!"

"You want my job so bad answer this question. What would you do when the FBI informed you that officers under your command had violated people's civil rights on orders from a lieutenant? And that same lieutenant used racial slurs in front of his subordinates and made sexists comments. What the hell would you do if you were captain?"

Busby didn't answer. His expression changed from anger to dismay.

"You must have gave the chief one hell of a blow job. Because he won't let me fire you or demote you. But he will let me give you a five day suspension without pay. That suspension started yesterday so this expense report for that meeting you attended in New Orleans goes in the trash. And you be billed for using a police vehicle.

"You will surrender your badge right now and then you will accompany me to the detectives' conference room. Where you will apologize to Sergeant Hadfield and Detective Taylor for your comments yesterday. And you will apologize to your detectives as well.

"And this next order comes directly from the chief. Reverend Theodis Cleckler is no longer a person of interest in the Hoffman homicide. Cleckler passed a polygraph yesterday."

"But we didn't give it him."

"No we didn't dickhead. Because our polygraph operator works for you. Give me your badge and get your ass in the conference room."

A contrite Busby gave the necessary apologies under the watchful eyes of Thigman, and then left. Thigman placed Hadfield in charge. He then told her and Taylor to come to his office.

They sat in front of Thigman's desk. He returned to his worn desk chair. Hadfield realized he had the oldest and worst furniture of anyone on the command staff. There were few mementos of pictures in the room. The menacing reminder of his street name lay on the desk blotter. Jolene visualized it being used on Busby, only she was the one using it.

"The door is closed. This conversation is cop to cop and off the record. Desmond do you understand cop to cop?"

The clean cut intelligent looking Taylor answered. "Yes sir, what's said in the car stays in the car."

"Excellent definition Desmond. And you did the right thing yesterday. Unfortunately it is going to cost you. Busby's punishment is just another score for him to settle. And his rabbi DePiano will help him. Jolene will tell you how that works. My advice to you is stay out of the way. And you don't want the reputation of running to the ACLU every time you hear the N-word.

"A new century starts in eight months. Things will be better. You don't have the need to know why.' Thigman paused and looked at the two detectives. His expression told them not to ask questions. 'I have to use ninety days of leave time between now and the end of the year. So I won't be around all the time to look after you two. I twisted Busby's tail pretty hard this morning. So watch your backs and roll with the punches.

"Jolene you and Desmond will be working as partners for the rest of this week. I expect Busby will change that assignment as soon as I'm gone. Next Monday I'm out of here for thirty days. So Desmond learn what you can from

Sergeant Hadfield. Do either of you have anything you want to say?"

"Sir,' Taylor asked tentatively as he pointed at the blackjack. 'What is that?"

"That is a J.M. Buckheimer Company blackjack. They called that particular size the Convoy." Thigman handed the leather covered club to Taylor. Who reluctantly took it with two fingers like he had just been handed a dead rat.

"That lady I took home last night, Miz Freda. She said she sewed your pants pockets thicker so you could carry this."

Thigman smiled at the memory. "That is one fine woman. She reinforced many a pocket for me."

Desmond politely handed the club to Jolene who wasn't expecting it weigh as much as it did.

"Miz Freda says you smacked the drink out and gospel in with one swing on a great big man named Abraham Mose."

Thigman laughed out loud. "I haven't heard that story in thirty years. I can't believe that woman still remembers that."

"She swears its true Captain."

"And that's a story I haven't heard Captain,' Hadfield said. 'Now you're going to have to tell it."

"I started here in 1961 fresh out of the paratroops and I wasn't afraid of the devil himself. Abraham Mose was a name the old guys used to scare rookies. They said he was a half breed red bone buck toothed cross eyed mulatto that was seven foot tall. Mose could whip a full shift of all the police in the county and nobody able to put him in jail. I thought it was all bullshit.

"It was in sixty two or sixty three that I found out how real he was. It was a full moon with that night. We were really busy and my partner was off. I was sent down to an old bayou neighborhood to sort out some kind of problem. I had managed to get a couple of blocks away from my car.

"I heard an awful bellow. I looked and saw the biggest human being I'd even seen no more than twenty feet away.

He was mad and yelling, 'I'm Abraham Mose and I ain't going to jail!' He ran my way. I drew gun and started shooting. I missed him all six times. He stopped and looked at me. I pulled my blackjack. I figured if I could get one good lick in it would slow him down enough that I could out run him. He let out another bellow and started my way.

"I jumped up and hit him as hard as I could right between the eyes. Mose stopped wavered back and forth then dropped to his knees. Then he fell forward on his hands. Suddenly he pushed back up and knelt there with his arms spread. He looked up at the moon and started shouting LORD LORD LORD!

"I took off running. I could still hear him hollering when I got to my car. I left that neighborhood and went home to change pants. A couple of weeks' later people were calling me Blackjack. I heard Mose started going to church. Now days a fellow like him would get a ball playing scholarship to LSU or Alabama. I never heard of any more trouble out of Abraham Mose."

Jolene handed Thigman the blackjack. Desmond said, "Miz Freda swears it's true. She acts like she saw it happen."

Lyle Thigman held the blackjack and smiled. "She would know. Her maiden name was Mose."

The rest of the week passed too quickly for Jolene. Working with Desmond Taylor was a joy. The young man was genuinely interested in police work and being a detective. If taught the right way Taylor would go a long way in his chosen profession. Too bad it wouldn't last. They were driving to Baldwin County Alabama to visit Andrew Burns. It was Friday and the Captain told them not to worry about coming back to the station before quitting time. He had told Hadfield earlier that Burns had passed a lie detector test and she needed to tell him that he was no longer a person of interest. Thigman also warned her once more to watch her back around Busby.

The deep sea fishing trip with Harrellson had been rained out the previous weekend. He had called her earlier and confirmed good weather for tomorrow and asked if he could pick her up at six AM and they would make a day of it. She had agreed. But as she and Taylor cruised across Mobile Bay on I-10 Jolene realized she was more interested in seeing Andy Burns than fishing with Harrellson.

Satisfied that Theodis and one of his church members had all the children fishing from his pier under control. Andy got back in the ATV and started toward the house He heard his dogs barking and saw an unmarked police Crown Vic in his driveway.

Unexpected visitors were not cordially greeted. However, Burns was pleased to see Hadfield get out the Ford. He was curious about detective with her. Both of them were dressed in casual Friday attire. She was wearing nice jeans and a button down collar shirt. Her red hair was pulled back into a ponytail. A holstered Glock pistol and a gold sergeant's badge clipped to her belt completed the ensemble. The man wore chinos and a neatly pressed sport shirt. Ditto on the Glock his badge was silver and read detective. Hadfield introduced Taylor. He and Burns shook hands.

The Pudelpointers greeted Jolene with enthusiasm they reserved for friends. There was a loud whinny from the barn as Major issued his welcome.

"What was that?" Taylor said his eyes wide as he looked around.

"My horse."

"You gotta a horse?"

"Yes"

"He not loose like them dogs is he?"

"No,' Andy replied with a mischievous smile. 'But the bull we caught this morning was. I hope he's back on his side of the fence."

Taylor looked like he was ready to bolt for the car.

"You mean there might be a bull loose out here?"

"He could have got back out. But don't run for the car. It might upset my dogs."

"Them dogs don't like dark meat do they?"

"I don't know. I never feed them fed any."

The dogs were sitting calmly next to Burns their tails thumping the ground in anticipation of Jolene playing with them.

"Desmond,' she said. 'One thing you are going to have to learn as a detective is how to recognize bullshit when you hear it."

"Are you shitting me Mister Burns?"

"No, but do you think I would let Theodis Cleckler bring a dozen kids out here to fish if there were any danger?"

"Is Reverend Cleckler out here?" Jolene asked.

"He's down at the lake with a couple of deacons and a bunch of kids."

"I've been to his church. He's a good preacher. I sure didn't know he came out in the woods like this." Taylor said.

"Actually you are safer here than you are in the projects. Y'all come on Theo will be glad to see you."

Burns led them to the ATV and they all squeezed into the small cab. The dogs remained at the house. As predicted Theodis greeted Taylor and Hadfield like long lost friends. He certainly knew how to forgive. Theo cajoled Taylor into trying his hand at fishing. It was apparent he had grown up in a city. Jolene assured Taylor it would be alright. She rode with Andy back to the house.

"That is really nice of you to do that for those kids and Taylor. He was scared to death when we turned off the paved road."

"I figured that was the case. I leave the dogs at the house and put Major in the paddock when Theo is out here with a group of kids. Animals terrify children who haven't grown up around them. When they get comfortable I introduce them to the dogs and the horse."

Burns stopped the ATV. Hadfield got out and started playing with the dogs. Major whinnied again.

"You didn't drive over here from Biloxi just to pet my dogs. What do you want Hadfield?"

"Officially you are no longer a person of interest. And I understand you passed a polygraph. Did you have anything to do with Reverend Cleckler taking one?"

"I did. Is that what made your boss come around?"

"That is what made my Captain come around. My lieutenant hasn't yet." She went on to recap the incident with Busby and what had happened since.

"When Theodis called me Monday I figured that lieutenant was behind it. Isn't he tight with that Captain that screwed Don and Mark?"

"Yeah, but I think they enjoyed it." She told him what happened at SWAT headquarters.

"Ouch.' He said. 'But you had better watch your back big time. Those two will be gunning for you."

"I know,' Hadfield said looking up from playing with the dogs.

"Where did you find these rare dogs Burns?" she asked.

"They sort of came with this place. I'd been here about three months when a guy showed up at the gate. He was the dog's breeder and trainer. Charlie Raifield purchased them before he died. Part of the deal was the dogs be trained, and the trainer teach Charlie to handle them. This guy didn't know Charlie had passed away when he called Mrs. Raifield and told her the dogs are ready to be delivered. She gave him directions to the gate and told him the dogs belong to me. He hung around a week and taught me to handle them."

Jolene smiled as she rubbed the dogs' brushy snouts. Another whinny interrupted her thoughts.

"Can we walk down to the barn and see Major."

"Sure you can ride him if you like."

"No, maybe another time."

They reached the barn and the buckskin had his head over the paddock fence. He nuzzled Jolene's neck and shoulders. She giggled and stroked Major's head and neck.

"Alright big guy quit putting the move on Hadfield it's play time." Burns opened the paddock gate. Major abruptly turned away from Jolene trotted through the gate and out of sight around the barn.

"Don't tell me he understood what you said."

"No he understood what opening the gate means. Come on."

They found Major was patiently standing at another gate. He looked around to see if they had followed. The thick green grass beyond the gate shimmered in the afternoon sun. The pasture was about the size of a football field and surrounded by trees. Burns swung the gate open and the horse galloped through his mane and tail streaming behind him. The sight brought a broad smile to Jolene's face. Andy closed the gate and rested his arms on it watching the horse frolicking in grass.

"When we moved here I had to build the barn and paddock. I turned him out in this pasture. I don't believe that big rascal had ever seen this much grass in his life. He ran, he rolled, he bucked, he kicked, and he was having a ball. I knew I couldn't leave him out there because he wasn't used to eating a lot of grass. It would make him sick. I tried for over two hours to catch him. I wound up having to rope him. Now he plays catch-me-if-you-can whenever I turn him out. I'll have to rope him this evening. It's a game to him and me too because I let him get away with it."

"I would like to see that." She said mesmerized by Major's antics in the pasture and trying to visualize Burns roping him.

"Hang around I'll catch him before I go to dinner."

The horse came by the gate running flat out. Jolene stepped back startled. Burns didn't move, he just smiled, watching the horse.

"Do you actually rope cattle if they get in here?"

"Sometimes. Most of the time we just push them back to their pasture. I had to get a rope a bull this morning. He was nasty. Couldn't have done it without Major. Working cattle from horseback is pretty much all horse. And he's got a lot of cow."

"Cow?"

"That's cowboy for a horse having a lot of cow sense. They can anticipate what a cow will do. It gets to be quite a ride sometimes. This morning was wild."

Jolene looked around uncomfortably. "You weren't bullshitting Taylor about the bull were you?"

"No."

"Could it get back in here?"

"Yes, I don't do a very good job of fixing that fence. It gives Major something to look forward to and its fun."

Jolene looked at him as he watched Major romp and play. "You really like that horse."

"Yeah. When you get one as good as him it is a lifetime commitment. I was told once that getting a horse is like getting married, you may have to try a few before you get the right one. Major will do anything I ask of him. One hell of a vaquero broke and trained him."

"Vaquero?"

"It means cowboy. Manny Collazo is the best cowboy and horseman I've ever run across."

Burns never stopped watching Major cavort in the pasture. He didn't turn his head when Jolene asked if he would tell her why he was busted from sergeant. He ignored the question until the horse stopped playing and began to graze.

"Let's walk." He said and she fell in beside him as they made their way toward the lake.

"I was running range training. We had a kid like your Officer Peterson. He had brought a new pistol and couldn't shoot it as well he thought he could. He pitched a temper tantrum and threw the loaded weapon on the ground.

"I confiscated his gun, and ordered him off the range. I filed conduct unbecoming an officer charges, as well as range safety violations against him. And I made a written recommendation that he be terminated. Somebody with that kind of temper doesn't need to be a cop, much less carry a gun.

"I lacked two weeks completing my probationary year as sergeant when that happened. During probation you can be busted back to officer rank just because they don't like you. And there is no appeal either. This kid was a lieutenant named Phillips' fair-haired boy. I'd never seen eye to eye with Phillips on anything. He convinced the chief that I was unstable and over reacted to the incident. He said the kid was acting out and expressing himself and I had no concept of how young people behaved. And I was incapable of supervising them. I lost my stripes. That really hurt. Fortunately I had enough time to retire. I never went back to office."

Jolene didn't want to pour salt in the wound by telling him about her conversation with Phillips. They walked the tree line to a section of the lake that could not be seen from the house. It held a large metal building with a concrete ramp extending into the lake.

"That's one hell of a boat house Burns."

"It's not a boat house, it's a float plane hangar."

"There's an airplane in there?"

"Not at the moment."

Her cell phone buzzed. The call ID showed Taylor was calling. When she finished the call she spoke to Burns. "Reverend Cleckler and his group are packing up to leave. Taylor wants to talk to me in person. We need to start back that way."

Burns said. "Follow the tree line, it is about three hundred yards."

When they reached the pier Jolene saw a nice boat ramp and a block enclosure holding a large Go Devil boat complete with poling platform and long shaft tiller steer motor with the same logo. These slick bottom boats were popular along the coast in the marshes and bayous. It wasn't exactly what she would have picked to fish from in this lake. Hadfield conferred with Taylor and rejoined

Burns. They both watched the group load up in two church vans. Taylor rode with Theodis.

"He wanted to ride back to Biloxi with Reverend Cleckler. I think they hit it off." Jolene offered.

"That guy strikes me as a good officer. He will do well with more experience. I believe you can count on him. Unless he's out in the woods." Burns smiled when he added the last part.

"Captain Thigman thought the same thing when Taylor asked to be transferred from patrol. Lieutenant Busby didn't like it, but he didn't have any say in the matter."

"Is this the Blackjack Thigman Mark Hildibrand talks about?"

"One in the same." Hadfield answered. She retold the Abraham Mose story without embellishment. "I've heard a lot of war stories but that is one I'm hesitant not to believe."

"For a cop from that era or anytime for that matter to admit missing six shots. I think there is more truth left out than fiction added."

"That's good point." They had reached the entrance to the shop. "Burns I'm just being nosey, what's in those two buildings on each side of the drive? I expect a guard to step out of on them every time I come in here."

"That's not a bad idea as much traffic has been in here the last two weeks."

"Are you saying what's in the building is none of my business?"

"No, you wouldn't believe me if I told you."

"Try me."

"Cannons."

"Cannons?"

"That's what I said."

"Bullshit Burns. First it was bull roping then it was an airplane hangar and now you have cannons in garages. Bullshit."

"You forgot about roping Major you didn't believe that either."

"You're a smartass too Burns!"

"Some people just bring that out in me. Would you like me to open the doors on the guardhouses as you call them? So you can see for yourself that I'm not lying to you."

"Please do."

He went inside the shop and unlocked a small cabinet holding two switches and a circuit breaker. He flipped the switches and turned off the breaker. He came out and motioned her to follow him. When they reached the buildings he stood back and watched.

Hadfield was speechless. Inside each building two massive civil war era field pieces stood deadly silent, the menacing muzzles pointed from the open doors.

"Cannons!" she said looking at Burns.

"Most people say shit damn or something more graphic. I would have preferred you to say thank you Mister Burns I believe you now."

"And I suppose they are real?"

"Yes they are full-scale replicas of 1860 Ordinance Rifles. Complete with all accessories."

Jolene walked into the building and stood between the guns. She touched one of the shoulder high wagon wheels. "These things actually shoot?"

"Yes."

"Do you ever shoot them?"

"They are great Fourth of July noise makers."

"These things look like they are aimed right at the gate."

"They are."

"Why?"

"Charlie thought they would be cheaper than full time guards."

"Bullshit!"

"Whatever."

"Burns!"

"You didn't believe me anyway. Now get out of there. I need to close these doors. And I gotta catch Major."

Hadfield was quiet as they walked to the barn. She watched Burns retrieve a lariat. Telling her to wait by the gate he put on leather gloves and strolled toward the buckskin. Andy stopped and shook out a loop with the rope. The horse watched this, then threw his head back and whinnied. He reared bucked a few times and ran straight for Burns. Jolene thought for a moment the Major was going to run down his owner. Andy stepped aside and flipped the rope underhanded as the horse galloped past. Major slid to a stop. He walked calmly as Burns lead him to the barn. After the horse was fed Andy joined Hadfield.

"Impressive Burns I thought you were about to be trampled. Do you have to do that every time you put him out there?"

"Only if I want to. It's a lot easier to open the gate. He will beat me back to the barn to get to that feed bucket."

"Bullshit Burns!"

"Hadfield you sound like a broken record."

They walked toward the house. Jolene played with the dogs and didn't say anything. He motioned her inside the shop, where he looked at a couple of the machines.

"You married Hadfield?"

"No."

"You have a boyfriend or are doing the seeing thing with anybody?"

"No Burns."

"You like men?"

"BURNS! Damn it! Yes!"

"You can't be too careful these days!"

"What the hell are you trying to say?"

"I would like you to have dinner with me tonight. I go to a place in Fairhope it's on the municipal pier. It's not much out of your way going back to Biloxi."

"I thought we were going through all that just so I could fish your lake."

"Same rules apply to you as everybody else. Except maybe the wear out your welcome thing. I'm going to clean up. I need about twenty minutes. Make yourself at home. Play with the dogs, whatever. If you need to primp or pee use the bathroom by the office."

He left the shop before she could reply. And she didn't recall saying she would have dinner with him either.

The small restaurant was almost half-way out the quarter mile long concrete pier protruding into Mobile Bay. Their table allowed them an unrestricted view of the municipal marina and the large sailing yachts docked there. The lights of Mobile's skyline twinkled in the distance.

"Is your marriage an off limits subject Burns?" Jolene asked between bites of shrimp.

"You've done a lot of investigating me Hadfield. Maybe I ought to interrogate you."

"I'm sorry, it's..."

He interrupted. "You were doing your job don't apologize for it. We're not sitting here in an investigative interview situation either. Or at least I hope we're not.

"My first Border Patrol assignment was in El Paso. I was checking a tour bus crossing back over from Mexico. A gal I went high school with was on it. She was vacationing between jobs. We had dated back then. After graduation I went to the Marines and she went to nursing school. Anyway she was infatuated with the west wanted to stay in El Paso for a while. We started seeing each other and wound up getting married. I was transferred to Naco in Cochise County, Arizona. Her infatuation turned into homesickness. Small town life in Cochise County Arizona is either love it or hate it. She hated it.

"The smuggler shooting business came up about then and I left the Border Patrol. We moved back home to Alabama. I took the police exams and got a job. The marriage went sour after that. The divorce was fair. I didn't have much going in or much coming out."

Jolene smiled and said, "That sounds like my first marriage."

"So you've been married more than once?"

"Twice, divorced the first one, widowed the second."

"I'm sorry. Is that something you talk about?"

"Tommy Hadfield was an Air Force fighter pilot. He was killed in a crash during the Red Flag War Games at Nellis Air Force Base in Nevada. I was going to leave the police department and be a full-time Air Force wife. Tommy had orders to Japan when he was killed. I came back to work. Without good friends like Mark Hildibrand, Don Smith and their wives, I wouldn't have made it. That was six years ago. I'm over it now with good memories. But I wish," she felt herself start to choke up and she paused regaining her composure. "I wish Tommy could have said good bye."

"I know the feeling," Andy said as he stared blankly at the marina and bay. Jolene watched him closely and as he spoke.

"I felt like my world had collapsed when I retired from the PD. Life as I knew it was over. I liked Arizona when I was in the Border Patrol. I didn't know if there was anything for me out there, but there was no reason to stay in Alabama. Charlie Raifield had offered a job, but he was too good a friend for me to work for him. Tombstone was centrally located enough that I could roam around and try find whatever I was looking for. But I expect you've learned the story already, so....."

Andy sighed and then said, "What the hell. That night in town me an Manny were loaded to the gills. And I was in a self-destruct mode. The pain was too great. I've never spurred a horse like I did Major that night. I wanted him to stumble and fall on me. Put me out of my misery. Somehow he made it back to that beat up mobile home I lived in, running full speed through the desert at night. I lived four miles out of town. He was standing in the corral still saddled the next morning. I woke up in the horse trailer and heard the phone ringing. I managed to get inside to answer it. Charlie Raifield's attorney was on the other end. He wanted me in his office in Mobile as soon as possible."

Andy paused and looked at Jolene; she saw the sadness in his eyes. "Somehow I managed to pack up what I had and get Major loaded in the trailer. I had just enough money for gas and horse feed. I was going to be hungry by the time I got to Mobile. But hell it hurt too damn much to stay in Arizona. Manny Collazo showed up just as I was pulling out. He hadn't been out of jail very long. Manny wanted to buy Major from me, right then. But I needed that horse too much. I still do."

He stopped talking and returned to watching the dark waters of Mobile Bay. After a few minutes Jolene asked softly. "Do you ever hear from Manny?"

"It has been a while now, I called him when I got settled on the place. We exchanged phone numbers. And we actually called each other a few times. I guess it has been well over six months since we talked. But I think about him and his daughter every time that big buckskin gallops across the pasture."

Jolene watched a tear slide down Burns' cheek. She reached out and put her hand on his forearm, and squeezed gently.

CHAPTER EIGHT

AS she drove west on I-10 Jolene Hadfield felt guilty. She wasn't sure why. Was it because she opened up and admitted she still hurt because Tommy Hadfield hadn't said goodbye? Or was it because she felt she betrayed Andy Burns by investigating him. The scary part was that both of them needed to put the past ghosts to rest. And what was more frightening was that she was completely at ease talking to Andrew Burns.

When Jolene crossed the Mississippi State line she was in range of the police department's radio repeater. The sudden burst of voices and static startled her. At this distance she could only receive bits and pieces of the transmissions and they didn't sound good. Police cars were being dispatched to back up other units already on the scene at something in the projects. Her cop instincts kicked in and she picked up the cell phone punching the communications supervisor's number on speed dial. The second shift radio room supervisor was a male who usually remained calm regardless of the situation. Tonight was an exception.

"Sergeant Hadfield,' the supervisor in a panicky voice. "We've had a double killing in the projects. We need everybody we can get down there now. That nigger preacher Cleckler is stirring up a riot!"

The radio traffic grew more intense with dispatchers trying to shout down the cops, and cops trying to shout down dispatches. Pandemonium ruled the communications system. Jolene didn't know where the field supervisors were or who was in charge. Something had to be done quickly or there would be a riot.

"David," she said calmly and firmly into the cell phone. "Listen to me, David, tell your people to stop talking on the radio now. They have to shut up now, David."

Holding onto the phone and listening to the radio Jolene turned on the emergency strobes concealed in the Ford's grill and headlights as she accelerated. Soon half the radio traffic was quiet.

David was breathing a little calmer now. "Now, David,' she said, 'you plug your headset into the console and start telling all units to hold radio traffic. Do that now, David." He did.

In a few minutes the radio was silent. "Now David,' she said, 'get the shift supervisor on the radio and have him call you on his cell phone. And you find out what is going on down there. I should be on the scene myself in about twenty minutes."

She hung up the phone and remembered Mark Hildibrand telling her during the first week she worked at Biloxi PD, 'that' when communications panics, the officers on the street panic.' Hildibrand had taught her well. Jolene felt like she learned how to police from that man. The only thing she had learned in four years at the Jackson was how to rebuff attempts from male cops trying to get her in bed. It occurred to her that Andy Burns would have done the same thing she just did. No, police sergeants like Hildibrand and Burns would not have lost control of the situation to begin with. She switched on the siren as she sped west on the moonlit interstate.

Jolene arrived in the projects. She switched her radio to the detective frequency and contacted the investigator on the scene. Web Griffin answered and gave her the address. When she approached the block of old brick apartment buildings she saw that the crowd outnumbered the police officers at least five to one. Fortunately the crowd was paying attention to Rev. Theodis Cleckler standing in the bed of a pickup truck. His baritone voice carried across the crowd.

Gesturing with his hands as he spoke, Cleckler held the gathering's attention. "Brothers and sisters, we are not here to fight the police! The politicians are responsible for the deaths of Brother and Sister Simpson. Their gambling halls caused these dear people to take their own lives in the misguided hope that insurance money would pay to feed their beloved son Melvin!"

Jolene thought Cleckler was well informed. And he didn't sound like he was inciting a riot. She saw the huge frame of Captain Bernard DePiano towering over officers as he directed the men at the rear of the SWAT van. Officers rejected by the former SWAT bosses as unsuitable were currently members of the special unit. Unofficially known as, DePiano's slugs and thugs, they were happily passing around gas masks, tear gas munitions, riot shields and long black clubs.

Hadfield drove past hoping the bright strobe lights would keep DePiano from recognizing her. She parked near the other unmarked units and went inside the apartment building. She could still hear Cleckler's words.

"Brothers and Sisters go peaceably back to your homes! Do not confront the police! They are frightened men who will overreact!"

That's for damn sure Jolene thought as she entered the building. She heard Cleckler tell the crowd to boycott the casinos. As she stepped into the apartment where the other detectives waited, Cleckler once more urged the crowd not to fight with the police.

"With DePiano and his SWAT thugs out there, those people ain't got a prayer's chance in hell of getting home without being gassed." Griffin said to the group while peering out the front window. He turned and greeted Hadfield. "Hi Jolene, you could have stayed away, ya know."

"I was out and it sounded like there was a problem down here."

"There is,' Griffin answered, 'and it is not likely to get any better."

"What happened?" she asked.

"Patrol got a shots fired call to this building. Three units responded, found the door open. They came in and found a black male and black female dead of gunshot wounds. Wounds apparently self-inflicted. The patrol guys found a note. The note says they were about to be evicted for non-payment of rent. We've found a notice to that effect and duns from every finance company in town. The wife apparently wrote the suicide note. It says they gambled away all their money trying to win big to pay the bills. Tomorrow they would have been on the street." Griffin paused, lit a cigarette and then continued the briefing in his monotonous matter-of-fact tone.

"The deceased are Johnny and Roberta Simpson, both in their early forties, or at least they were. There was something in the note about a life insurance policy. We found that, and apparently they didn't know it won't pay off in suicide cases. Coroner agrees it was self-inflicted gunshot wounds that caused the deaths. The weapon they used was a twelve gauge double barrel shotgun. One barrel for each of them it appears Johnny stuck the gun in his mouth first and Roberta went second. She must not have trusted him to go through with it because I always thought it was ladies first." Griffin grinned for the first time since Jolene had arrived.

She rolled her eyes at his last remark. Before she could ask another question, Griffin went for his second punch line. "They used bird shot shells in that gun. Cause the backs of their heads are still intact. No mess, just black eyes. Now we can use their heads for one of them Mexican noisemakers. What da ya call 'em?"

"I call them I've heard enough." Jolene snapped, aggravated that she let Griffin's comments get to her. "How does Reverend Cleckler know so much about what's going on?"

"One of the first officers on the scene is a member of Cleckler's church. Apparently he filled him in before we got here. Melvin Simpson the deceased's kid hasn't been located. The patrol guys know him. He's a local gang banger fourteen maybe fifteen. His street name is real original, OJ. Last time patrol shook him down he had quite a bit of cash on him and a couple of crack rocks. Maybe momma and daddy should have borrowed the rent money from him."

Jolene was about to comment when the crowd outside went wild, their screams punctuated by the pops of tear gas canisters exploding. She went to the window and watched the mayhem outside as the gas masked equipped cops waded into the crowd wildly swinging their riot batons. Before daylight forty seven people, none of them police officers, would be treated for injuries at the local hospital.

Two hours after the project riot, most of Smith and Hildibrand's third shift officers were waiting for police cars to drive. Two of them, partners Gresham and Graham, were standing impatiently in the parking lot when their assigned unit arrived. They looked at each other with raised eyebrows when Officer Peterson emerged from their cruiser.

"Little Big Balls nuts musta shrunk." Graham whispered.

"He's walking a little spread legged. I hear his proxy brother in law kept a riot shield close to his jewels this evening." Graham answered.

"You night watchman pukes don't go to sleep and run over any curbs tonight. Us real police have to chase people with those cars." Peterson sneered as he awkwardly walked into the station.

"Check it close, Partner," Gresham said. "Make sure that little prick didn't leave any hand grenades or bazookas under the front seat."

To the veteran street cops, checking the squad car thoroughly at the beginning of a shift was akin to the holy gospel. Each man went about this task as if his life depended on it. Graham inspected the video recording system mounted in a console between the front seats. He wasn't surprised Peterson left the unit recording. Punks like him wanted real time videos of their adventures. Graham played back the tape looking for anything showing the so called project riot. And he hit pay dirt. In living color glory on the five-inch screen was serious video-taped evidence of large-scale police misconduct at the direction of the Big Dago himself. DePiano was shown getting a lick or two in on Rev. Theodis Cleckler, then walking delicately away protecting his privates.

Dark clouds have silver linings. A less than perfect detail was assigned to Gresham and Graham. Lt. Smith send them to keep peace at the hospital. After replacing the videotape, they promptly responded to their assigned task.

Getting to the silver lining was challenging. A large impenetrable dark cloud covered the emergency room entrance. Blocking the portal was the considerable bulk of Adonis Purcell. A hardened mass once encountered by NFL rushers before the giant lineman failed to make the season cut. He was working his part time job as hospital security officer to supplement to his full time income as chief bailiff and bouncer in the court of Judge Emory C. Richmond, a jurist with no tolerance for lawyer nonsense and exceptional fairness to anyone appearing before his bench. Richmond helped Purcell trace his family tree. They learned their ancestors were slaves on the same Mississippi Delta plantation.

At the moment Adonis' smooth shaven head, as slick as a bowling ball and close to the same size, was turning toward the street cops. Purcell's dark eyes radiated hate. A faithful member of Rev. Cleckler's church, Purcell knew it was wrong to hate. But tonight he felt there was a divine exception for members of Biloxi PD.

"You stupid honkeys must have balls bigger'n yo brains. But that ain't say'n nutten cause neither of ya gotta a brain bigger'n a peanut."

"One of our officers said Reverend Cleckler left this in his car. We would really appreciate your seeing that the Reverend gets it." Gresham said as he handed over the tape. Graham stood by his partner looking as humble as possible. Which was hard to do knowing Peterson's badge number would be displayed on the screen whenever the video was played.

The sky was gray with first dawn light when Tucker Lee Harrellson knocked on Jolene's front door. She was wide awake. Her eyes were still red from exposure to the tear gas. The adrenaline from the previous evening robbed her of any sleep. She'd tossed and turned all night worrying about what happened. DePiano ordered the police to attack the crowd. They launched tear gas and non-lethal projectiles at people willingly walking away. The non-lethal projectiles, hard rubber and wooden blocks with rounded off edges hurt like hell. Using them guaranteed a fight started. Arresting Theodis Cleckler for inciting a riot and assault was ludicrous. If anybody needed to be arrested it was Captain Bernard DePiano.

"Good morning, Tucker," Jolene said. Perhaps the fishing trip would ease her mind about the night before. When Harrellson politely opened the door to his dark green Land Rover, she thought of Andy Burns and dinner that seemed long ago instead of hours.

Jolene noticed Harrellson was driving away from the docks where most ocean going boats were moored. He answered her question before she could ask it. "I live on Bay View Avenue on the Back Bay. I have my own dock. It is calm today. We'll have a good boat ride out to the Gulf."

Harrellson's contemporary house blended into the bay side setting. He didn't offer to take her inside and led the way to the boathouse. It was light enough for Jolene to make out the lines of a large fishing yacht. Harrellson told her to climb aboard as he untied the bowlines. Ten minutes later they were cruising the Back Bay of Biloxi on course for the Gulf of Mexico. Jolene stood on the fly bridge watching Harrellson handle the craft. He had given her what she assumed was the standard safety briefing he would give anyone who came on board. Jolene asked about the boat. Harrellson told her it was a Hatteras thirty six-foot twin diesel fishermen. She nodded her understanding, and said, "I'm impressed."

Harrellson smiled slightly and seemed to be a little embarrassed at her comment. Many people along the Gulf Coast lived in houses that didn't cost what his boat did. Tucker Lee Harrellson was rich. He lived in a nice house, he drove a luxury car and always dressed well. He didn't seem the least bit portentous. And she was standing on the flying bridge of a boat that if you had to ask the price you could not afford it. Hadfield she wondered if he read her mind as he steered the craft between two marker buoys.

"The saying about if you have to ask what they cost you can't afford it isn't true,' he said. 'You have to know how much to write the check for."

Jolene smiled, the only figure she wanted to know when she'd purchased her bass boat was how much was the down payment. They shared coffee from her thermos and she watched the sun rise as they headed south toward the Gulf. Harrellson pointed out the coastal islands as they passed them. An hour later there was only the horizon off the bow. It was warm and breezy on the fly bridge. She dozed off for a much needed nap when Harrellson cut the engines back to idle and announced. "It's time to fish."

He removed several large rods and reels from the equipment locker and then set about rigging the hooks. Jolene confessed to this being her first deep sea-fishing trip. Harrellson looked surprised at that revelation. Jolene watched him bait the hooks. The bait, cigar minnows, were the size of small bass she sometimes caught and always threw back. After rigging four rods, Harrellson cast the bait into the water and placed the rod in a holder.

"I'm got the boat set to drift over an artificial reef, there is an old liberty ship sunk down there." Harrellson said gesturing at the water.

"We are bottom fishing, for Amberjack, Triggerfish, Grouper and Snapper. And there is the always the possibility we could catch a shark. You can sit in one of the fighting chairs and watch the lines or you can hold a rod. I'm really amazed that anyone who fishes as much as you do has never been deep sea fishing."

Jolene removed her windbreaker and was applying sun block to her arms as she listened to the fishing lesson. The reason she had never been deep sea fishing was that she couldn't afford it. And she was glad she had chosen to wear baggy trousers and not shorts. They were comfortable and didn't show off her rear end. Harrellson was dressed in an expensive T-shirt, faded khaki slacks and boat shoes. He wore aviator style sunglasses and had a cloth cap with the Orvis logo perched on his head. She exchanged her sun block tube for the Ranger Boat's hat in her bag. She had just gotten her hair tucked in the cap when of the reels started playing out line.

Harrellson grabbed the rod and set the hook. "First strike this quick means we may have a good day." The line started running on a second reel and Jolene grabbed the rod. Before they could land the fish they'd hooked the lines began to run on the other rods and reels. The next minutes were hectic for Harrellson as he reeled in fish and deftly used the gaff and net to bring them into the boat. Jolene, with Harrellson's help landed two Grouper herself. Harrellson pulled in a big Snapper. He brought the boat around and anchored. Jolene had already cut bait and had three lines back in the water.

"For a first-timer on a deep sea boat you catch on fast." he said.

"Fishing is fishing anywhere I guess, Tucker. Unless it's fly fishing and I can't use a fly rod." Jolene said thinking about Andy Burns reeling in Nigel Hoffman's body with a fly rod.

"I'll teach you to use a fly rod. We can take the flats boat out and fish the shallows. That's a lot of fun," Harrellson said.

"How many boats do you have?"

"Four," he answered sheepishly. One of reels began to sing as the line played out, when Jolene moved to pick it up, another one started. Soon there were six fish on the deck. Two of the double rigged lines had yielded a second fish. Two Snappers were too small to keep and Harrellson threw them back. Hadfield landed a nice Triggerfish. As soon as the lines were back in the water, reels begin to whine. In minutes there were two more Grouper on ice. Jolene was baiting the hooks and Harrellson pulled in a two-foot-long Amberjack.

"We're are going to have a great lunch," he said holding up the gaffed Amberjack. "Don't put those lines in right now. There is a charter boat coming this way. We'll move to another place and let the charter skipper have this one. He takes people fishing for a living. He needs this spot more than we do."

Jolene looked in the direction Harrellson was looking when he mentioned the charter boat. She could make out the approaching craft. She had no idea how he knew it were charter boat. But his moving off a good hole to allow the charter boat access was commendable.

Harrellson anchored once more after running west for an hour. This time only two lines went in the water. Jolene watched these while he set about cleaning and filleting the Amberjack. This spot in the Gulf of Mexico wasn't yielding fish like their previous location. Jolene only reeled in one Snapper by the time Harrellson lit the gas grill. She walked back to the grill and watched as he swabbed the Amberjack fillets with a secret concoction from an old family recipe. He was about to place the fillets on the grill when one of the reels started running. Jolene grabbed the rod and it was almost jerked from her hands. She lost her balance and fell across the stern. Hadfield managed to get her knees on the deck and her thighs against the transom rail. Whatever was on the hook almost yanked her overboard.

The rod was bent to almost ninety degrees. "Let 'em run. Don't try to reel him in right now. The line won't break." Harrellson said.

He effortlessly lifted her into a fighting chair. She braced her feet against the stern. He buckled the chair's seat belt across her lap without copping a feel. He adjusted the drag on the reel as she held the rod tightly.

"Put the rod butt in the chair socket it will be easier to handle."

She was able to relax her arm muscles some and watch the line.

"Whatever the hell it is it almost jerked me overboard! What have I caught?"

"We'll know when it surfaces. It could be a shark." Harrellson said, smiling. "Thanks for not letting go of the rod."

"Thanks for not letting me fall overboard."

She fought the fish and begin to reel it in to the boat. The massive vertebrate broke the surface and dove back into the gulf.

"Jew fish, at least a hundred and fifty pounds!" Harrellson exclaimed.

"What is a Jew fish?"

"An oversize Grouper. It looks like you have a good one too. Unfortunately it is a protected species. We'll take a picture of it and throw it back." He said as he picked up the gaff hook. Fifteen minutes later the monster was on the deck. Jolene was amazed at Harrellson's strength. He handled the fish with the same ease she used to pick up her briefcase. He hooked the fish onto the scales and she screamed, "Yes!" When he announced the fish weighed one hundred and ninety seven pounds.

It was twilight when Harrellson conned the Hatteras into the boathouse. Jolene jumped onto the dock and secured the bowline around a cleat. He shut down the boat's diesels. Jolene handled the lines. He smiled handing her, her tote bag. "You're good crew."

"I've enjoyed this, Tucker. Thank you for asking."

"You are welcome."

The lack of sleep the night before was beginning to show. They rode in silence back to her house. She was glad it was dark and he could not see much of the place. She thought it a rather ratty comparison where she'd been. At the door she squeezed his hand firmly.

"Thanks again. And let me tell you one more time, lunch was great."

"I do better in the house kitchen. That was just something easy to fix on the boat," he said.

"Good night Tucker."

The alarm sounded a few minutes after Hadfield awaked. She rolled over and turned it off, glad she remembered to set it in the first place. Jolene headed for the shower. She slept most of Sunday and Friday night was a distant memory. Saturday was a different story. Despite the sun block, she suffered mild sun burn on her face and arms.

At seven thirty a.m. Hadfield was not surprised to see Lt. Busby in the hall on the way to her office. The events of Friday night flashed into her mind. She did not like Busby's expression when he stepped in front of her.

"Hadfield I need all your reports and case files in my office before nine o'clock."His tone caused her paranoia gauge to peg giving her a sense of foreboding. "Yes sir."

She drew a deep breath as she walked into her small office. Something was up. And she wasn't sure she wanted to find out.

Thirty minutes later she was in Busby's office. He took her paperwork without comment.

"Sergeant Hadfield, you are as of this moment relieved of duty pending investigation into your misconduct this past Friday night. Specifically you gave orders you had no authority to give. You may remove any personal effects from your desk. Leave your cell phone on your desk. Griffin will carry you home. We will notify you when to report for a personnel hearing. Turn your badge and city car keys now."

Busby hadn't so much as looked up from his desk during this proclamation. Jolene threw her car keys causing him to look up. Her badge hit him between the eyes.

"THAT IS THE MOST CHICKEN SHIT FUCKING THING I HAVE EVER HEARD OF!" she screamed as she turned on her heel slamming the door of his office behind her.

CHAPTER NINE

JOLENE remained quiet during the ride home. She was hurt, yet she knew talking wasn't a good idea. Web Griffin's offer of 'let me know if I can help' was a gesture. Anything she said would be reported to Busby. Griffin likely had a tape recorder secreted in his jacket pocket. She broke down losing composure talking to her father. He told her to call a lawyer and offered to pay the bill.

Desmond Taylor called and offered his help. She didn't know how soon she would need it. Hadfield answered her door and found a two Biloxi cops standing on her porch and four more in the yard. They were slugs and thugs from DePiano's SWAT team.

"Jolene Hadfield!" An overweight red faced cop with bad teeth announced. "We have a warrant for your arrest!"

Before she could reply Jolene was grabbed and thrown to the ground. Her arms were wrenched behind her and she was cuffed. The two cops searched her for weapons. They groped every part of her body. One with really bad breath hissed in her ear as he squeezed his hand between her legs. "Complaining won't do you any good bitch."

The other four cops strolled into her house.

The piece of steel glowed red. Burns hammered it against the anvil. The phone rang. He quenched the steel removed his heavy gloves and picked up the phone. The caller ID showed a Mississippi area code.

"Burns." He answered.

"Mr. Burns, this is Desmond Taylor we met last Friday. Reverend Cleckler gave me your number. He said I should call you ASAP."

"What's going on Desmond?"

"They relieved Sergeant Hadfield of duty this morning and sent her home pending disciplinary action. They booked her into the jail about fifteen minutes ago."

"What the hell for!"

"She's charge with misdemeanor assault. They holding her on a two thousand dollar cash bond only. Captain Thigman is on vacation. I've called him and left a message. I left messages for Lieutenant Smith and Sergeant Hildibrand too."

"Good work Desmond. Now you stay out of the line of fire. Don't give them any excuse to come after you. Call me as soon as you learn anything else."

Burns hung up the phone. He took a deep breath and dialed another number. After telling B.J. Hassinger's secretary the problem he waited. He turned off the gas forge inspected all the running CNC machines and turned Major out in the paddock. He was growing more frustrated by the minute. Burns was sitting at the desk in his office when the phone rang.

"Andy this doesn't sound good." Hassinger said. "Hadfield was picked up on an assault warrant and the bail is excessive. They won't furnish incident and arrest reports without subpoenas. The bank called and your wire transfer for the bond and retainer came through. One of my associates is at the jail posting the bond. He has subpoenas for the reports. We'll will keep you anonymous like requested. What are you going to do if she insists?"

"She can insist all she wants. Let me know when you have her out. I've got another call coming in. Gotta go." Burns clicked the phone and answered the waiting call. Desmond Taylor was on the line.

"Bad news Mister Burns. Those assholes searched her house and it is totally trashed. Her truck is trashed and so is her boat. The truck and boat trailer tires have been slashed. Captain Thigman is here already Lieutenant Smith and Sergeant Hildibrand are on the way. I've taken off the rest of the day to help. Do you know when Sergeant Hadfield will make bail? They won't let us post it."

"The lawyer is getting her out now. Make sure somebody gets pictures of what that place looks like. Thanks for your help and keep me posted."

"One more thing Mister Burns. I called Reverend Cleckler. He is on the way with a group to help clean up this mess."

"That was a great idea Desmond thank you."

Burns called Hassinger back.

"The police searched her house her truck and her boat and they trashed everything. There's people she knows there cleaning up and more on the way. Make sure your man breaks the news gently."

"His name is Wayne Brown, he will call you when he gets her home. Andy I'm sorry this has happened. Something is really bad here. We'll get to the bottom of it."

Burns hung up. Five minutes later he dialed Jack Jackson's number at the FBI. The agent answered the fourth ring.

"Jack, Andy Burns, something the other day gave me the impression you guys have an interest in the Biloxi Police Department. If that is correct, something is going on you might be interested in."

"What is happening?"

"They arrested Jolene Hadfield this morning."

"Hold one I'm going to get H.H. on the line with us."

When he finished telling the particulars he heard silence. Burns wondered if the agents were still on the phone when Jackson spoke.

"We need talk to Hadfield. H.H. is calling the Gulfport Field Office. We may have a Section 242 Civil Rights Violation. Hadfield doesn't strike me as someone who complains their rights have been violated. I don't know if she will follow though."

"I agree. Maybe this experience will change her mind. Don't tell her I sent you."

"Sure thing and Helium Head wants to know if her rifle is ready and will you go her bail if she needs it?"

Burns laughed, it felt good for the moment. His cell phone began to vibrate. Mark Hildibrand's name was on the caller ID. Andy cleared off the FBI call and answered the cell.

"What's up Mark?" He answered.

"Andy, me and Don are Jolene's house. I can't believe how bad those assholes trashed it. Don has video and still pictures of everything. I hate for Jo to have to see this. My wife is on the way to help and Desmond Taylor is here so is Lyle Thigman. And he is pissed beyond mad. Jolene's daddy is on the way. Preacher Cleckler just showed up with a van full of women to help. Is she out yet?"

"Her lawyer should be bringing her home soon. Mark don't spare any expense cleaning up. I will pay for it. Just keep it between us."

"Sorry Andy you gonna have to get in line to do that." Hildibrand said as he disconnected.

Burns sat drumming his fingers on the desktop. The phone rang, he grabbed it.

"Mister Burns this Wayne Brown with Mr. Hassinger's office. I'm calling..."

"How's Hadfield?"

"She is devastated. The arrest was bad enough. They body slammed her on the ground. And male officers searched her an inappropriate manner. Her house won't hold all the people who turned out to help. Sergeant Hadfield's father is here and he is madder than a wet hen and so is his buddy Lyle Thigman. I'm trying not to hear what they are plotting."

"What are the circumstances with this so called assault?"

"She was relieved of duty pending a personnel action to demote or terminate by Lieutenant Alan R. Busby, world class asshole if you pardon me. When he asked for her badge Jolene bounced it off his head."

"What are the charges relieving her from duty?"

"She allegedly gave unauthorized orders during the project incident last Friday night."

"So what's her situation now Mister Brown."

"My name is Wayne, Mister Burns. We would like to get her out of here so she can recover. I expect all hell to break loose in the PD tomorrow. That is another reason she needs to be gone. My uncle has a place in Mentone AL with a fishing lake and an airstrip that he leases by the week. It is available for the next month and he will give us a deal. It is almost in Tennessee so it is far enough away. Only problem is who pays for it. The cost might be recouped from litigation."

"Book it for the entire month. I will pay for it. Tell Hassinger to run the billing through your office. My business lawyer and accountant will contact him and arrange the details. Get him all the details on that place. Get Hadfield out there ASAP."

Miles Cromwell, Burns lawyer and accountant was his usual wealth of information. "Andy I know the place in Mentone. I've spent a week there. Drop dead beautiful log house and several guest cabins. Paved runway with remote activated lights. Navigation beacon. Charlie went up there from time to time. He made several offers to buy it. I got a polite query last week from the firm handling it. It is a bankruptcy asset and needs to sell. I think it is worth looking into. It would be a good investment for you."

"Look into it, my cell phones buzzing gotta go."

"Andy, Mark, we've called the Sheriff's Department to make reports on the damage to Jo's house. Her Glock is missing. Those assholes probably stole it. One of them left his business card stuck on the door. He wrote on back, 'search incident to arrest enjoy.' They know they can't do that shit. The FBI is here and so is the Sheriff's Department watch commander. She called the District Attorney. He is sending somebody out here. This bullshit has pissed some people off. They're not going to get away with this. Captain Thigman is past ballistic. Jolene's dad wants to talk with you."

Before Andy could say anything a different voice was on the phone. "Mister Burns my name is Joe Hadfield, I understand you know my daughter."

"Yes sir, how can I help?"

"I'm going to get her truck and boat fixed tomorrow. These boys here tell me you've got a real secure place. Would you mind if I bought her truck and boat over there for safe keeping?"

"A couple of things. First call me Andy. Second you take care of Jolene. I'll have somebody come get the truck and the boat this evening. Don't worry about the repairs. When she's ready for it y'all come get it and plan on fishing."

"Andy I appreciate that. You call me Joe."

Bob Rabun's cell phone rang he answered. "Hi Andy good to hear from you. What can I do for you?"

"Sergeant Hadfield has a problem."

Twenty minutes later two roll back tow trucks and a Baldwin County Sheriffs van left for Biloxi Mississippi.

The day was not over by a longshot. Andrew Burns answered his phone again. "Andy, Jack Jackson, we need some pro bono off the record help."

Bernard DePiano looked at the reports on his desk. The post it note said they were important. The two officers that arrested Hadfield were hospitalized with injuries sustained in an off duty bar fight. He stood and primped in front of a full length mirror installed in his office. Maureen Peterson in communications would know what was going on with the two cops. And his nuts were getting close to normal. At least until he turned around and saw Lyle Thigman.

"What are you doing here you gray haired old fart? You're on vacation."

Thigman kicked a chair into DePiano's crotch. When the old fart finished using his blackjack. He stepped into the hall and spied Busby. He was strolling toward his mentor's office carrying two cups Starbucks and a box of doughnuts. The lieutenant dropped his burden and turned tail running. Thigman gave up the chase when Busby ran out the door.

Two rumor monger cops quickly located doughnuts that had not rolled on the floor. While they stood munching on their find one asked. "What the hell was that all about?"

"I don't know," the other answered with his mouth full glazed nut. "But it sounds like somebody is shooting outside."

The Biloxi Chief of Police and his Deputy Chief had arrived at the weekly Rotary Club meeting. Before leaving their car a radio dispatch was broadcasted. "All units in the vicinity of the station. We have a report of a detective running through the parking lot shooting over his shoulder."

The Chief turned to his Deputy. "Harold call that drug test outfit and get them in here today. They need to test everybody working."

"I'll handle it right now Al." The Deputy Chief deployed his cell phone.

Before the Rotary meeting was over, two Biloxi units were dispatched to assist the Sheriff's Department with warrant service.

Once back from their weekly civic meeting the Chiefs found no one available for the daily staff briefing. The Chief summoned his secretary. "Margret where are DePiano and Busby?"

"The EMT's took Captain DePiano to the hospital. He fell in his office. Lieutenant Busby doesn't answer his cell phone or radio. Dispatch said the Mayor called wondering why Busby was running down the alley with his gun out. And the Sheriff is holding on line two for you."

Perplexed the Chief sat down at his desk and picked up the phone. "What can Biloxi Police Department do for our esteemed Sheriff today?"

"Al, we arrested four of your officers for burglary this morning. I need a purchase order number for the towing and impound fees on two of your patrol cars."

The Chief hung up the phone and screamed, "HAROLD!" Before falling out of his chair. The EMT's made a second run to Biloxi PD.

Jolene awoke groggy smelling fresh coffee. She remembered being taken to the hospital. She thought she had been in an airplane or was that a dream. It seemed like she'd heard Andrew Burns talking to air traffic control. The room she was in was really nice. It was very dim, heavy drapes kept out the daylight. She sat up in bed and looked around. A coffee carafe and cup were on the night stand. How did they get there?

Hadfield sat on the bedside and sipped coffee. Once she felt stable enough to walk, she venturing to the drapes and opened them. Jolene gasped at the splendor before her. The window overlooked the brow of Little River Canyon. While she was locked up she prayed wondering if God answered prayers of those who seldom prayed. Maybe the prayers were answered when she released and saw the strangers putting her house in order. As the warmth of the sun washed over her there was no doubt He had answered.

"I see you're up," Havelee Harris said as she entered the room. "The smell of fresh coffee always works for me. Come on down breakfast is ready. And it looks so good that it's probably sinful illegal and immoral to eat it. Let's go pig out." Jolene allowed the vibrant agent to lead her.

Andy Burns and Theodis Cleckler rode in the ATV back to the lake. Where Theo's boys and a deacon were watching over kids fishing. Bob Rabun and a couple of other off duty deputies had returned Hadfield's truck and boat. Both were now in pristine condition. The truck and boat trailer now carried matching wheels and tires. Burns offer of what do I owe you was met with a flat refusal.

Burns looked over at Theodis, whose head still carried bandages. "Theo I really appreciate what you and your congregation did for Sergeant Hadfield. I'm surprised really surprised after what y'all been through with Biloxi PD."

"Andy I taught you long ago what being a Christian is all about. Helping people is what we do. And I heard them lawyers whispering about Andy doing this and Andy doing that. I hope one Sgt. Hadfield knows what all you've done. She'd be a great woman for you."

Burns jabbed Theo in the ribs with his elbow. "You can walk too."

As they approached the lake Andy said two of the older kids were missing. "Those gang bangers you brought aren't on the pier. You need to find them. I've got to go unsaddle Major, he's tied to the paddock fence." Burns remembered the two sullen young men in baggy clothes giving him the evil eye. They started casing the place the minute they stepped out of Theo's van.

"Andy please don't be hard on Melvin Simpson. His parent's death caused that tragedy last week. The boy does have an association with a gang but the Lord wants me to salvage him." Theodis said emphatically.

Burns heard Major whinny loudly something was frightening him. The two dogs made a sound between a bark and howl. He snapped his fingers and said, "GO!"

The dogs leapt from the vehicle and dashed toward the barn.

Hang on Theo, Major is throwing a fit!" Theodis grasped a passenger hand hold and started praying as Andy spun the ATV around.

Melvin Simpson and his partner, Lemont Jones, were both fifteen and full fledge members of a street gang. Melvin now lived in the Cleckler household. He delivered four crack rocks to the undertaker's assistant while attending his parent's funeral. The Cleckler house was cool Melvin told Lemont, 'cause the 'stupid ole Uncle Tom nigger ain't got a clue.' And there was always church offering money to steal.

Lemont, who the cops knew as Yardman because he pretended to do yard work while serving as lookout during house burglaries, left the pier with Melvin as soon as Andy and Theo drove off. All the doors at the house and the sheds were locked. They were looking for something to steal when they found Major. Neither had ever seen a real horse before. They began throwing rocks at the gentle buckskin.

Both punks were amused at the horse's frantic actions, rearing and yanking back at the tie rope, trying to escape the fusillade of stones. Without warning two snarling dogs with teeth bared appeared.

The hoodlum's baggy clothes saved their hide. The crotch was ripped out of Melvin's trousers. Lemont lost his left pants leg while he was drawing a twenty-five caliber Raven pistol out of his pocket. It fired launching a bullet through an unlaced tennis shoes without hitting his foot. Fortunately the pistol jammed before he could try again.

Melvin tried to get his gun out and protect his manhood at the same time. Fortune smiled again. When his Lorcin . 380 slid down his pants leg and caught in the bunched up fabric around his unlaced Reeboks.

As he braked the ATV Andy knocked Melvin Simpson to ground. Burns bailed out and broke four of Lemont's fingers when he twisted the pistol out of his hand. The gangster hit the ground screaming. With the dogs standing watch. Andy searched the thugs for weapons providing a punch or two in process. After recovering Melvin's gun Andy secured both weapons in the ATV.

"Andy! Please don't be so harsh with the children! That don't know what they do." Theodis pleaded.

"Bullshit!" Burns said jogging toward Major, who was frantically pulling at the tether rope.

The horse settled down as Andy spoke softly and stroked the animal's neck. He carefully walked around him moving his hand along the horses' body looking for injury.

He closed his eyes for a moment and took a deep breath as he patted the horse's head. Major was calming down. Andy wasn't. He untied the horse and led him to the barn.

Melvin was sitting up and Lemont had quit screaming. Both remained still because the Pudelpointers growled baring teeth at any move. Theodis begged Andy to call off the dogs between prayers.

Burns went in the barn and grabbed a handful of heavy hay bale twine. He turned to Major, tightened the cinch and swung into the saddle. He shook a loop out of his lariat as he rode out of the barn. Andy called off the dogs and kicked the buckskin into a lope.

The sight of horse and rider motivated Melvin and Lemont haul ass. Theodis dropped to his knees and requested divine intervention. The gang bangers were already in high gear. The bad news honkey riding the horse was swinging a rope.

They ran side by side. Burns loped Major past them and pitched the loop over their heads. Letting the rope play out he took a couple of dallies around the saddle horn.

The loop snapped tight just below the thug's knees jerking them off the ground. They landed hard the breath knocked out of them. Andy spun the horse around on its hind legs and started for the church van. Major trotted along dragging the two punks behind him.

Burns secured both boys wrists and ankles with the hay bale twine. Then he bound their wrists and ankles together hog tying them. He opened the back doors of the church van and deposited the teenagers inside. Kicking the door closed, Burns turned a deaf ear to the hoodlum's curses and Theodis pleas and admonishments. Andy mounted Major and began coiling his lariat."

"Theodis do not bring those punks here again. Do not untie them until you leave this property."

Burns turned and loped Major away before Theo could answer.

Chapter Ten

FOR Jolene three weeks respite atop Look Out Mountain in North East Alabama was a blessing. Once she understood there was no cost involved she relaxed and enjoyed the place. A trio of women FBI agents rotated being there with her. When she learned there was more to the investigation that what she would told. Hadfield agreed to file a civil rights case against her employer. Her father assured her that her house was cleaned up and everything back in its place when he'd delivered her bass boat and truck with Lyle Thigman following in his SUV. She didn't fail to notice that Thigman was sequestered with the FBI agents for several hours. Fishing with her father helped heal the emotional wounds she's suffered. The day before he and Thigman left an impromptu fishing tournament was arranged. The lineup pitted Jolene and her old man against Lyle Thigman and Havelee Harris. The official observers were the other two FBI agents and the judge was the lodge manager.

"The Feds are gonna rig this!" Joe Hadfield yelled, the moment Jolene gunned the Ranger away from the dock.

"You got that right!" H.H. answered as she powered up a lodge boat with Thigman hanging on for dear life.

None of the fishermen paid any attention to a plane landing. And taking off again three hours later.

The lodge manger declared the tournament a tie. And house staff prepared and excellent meal including fresh bass. They were happy campers again because the pending doom of losing jobs was over. The property sold and the new owner retained the full staff.

Before she returned to the Gulf Coast, Jolene spoke with her lawyers several times. They were always encouraging even though she found the news bleak.

Hassinger and Brown were on the line with Hadfield.

"Jolene we have stipulated appeals on the personnel action and on the criminal charges. These will be heard in county court. We are on Judge Richmond's docket next month. Unfortunately you will be without a pay check for some period of time. The police department demoted and terminated you."

Hadfield choked up tears beginning to flow. "I can't afford that.

"Don't worry Jolene you have more help that you know of. We will prevail in court." Hassinger said. "Normally I won't make a prediction like that. But we have an excellent case and a fair judge. We are not going to gamble on jury. We will let the judge make the decision."

"All of that is easy for you to say. It's my livelihood and future on the line."

"Believe me we know that. I'm going to hang up, Wayne has some information for you. You take care."

"Jolene, I hate to give you more bad news. You were found guilty of assaulting Busby in Biloxi City Court. I don't believe Judge Richmond will up hold that. The four officers arrested for burglary and damaging your house were indicted by the grand jury. That is good news. Unfortunately the police department refused to suspend them from duty. They are still on the street working as cops. We have lodged complaints, so has the DA and the Sheriff. But the Mayor and the Chief won't budge.

"Your Glock turned up in a Pass Christian Pawn Shop. One of the burglars sold it to them. The Sheriff's Department has it. You can pick it up from them. Also we are filed a damage claim against the city for your house. That is on Richmond's docket as well. And we've got Reverend Cleckler on that docket the same day. We have some powerful evidence on Cleckler's behalf that will bode well for you."

"What is that?" Jolene asked.

"It would be better if you didn't know until court."

"It must be good."

"It will be a real Perry Mason moment in the courtroom. One more thing before we hang up. The two cops that arrested and searched you. They were disabled in an off duty fight. It will be a long time before they return to work, if ever.

"I know this call hasn't been all good news. Hang in there Jolene. We are going to win."

Hadfield thanked Brown and hung up the phone. She walked out of the lodge house and took refuge in a gazebo on the canyon rim. It was her favorite spot. She cried.

Biloxi City Attorney Bradford R. Palmer III entered Judge Richmond's courtroom late. He arrived at his table in time to remain standing when Adonis Purcell commanded, "All Rise. This court is now in session. The Honorable Judge Emory C. Richmond presiding."

Richmond ran a candid and somewhat unorthodox courtroom. He was known for his fairness toward defendants, abuse of prosecutors, and never having a decision overturned by a higher court.

It was Palmer's job as city attorney to look out for the best interest of Biloxi. Not to fill in for the city prosecutor who was out of town on a family emergency. Or handle personnel appeals for a vacationing associate. Thirty minutes ago his secretary handed him the files and the courtroom number. Bradford R. Palmer III had never had the privilege of practicing law in Judge Richmond's domain.

Hadfield and Theodis Cleckler sat the defense table with Lawyer's Hassinger and Brown. Joe Hadfield was seated across the bar behind his daughter. Lyle Thigman sat next to him. Don Smith Mark Hildibrand and Desmond Taylor sat behind them. Bradford Palmer didn't know the three people sitting on his side of the courtroom behind the bar. One was the DA's chief investigator. The other two were FBI agents. Adonis Purcell and his assistant bailiff, the court reporter, and the court clerk were the only other people in the room. A large TV with a video player sat near Richmond's bench.

Seated behind his Judge Richmond attired in his black robe opened the proceeding. His bass voice did not need a public address system. In his college days the Judge played left guard at Louisiana Tech University more commonly known as Grambling. His size matched his voice.

"We have four cases before this court the City of Biloxi. Two are criminal matters, two are civil matters. Defendant's attorneys have filed several motions in these cases. I will grant the defense motion to have these four cases heard together. After studying all of the defense motions and affidavits I find them troubling. Sergeant Hadfield has testified in this court numerous times. I know her to be a diligent and professional police officer. In his motion for dismissal and reinstatement Mr. Brown states Sergeant Hadfield was acting in the best interest of the police department and citizens of Biloxi Mississippi when she gave the orders that led to her demotion and termination documents state she was not authorized to give. I would expect Sergeant Hadfield to always act in the best interest of all concerned.

"Furthermore, Mr. Brown states the charges are unwarranted and a product of gender discrimination. That statement greatly disturbs me. Mr. Brown states the police department has refused to comply with repeated subpoenas for copies of radio and telephone communications tapes that will prove the claims against Sergeant Hadfield are without merit. And he has provided documentation that said subpoenas have been delivered and signed for five different instances. This makes me inclined to grant all motions in this case. MR. PALMER! Do you have anything to say about this? Do you have the subpoenaed material in court at this time?"

Judge Richmond paused and glared at Bradford Palmer who was busy shuffling papers on his table. Red faced Busby hesitated looked at his papers and answered.

"No Your Honor uh I think Captain DePiano has that information."

"Mr. Palmer you immediately summons Captain DePiano and said information to this court forthwith. In the matter of a misdemeanor assault charge against Sergeant Hadfield, a Lieutenant Alan Busby is subpoenaed today. Is Lieutenant Busby in this court?" The judged looked around the courtroom.

"Mr. Palmer you summons Lieutenant Busby to this court. And you also summons the personnel director for the City of Biloxi as well. I expect all these people and the material under subpoena to be in this courtroom in one hour. If they are not here at that time I will dismiss all the cases with prejudice. Get your calls made and get back in here. I believe we have some video evidence to review. Mr. Purcell please prepare the TV."

"Judge why the personnel director?"

"Mr. Palmer seeing the indifference to subpoenas displayed by the Biloxi Police Department. I want to make sure any order I give reinstating Sergeant Hadfield is understood and obeyed. If you are not out that door in five seconds and on that cell phone. I'll dismiss everything. Five..."

Palmer knocked over two chairs as he bolted for the door. Brown squeezed Hadfield's arm and whispered. "I think the judge is on our side."

Jolene smiled.

The hour dead line had passed when Judge Richmond finished viewing the tape and listening to the recorded voice of DePiano from the confrontation at SWAT headquarters. Purcell gave the judge a note indicating the arrival of DePiano and Busby. They were sequestered in the witness room.

"Your Honor I object to that video. It is clearly marked police department property."

"Overruled Mr. Palmer. If you read your subpoena it states all video and recorded tapes of the night in question. The tape is covered by that subpoena. And not only do I find it disturbing I am angry over what I have seen and heard. This court is in recess for thirty minutes. Mister Purcell please bring the TV and the tape into my chambers."

Seated at his desk Judge Richmond made a phone call. When the other party answered Richmond got to the point. "Amos I hate to intrude on your morning. I have something in my office that needs your immediate attention."

Five minutes later the District Attorney entered Richmond's chambers.

Court reconvened at the precise time. Judge Richmond looked over the courtroom. "Reverend Cleckler, will you please rise. In the appeal of the criminal charges brought against you and subsequent finding of guilt by the city court of Biloxi. I do not see any evidence to support these charges and the lower courts finding. I find you not guilty on all counts. Furthermore I order all record of your arrest be expunged. Mr. Palmer before this court closes today you will bring the original reports of regarding this incident and arrest. And you will bring all mugs shots their negatives or original file and finger prints to this court. I will have an arrest order prepared for you if those documents are not within the stated time. Do you understand me Mr. Palmer?"

"Yes Your Honor," Palmer replied meekly.

"Reverend Cleckler you are free to go."

"Thank you Your Honor. If I may, I would like to stay on in support of Sergeant Hadfield."

"You may. Sergeant Hadfield take the witness stand please."

After he swore Jolene in Richmond addressed the lawyers. "I will ask the questions. Sergeant Hadfield will you tell me in your own words what you did on the night in question?"

Jolene told her story including her visit to the scene and what she witnessed in the projects. She concluded with the events in Busby's office admitting throwing her badge at him.

"Sergeant Hadfield does the video we watched accurately portray the events of that evening including the radio traffic we heard?"

"Yes Sir it is accurate on both video and radio."

"Is there any written order or directive including policy and procedure manuals in the Biloxi Police Department stating that you as a police sergeant cannot give orders to a police department civilian employee?"

"No Your Honor."

"Thank You Sergeant Hadfield you may step down. Counsels may not recall this witness. The court calls Bernard DePiano."

DePiano strolled into the court room giving Hadfield and Cleckler a nasty look. He turned his head when he spotted Thigman.

"Are you Bernard DePiano," Richmond asked.

"I'm Captain DePiano."

"Raise your right hand."

After being sworn DePiano started toward the witness box. He didn't see the Judge motion his bailiffs forward.

"That won't be necessary Mister DePiano you won't be here long. Where are the tapes subpoena for your agency?"

"They aren't necessary for this?"

"Is that so? Please tell the court why?"

"The only persons allowed to give orders to my dispatchers are me, the communications supervisor, and the lead workers on each shift."

"Really, and is that published directive to all members of the department?"

"No, I'm a captain I don't have to publish or whatever."

"And did you have occasion to verbally abuse Sergeant Hadfield at SWAT headquarters?"

"She's never been in SWAT headquarters while I was there."

"And she was not present at SWAT Headquarters when you threatened Lieutenant Don Smith and Sergeant Mark Hildibrand?"

DePiano shot a mean look at Smith and Hildibrand. This was not lost on Judge Richmond.

"I remind you that you are under oath Mister DePiano."

"That's Captain DePiano and she wasn't there."

"Very well. Remain standing there while render my decision. Sergeant Hadfield please rise."

DePiano glared at the judge and then at Hadfield, he had no ideal Adonis Purcell and an equally large colleague were behind him.

"Sergeant Hadfield it is the ruling of this court that you be reinstated to the Biloxi Police Department at the rank of Sergeant. And any personnel action except promotion that involves you will remain under the jurisdiction of this court until you or I retire. Furthermore I order you to be paid all lost wages and compensation for benefits lost during this time. Such payment will be made by close of business this date and an accounting of such payments will be delivered to this court by the end of this day. The City of Biloxi is ordered pay all Sergeant Hadfield's legal fees, medical fees and any other expenses incurred by this debacle. Such expenses will be paid within thirty days from this date. A copy of the check and receipts paid with be delivered to this court on that date. Failure to do so will result in the issuance of contempt warrants for you Mr. Palmer, the gentleman beside you, the Chief of Police and the Mayor of Biloxi. Do you understand this ruling?"

"Yes Sir Your Honor, May Mr. Bryant leave the court now to make sure this gets done."

"Get on your way Mr. Bryant."

DePiano muttered, "Shit." And the Judge heard it.

"Mr. Purcell disarm Captain DePiano, take him to county jail on charges of contempt of court. He is to be placed in the general population."

"WHAT THE HELL..." DePiano yelled and then gasped when a massive fist struck him in the kidney. One of the places worked on with a blackjack a few weeks before. The Big Dago sank to his knees. The bailiffs lifted him up and carried him out of the court. Adonis played some catch up ball during the elevator ride to the jail. They had to drag DePiano to the booking desk.

Judge Richmond looked around the court satisfied. "We have two other matters involving Sergeant Hadfield. They will be disposed of before lunch. The Court calls Alan Busby."

Once sworn Lt. Busby sat on the witness stand. He held a manila envelope with red evidence tape around it.

"What have you got in that envelope Mister Busby?" Richmond asked.

"Uh it's what I was assaulted with."

"Open it up, hand it to me. I want to see it."

Busby torn open the envelope and removed the badge. He handed it to Judge Richmond.

"Let the record reflect the witness handed me a gold sergeant's badge from the Biloxi Police Department. It is attached to a leather holder with what appears to be a belt clip on the back of that holder. Mister Busby would you tell the court how you came to be assaulted by this badge."

"Hadfield threw it at me."

"Where did this badge hit you?"

"Between my eyes."

"Terrible a badge between the eyes. Do you have any receipts for plastic surgery or medical bills incurred as a result of this assault?"

"No Your Honor."

"Well what did you do after you were assaulted by this flying badge?"

"I went to the bathroom and looked in the mirror."

"Did you see any injury?"

"It left a mark."

"The flying badge that assaulted you left a mark?"

"Yes Sir."

"Did Sergeant Hadfield make any threats when she tossed this badge at you?"

"She made an obscene comment."

"You are under oath Mister Busby what did she say?"

"Uh this is the most fucking chicken shit thing I've ever heard of."

"And this occurred immediately after you relieved her from duty pending disciplinary action?"

"Yes Sir."

"And you swore a warrant out for her that same morning?"

"Yes Sir?'

"And ordered a two thousand dollar cash bond?"

"Yes Sir."

"In hindsight wouldn't you think that was excessive and perhaps illegal?"

"No Sir."

"One more question Mister Busby?"

"Sir I'm a police lieutenant."

"Yes and I'm a Judge. I am entitled to the courtesy extended me. Police officers may be required to refer to you by your rank. I am not. I do address officers by their rank. But for me it is a matter of respect. Do you understand that Mister Busby?"

"Yes Your Honor." Busby's cheeks began to color.

"Did you a few days before this incident refer to Sergeant Hadfield in degrading manner in a meeting attended by other detectives?"

"I don't recall?"

"Very well. I recall an affidavit that says you did, no further questions. Counsels may not recall this witness. Witness will remain seated while I render my decision. Sergeant Hadfield approach the bench please."

Jolene walked forward and stood in front of Judge Richmond. Busby stared hatefully.

"Sergeant Hadfield I believe this is yours." The Judge handed the badge back to her.

"I find you not guilty of misdemeanor assault. The City Court of Biloxi will return the two thousand dollar cash bond by close of business this afternoon. Or contempt charges will apply. Do you understand me Mr. Palmer?"

"Yes Your Honor."

"You may leave Mister Busby."

"Not guilty?" Busby questioned.

"If she had drawn her weapon and shot you under those circumstances. I would have found her not guilty. You have five seconds to get out of my court room or go to jail for contempt. Five!"

Busby almost fell getting off the stand. Regaining his balance he ran down the center aisle. Joe Hadfield tripped him.

"There is one more matter before this court. Sergeant Hadfield has filed for compensation for damages to her home her vehicle and her boat. This damage was done by members of the Biloxi Police Department during a warrantless search that has been ruled illegal. I will assign Sergeant Hadfield damages in the amount of $10,000.00."

"YOUR HONOR!" Bradford Palmer jumped out of his chair.

"The damage award is $15,000.00. You want to go for twenty Mr. Palmer?"

The City Attorney sat back in his chair shaking his head.

"This claim will be paid in thirty days. Or the same contempt charges as before will be applied. I caution you Mr. Palmer not to allow the City of Biloxi to ignore any of these rulings.

"The docket is now clear for this morning. This court is adjourned."

"Your Honor?"

"What now Mr. Palmer?"

"How long will Captain DePiano remain in jail?"

"Until he farts in a different key."

CHAPTER ELEVEN

IN the weeks following her hearing Jolene worked nonstop averaging one off day every couple of weeks. Busby gave her every assignment he could and all the on-call duty. Desmond Taylor received similar details. The other detectives were assigned to internal integrity investigations. Other words, a witch-hunt to find who turned over the videotape to Cleckler's lawyer. Peterson was grilled and re-grilled. They proved he was the dumb ass that left the videotape running. Busby's order to polygraph test the entire patrol division was not the straw that broke the camel's back. It was Hadfield's time sheets he'd sand bagged in his desk drawer and the return of Lyle Thigman. The Captain promptly approved the payment of over forty hours overtime for Jolene. The rumor mill reported the Chief threw a running fit.

DePiano was released from jail on contempt charges after his wife secured a second mortgage on their house. That was needed to post bond on the Felony Assault Charge against Rev. Theodis Cleckler. The Big Dago had spent over thirty days in the county slammer. Two officers were ordered to bring him to the Chief's office when he walked out of the lockup.

Unkempt in wrinkled clothes that were stored in a paper bag while he was jailed. DePiano stood beside Busby in front of the Chief's desk.

"Captain DePiano you are relieved from duty pending the outcome of the felony charges against you. This is an indefinite suspension without pay. If you are found not guilty you will be reinstated but you will not be granted back pay. The debacle you and Busby arranged has cost the City over $60,000.00 in legal fees, medical fees, rehab facility fees and back pay. If you have a badge in that mess you're wearing leave it and get out of here."

"Lieutenant Busby you are suspended without pay for ninety days for your handling of the Hadfield matter. You can take a voluntary demotion to patrol officer and avoid another suspension on your record. That will allow you a fresh start. You come back in ninety days as lieutenant, you won't have any chances left. One misstep and you will be fired. I suggest you take the demotion."

"Uh uh I can't do that. I will take the suspension."

"You and the Dago have cost the department a lot of money. I should fire you now. The FBI is crawling all over us with Section 242 investigation. The deputy chief put his retirement papers in this morning. I'm going to have pay Lyle Thigman for sixty days unused leave time. I can't let him take off now. Turn in your badge and get out of here."

Jolene wondered what now after an immediate summons to Lyle Thigman's office. Lt. Don Smith was in the office when she got there. Thigman motioned her to the chair beside Smith.

"There have been some major changes this morning." Thigman said. "I will not be taking sixty vacation days as planned. I am now Acting Deputy Chief. Harold turned in his papers this morning and packed up his office. DePiano has been relieved of duty and Busby received a ninety day suspension.

"Don you are now Acting Captain in DePiano's slot. This carries an extra five percent on you pay check. You are on the Captain's promotion list. It is unlikely DePiano will be back. So expect to be a provisional captain when I finally retire.

"Jolene you are now Acting Lieutenant over the detective unit. You'll get the five percent as well. You will also have division responsibilities as well. The next captain's exam is in thirty days. Stay out of the field and out of that Ranger boat. Use the time to study. This will be your office. Don gets the one next door."

Thigman pulled two badges from his desk drawer. "Lieutenant Hadfield, this one is yours. Captain Don Smith this one belongs you. Now go back to work."

The rank and file folks knew the acting designation was as good as the real thing. All were wary—new promotions could change people. A sign of change was forthcoming. Don Smith relieved the four cop burglars from duty. Nobody missed them. The third shift guys were happy. Don Hildibrand was promoted to Acting Lieutenant. And the real SWAT team was back on the job. Hadfield put the on call rotation back in force. It was Desmond Taylor's turn. She did add that if he got anything major, to call her out with him.

Another casino CEO was reported missing.

The patrol officers taking the missing person report called Lt. Hadfield and Desmond Taylor to the spacious home of Robert H. Austin, Chief Executive Officer Silver Beach Casino. Austin was four hours late. His distraught wife called the police. And begged them to start searching for her husband, fearing he might suffer the same faith as Nigel Hoffman. Jolene thought time might work in their favor this time. Hoffman had been unaccounted for thirty-six hours before police were notified. His family was out of town, and his staff thought he had joined them.

It was midnight when Jolene and Desmond left the Silver Beach security office. The head of security told them Austin was a straight arrow and a dedicated family man who didn't drink. The only lead was a security camera tape covering the parking lot. It showed a valet getting into Austin's company car, a dark blue Lincoln, and delivering it to the private executive entrance. A young black male in baggy clothes was seen near the car before the valet reached it. The tape was not clear enough to identify the subject. The security chief said he would send out for enhancement. She questioned the valet driver. He said he'd noticed a gangster looking kid near the lot. He doubted could identify him.

The dispatcher called Jolene's radio number, she was asked told to call the office immediately.

"Sarge, uh excuse me Lieutenant Hadfield," the radio room supervisor said. "The highway patrol found Austin's Lincoln near Hattiesburg with a body in it. They're working it as a homicide. Its five miles south of Hattiesburg on the north bound side of I-59."

"Thanks David. Taylor is with me. We'll be on the way."

"I'll advise the highway patrol."

Traffic on I-59 slowed to a crawl. Impatient drivers moved from one lane to another hoping to get ahead. An array emergency lights flashed in the distance. The right lane was blocked by police cars.

Hadfield wanted to get to the scene as much as other drivers wanted around it. She pulled to the right shoulder, activated the emergency lights and proceeded to pass the stalled traffic. Desmond grinned and said. "Lieutenant Jolene you just pissed some folks off."

"This is a crime scene. No one is admitted to this area!"

Jolene saw the imposing figure of a large uniformed state trooper backlit lit by flares and emergency lights.

"Lieutenant Hadfield, Detective Taylor Biloxi Police Department."

Jolene saw another uniformed officer approaching.

"Stand easy Trooper I'll take care of this." The new comer said as he stepped outside the flares and orange cones.

"I'm Lieutenant Vereen, Mississippi Highway Patrol. Your names again please?"

"Lieutenant Jolene Hadfield and Detective Taylor Biloxi PD. I understand you have a crime scene involving one of my missing persons."

Vereen looked at her briefly his eyes stopping on the gold badge clipped to her belt. "It's the car you're looking for Lieutenant. The deceased matches the description of your missing person. The crime scene technicians are still processing the scene. The body hasn't been removed. They will move it when they are good and ready."

"Any chance we can take a look?" Jolene asked.

"Lieutenant Hadfield for some reason the head of the Forensic Science Department responded to this call. Doctor Higgins is in charge of the scene. Nobody gets in there without his approval. Give me a good reason."

"Lieutenant Vereen, Austin is the second casino CEO from Biloxi to turn up missing in the past few months. The first one was found dead in a lake in Alabama. If that's Austin in the car we may have the second victim of a serial killer."

"That is a good reason Lieutenant Vereen." A rumpled looking man in civilian clothes said. Jolene hadn't noticed him arrive.

"I'm David Higgins. What were the circumstances involving your other case detective?"

Higgins looked like a cross between an absentminded professor and the TV detective Colombo. Jolene related the details of the Hoffman murder. Higgins motioned them to follow him. It was at least a two hundred yard walk amid police cars flashing emergency lights and traffic cones. They reached an area within the blockade of cruisers that was roped off with crime scene tape. A technician stood by with a clip board. Higgins told her to log Hadfield and Taylor into the scene. With their names noted the tech reached into a nearby box and gave each of them disposable gloves and booties to cover their shoes. Higgins donned the same items. They followed him to the Lincoln. He turned on a flashlight illuminating the grotesque scene inside the car.

Austin's body sat up right behind the wheel. His shoulder harness and seat belt fastened and his hands rested in his lap. The pupils of Austin's eyes were fixed glazed in death. Dried blood that had flowed from his gaping mouth down his chin over the handle of a knife protruding from his throat staining his white shirt and neatly knotted tie. The odor of released bowels reeked from the Lincoln's interior.

Desmond Taylor gagged and stepped away.

Higgins asked. "Does that appear to be the same type of knife Lieutenant Hadfield?"

"Yes, "Jolene sighed, afraid that it was identical to the Hoffman knife.

"I think the blade is stuck clean through Mr. Austin and into the seat back. It would take a very strong person to inflict a wound like that." Higgins said. "If that knife is made by your Reverend Cleckler, we have a very interesting case."

Jolene examined the car and the scene for another twenty minutes under Higgins' watchful eyes. Taylor followed but avoid looking into the car.

"Doctor Higgins, thank you for letting us have a look. Please fax me a picture of that knife when you get it out. I will send your office copies of everything we have on the Hoffman homicide."

She handed him a business card. Higgins promised copies of everything they found. He escorted her out of the crime scene. The woman scribe duly noted the time. Jolene stayed busy with paperwork the next morning, amazed at what Busby left unattended and what Thigman dealt with. She accepted a lunch date with Tucker Lee Harrellson and was now afraid she was going to have to cut it short. David Higgins called. The knife removed from Austin was an exact match to the Bowie knife taken out of Nigel Hoffman's corpse. The knife yielded a partial fingerprint. There was not enough points to compare for a positive identification. Shoe prints from a sneaker and what appeared to be hiking boots were found, as well as some tire tracks. State investigators were planning to interview Rev. Cleckler first thing after lunch and they invited Jolene to sit in. One knife was a coincidence they thought and two knives were considered probable cause for a search warrant of the Cleckler residence and his shop. She told them the results of her investigation of Cleckler and the results. She called the district attorney's office and ran the scenario by them for advice. The answer was not without a lot more probable cause. And not at all because Judge Richmond was signing off on search warrants this month. Jolene called Tucker Harrellson back and asked him if he could meet earlier for lunch.

Burns watched Havelee Harris gallop Major down the tree line. He called the FBI office the day before and said the rifle was ready. Surprisingly she'd showed up alone, dressed in worn jeans and old shirt. H.H. asked if she could ride and even brought her own saddle. A barrel racing rig much lighter than his A-fork Wade. He'd told her to ride all she wanted. He knew Major was in good hands with the lithe FBI agent.

"Now I smell like horse sweat and my sweat that was fun!" H.H. said walking into the shop. "I'm going to need some gun oil or a shower. The gun oil first please."

Andy looked up from his bench and smiled. "Apparently you had a good time."

"Yes Major is an awesome horse! My old barrel horse could out run him. But he's fast."

"You ride him well."

"I'm from an Oklahoma. I grew up on ranch riding horses before I could walk and shooting as soon as I could hold a gun."

"And you told them that when you got to the FBI academy."

"No," she grinned. "I let them find out the hard way. Now where's my rifle?"

"It's in the black case by the door. Take it out to the bench and look it over. There are fresh targets up at one and two hundred yards. It is a half-minute rifle. When you're through slobbering over it. Adjust it to suit you. Then come get some ammo."

She stuck her tongue out at him like a petulant child and hauled the heavy black case outside. Burns listened for her to pop the latches on the case. A second of two later he smiled at the commentary. "OH MY GOD! OH MY GOD! I'VE NEVER SEEN ANY THING LIKE IT! Oh shit! Damn it's beautiful! Oh damn I bet this thing will drive tacks!

Andy thought the sinister looking black and grey rifle was anything but beautiful. Still beauty is in eye of the beholder. He liked the goofy girl FBI agent. The rifle was above and beyond what he would normally build. It was for her taking care of Jolene Hadfield.

The screen door slammed open. "Burns its awesome! It fits like my butt in a saddle! Give me some bullets!"

All he heard from the range was a string shots followed by a squeal of delight. This was repeated for forty rounds of match grade ammunition. The screen door slammed open like a herd of runaway kids ran in. H.H. ran over and hugged Burns and planted a kiss on his cheek. "It is awesome! It's out of this world awesome! Ten shots inside a half an inch. HRT pukes eat your hearts out!"

"That rifle is built over and beyond the normal field office sniper rifle. I wanted to build the rifle exactly for you. Jackson assured me the rifle would become part of your permanently assigned equipment list."

"Why me?"

"You're smart. You know what you're doing. You shoot really well. And the past that goofball façade you put up is a very dedicated agent. On a personal note, I appreciate what you did for Sergeant Hadfield."

"She is an Acting Lieutenant now. I expect the rank will become permanent."

"I did not know that." Burns said surprised.

"You like her don't you?"

He hesitated a moment. "Yes, I thought there might have been some attraction on her part. But I haven't heard from her since her trouble. So I guess I was wrong."

H.H. picked up on his sadness. She went over and hugged him. This time giving him a chaste kiss on the lips. Burns appraised her for a moment when she stepped back. "One other thing Helium Head." He paused. "I expect ten percent of what you win off other agents with it."

Smiling, she slapped Burns on the shoulder.

"Where's the suppressor that's supposed to go with it? I don't want it without a can."

Burns handed her a two boxes of subsonic ammo. "Shoot this in it and tell what you think first."

A few minutes later he heard the signature cough of a suppressed weapon firing. He didn't have to wait long for her reaction.

"SON OF A BITCH! BURNS HOW IN HELL DID YOU DO THAT?"

She stormed back inside. "Burns it's not supposed to work that way! What the hell did you do?"

"That is something you don't need to know. It is extremely expensive to build. And that is why you are assigned that rifle. Do not allow anyone to attempt to take it apart or try to work on it. In the event of a failure it comes back here. And it comes back here when it's fired 10,000 rounds. You will keep a data book with the gun. Now go shoot and don't ever forget to clean it."

Harris walked back outside. A moment later the screen door opened and she threw an empty ammo box at him.

Later after packing the gun case in her car Havelee came back into the shop. "Burns, I'll buy dinner tonight if I can use a shower and clean up. I've got better clothes with me."

"OK, I've got to clean up as well. Let me show you a guest shower."

"A guest shower?"

"There are four guest bedrooms each with its own bath."

"A little bit different from the ranch back home?"

"Did y'all have indoor plumbing?"

That earned him a jab in the ribs. Later while he was showering. The shower stall door opened and H.H. stepped in. She put her finger on his lips. "My underware is in your dryer." This time the kiss wasn't so chaste.

After dinner Havelee looked at Burns and asked a question. "Do you land the Skywagon on that grass strip you have next to the barn?" The Skywagon was his Cessna 337 twin engine he'd flown her and Hadfield to Mentone in.

"You're the first person to notice that."

"And there is a Cessna Floatplane as well as a nice airboat in that lakeside hanger. You better start talking Burns you're busted on excessive toy violations."

"The dirt strip is for a Piper Super Cub. It is at the Bay Minette hanger with the Skywagon. Charlie Rayfield taught me to fly fifteen years ago. Along with the place he left three airplanes, the private hanger a private boat house at Bon Secour with two large boats in it. And the means to keep up all of it. When he taught me to fly he arranged for the Super Cub to be based in Shelby County south of where I worked and lived. That way I could fly down here and we would take one of the other planes to matches."

"Didn't he have family to leave all that to?"

"I got the part they didn't want and the stuff they didn't know he had. I met Charlie at a rifle match right I after I moved back from Arizona. He'd been in the Marines so that, shooting and rifle building became the foundation for a great friendship. He had a wife and two daughters. They live in a manner I can't even comprehend. Only a couple of lawyers know what he was really worth. Neither one knew all of it."

"Yeah but you got three airplanes and what all else. I wouldn't complain."

"I don't. It is a blessing."

They walked in parking lot her car was parked next to Burns truck. She stood close in front of him touching his chest. "Don't take any of this the wrong way." She said. "But this afternoon was wonderful. We both needed it. And it will stay between us forever. I'm transferring to Quantico in January. I will be near an old off and on again romance. We're going to try and make it work this time."

"I hope it works for you." He said.

"And I wasn't going to say anything about this. But I don't want to see you hurt. Jolene is apparently seeing a very wealthy guy over that way. His family owns most of lower Mississippi from what everybody says."

Havelee hugged him tightly and kissed him goodbye. Once in her car she rolled down her window and said. "I'll take care of the rifle. It's special."

"I know you will and I'll expect my ten percent."

She flipped him off as she drove out of the parking lot.

When he got back to his place. Burns walked down to the barn and sat with Major for a while.

Jolene was working in her office when Desmond Harris knocked then politely entered. "Lieutenant Hadfield, can I talk to you for a minute?"

"Sure Desmond, close the door." She said wondering what brought about the formalness this morning. "What's happening?"

"Lieutenant, you told me I could use Busby's office and computer if I needed."

"Yes, I told the others the same thing."

"I've got an associate degree in computer science besides my criminal justice degree. There are some anomalies on his computer."

"Don't tell me somebody is watching porn on a city computer."

"No ma'am. I suspect worse. That computer needs a forensic geek look at it. And it probably needs to be a fed."

"OK. I will have that done. Thank you Desmond. Close the door when you go out."

When Taylor was gone Jolene picked up her phone. Havelee Harris answered the ring. Hadfield recounted the conversation with Taylor. The FBI agent thanked her. An hour later a computer technician picked up Busby's computer and left another one in its place.

Chapter Twelve

"I got two AK's and three Uzi's, Bro. We gonna take down dat muther fuck wid dem dogs dat dragged us," Melvin Simpson bragged to Lemont Jones.

"Yo listen Bro I capping that muther fucker. Yo ain't. Sides I's da one dat knows how da get there," Lemont answered as the gang bangers strolled through the projects. Of the two Lemont had the most intelligence and memory. Yet he allowed Melvin to lead the way into the street life and easy money. They both saw the approaching police cruiser.

"Yo holding' Bro?" Lemont asked.

"I got my nine in ma drawers."

"Yo ain't got no nine in yo pants nigger. Yo holding any rock?"

"I holding nine inches of big black dick," Melvin grinned as he fondled his crotch and extended his pelvis toward the cruiser baiting the cops. The squad car passed its occupants ignored the hoods.

Melvin led Lemont into a dilapidated metal storage shed in Theodis Cleckler's backyard. Stepping around two lawnmowers that had seen better days, Melvin went to a corner and moved some boxes. He picked up a dirty rug. Unrolling the rug he presented his stash of weapons to Lemont. Lemont's eyes widened as he looked at the hardware before him. The two rifles were semi-automatic

AK-47 assault rifles that would spit a bullet with each pull of the trigger. There were two magazines holding thirty rounds for each rifle. The three smaller weapons were the gang bangers choice. Melvin called them Uzi's. They were not the famed Israeli submachine gun. The Tec Nine pistols looked similar, but that was all. The nine millimeter semi autos each had two thirty round magazines. An unskilled gang member had converted these guns to fire full auto. With this conversion they would reliably jam after the first few shots. Nevertheless, they were deadly.

"Where you get these?" Lemont asked incredulously.

"I paid twenty five hundred for 'em."

"Where you get that kinda bread Nigger. Yo dealing rock again?"

Melvin inserted a magazine into one of the Tech Nines and pointed it at Lemont. "I'm gonna tell yo some'em, Nigger,' Melvin hissed. 'Yo tell dis an yo dead. Yo unnerstan?"

"Yea I unnerstan Nigger whatcha gonna tell me." Lemont said indignantly.

"I helps a rich white fucker catch people and kill em. He pays me, and I get to keep any money dey have on 'em."

"Yo lying Nigger. Yo ain't doin dat shit."

"Where in hell yo think the bread came from fo this Bro? Cuttin' yards?"

Lemont didn't know what to think. The guns were real. They were the means to get back at the man who broke his fingers. All they needed now was some wheels. That was the easy the part. He hefted one of the Tec Nines and grinned. "Dat's a dead mo fucker over dere in Alabama."

Melvin rolled the guns back up in the rug and stashed them behind the boxes. He picked up a large rusted screwdriver and then pushed one of the mowers from the shed. "Grab a mower, Nigger. Let's do some houses."

The gang bangers were soon going house to house in an upper middle class neighborhood knocking on doors and pretending to want yard work. At the first likely looking house where no one was at home there or the houses next door, Lemont cranked the lawnmower and began cutting the front lawn. Melvin went around back of the house and used the screwdriver to force open the door locks. His only interest once inside was jewelry, guns and cash. Within four hours the burglar and his lookout netted a Smith & Wesson nine millimeter pistol, a Colt thirty eight special snub nose revolver, a Raven twenty five automatic, fourteen rings of which two were worth fifty bucks each at a fence, and two hundred fifty dollars cash.

Lemont complained about only getting the Colt and a hundred dollars for his trouble. He really wanted the nine Melvin held. Lemont accepted the Raven twenty-five and shut up. He knew a twelve-year-old in the projects who wanted a twenty-five and had a Glock to trade. Lemont found the twelve-year-old kid and within an hour had a Glock nine-millimeter. Now he had a nine in his drawers. And he didn't Melvin think had no nine-inch dick.

Police departments cannot function without paperwork. Lt. Mark Hildibrand usually cleared out the paperwork as soon as possible and hit the streets. The administrative load was light which was good because his sergeant was off. The intercom from communications interrupted his work.

"Lieutenant the fire department medics are rolling on a shooting in the projects. Two units are on the way." Hildibrand said.

The unmarked police unit assigned to Hildibrand would be one less set of emergency lights to attract attention in the projects. With the exception of the blinking lights on the fire medic's truck and the ambulance the street was not lit with beacons of red and blue. Two police units were on the scene. The backup officers were preparing to leave. They recognized the unmarked Ford and walked up as Hildibrand got out.

"What's the story?" He asked.

A cop who hardly looked old enough to drive answered. "Accidental, a twelve year old kid was playing with a twenty five auto and shot himself in the balls. I'd hate to get that kind of a vasectomy."

"Anything on the gun?" Hildibrand asked.

"Henderson is taking the report. I expect the gun is stolen, the mother said she didn't own one. The kid is screaming he knew what he was doing. And he's milking it for all that its worth."

"You would too if you'd been shot in the balls." The partner added.

Two female officers, Henderson and Scott, came up. They were the primary unit. Henderson gave a preliminary report.

"Otis Wilson, a black male twelve years of age, accidentally shot himself while playing with a Raven twenty five caliber automatic. According to the fire medics the entrance wound was in the scrotum exiting the testicles and then into this left leg barely missing the femoral artery. Otis stated he thought he knew what he was doing. Apparently he didn't. Otis did tell us he got the gun from a black male street name Yardman."

"Yardman is Lemont Jones," Officer Scott added. "He is the lookout for a house burglar Melvin Simpson, street name is OJ. Both of them are Biloxi Crips. I saw a recent report where a twenty-five auto was stolen in a burglary. The MO fits Yardman and OJ. But the victim didn't have the serial number on the gun."

"One thing for sure, Lieutenant." Scott said with an impish grin.

"What's that?"

"Otis ain't likely to sire any more of 'em."

The two backup cops groaned in unison. Hildibrand admonished the female officer simply by saying 'Scott' in a disgusted tone. The two women cops giggled as they fled to their cruiser.

The male/female buddy tournament Jolene Hadfield fished with Tucker Lee Harrellson the previous weekend was great. They had won first place. An unusual lack of bad weather during hurricane season made for great fishing.

There was one more tournament she could qualify for on the women's pro bass fishing tour this year. She had placed in the top three in another tournament two weeks before. A top three finish in the last season tournament would allow her to fish the whole next year if she could afford it. A sponsor or two would be nice. Daydreaming about fishing was more frequent these days. She had passed the captain's exam with flying colors. Lyle Thigman told her promotion to his slot was likely if she could lose the acting status and was confirmed as lieutenant. Mark Hildibrand had also passed the test. The problem was Busby's suspension was over and he would return to work tomorrow.

The city HR director would not let the Chief move her back to sergeant rank citing the order of Judge Richmond. Acting Deputy Chief Thigman solved the dilemma.

"Hadfield stays Acting Lieutenant in the division head's slot. She's been that job and the detective lieutenant's job for three months. I bet Busby won't make it a month before screwing up." Thigman told the Chief.

The next morning Busby was summons to the deputy chief's office. He was surprised to see Thigman behind the desk and Hadfield sitting in a nearby chair.

"Busby you will resume your duties as detective lieutenant. Acting Lieutenant Hadfield is charge of the division. You report to her. I strongly suggest you do your job very well. Now get lost."

Once he left Thigman turned to Jolene. "You are in a precarious position in this. If he gets out of line report him to me immediately and I'll handle it. Have you heard anything at all about his computer from the FBI?"

"No and Taylor won't say anything about what he found. I know their best people have it. We'll hear when they tell us."

Things went smooth that morning until Web Griffin and his partner bought in Melvin Simpson and Lemont Jones.

A shout from Lemont Jones got everyone's attention.

"I AIN'T BROKED IN NO FUCKING HOUSE! I GOT RIGHTS! YOU CAN'T DRAG ME IN HERE LIKE DIS!"

Jolene heard Web Griffin's calm reply. "Lemont, what are you talking about? I just asked you where you were last Thursday."

Lemont was quick enough to realize he had screwed up. "All you fucks ever ax me is about breaking in houses."

Melvin Simpson's answers to Griffin's partner were just as loud. The shriek from a hysterical female in the hallway brought Jolene out of her office.

"MY BABY LEMONT! WHERE YOU GOT MY BABY!"

A uniformed cop was doing his best to restrain the woman and ward off blows from her purse at the same time. A solidly built man with her was trying to reach the cop. A second officer grabbed the man's arm and ducked a vicious swing. As the cop dodged the blow Jolene saw him remove the pepper gas canister from his belt.

Lemont wailed. "MUTHER DEAR DEY BEATIN' ME MUTHER DEAR DEY BEATIN' ME!"

Those words caused an adrenaline dump in Lemont's mother. She broke free from the cop and kicked him in the balls. At the same time a burst of pepper gas struck Lemont's step daddy in the face. Desmond Taylor grabbed the screaming mother in a chokehold and shoved her hard against the wall. The impact calmed her for a moment. Jolene's eyes began to burn from the over spray of pepper gas.

Lemont was putting up a good fight in an attempt to reach his mother. The overweight Griffin won by slamming Lemont's head into the metal desk a couple of times.

Lt. Busby rushed into the hallway fray. Lemont's mother recovered and started screaming again. Her husband was cursing the cops and pepper gas as his arms were twisted behind him and cuffed. Busby decided to join the ranks of the indignant.

"TAYLOR RELEASE THAT WOMAN!" Busby commanded.

"Lieutenant that is not a good idea," Taylor gasped affected by pepper spray.

"I SAID LET HER GO! OR YOU WILL FACE CHARGES!"

Jolene saw Busby's face turn an angry red color. She started to say something when Lyle Thigman touched her arm and shook his head. Taylor let go of the screaming woman. Busby became the second cop writhing in the floor holding his balls. Taylor shoved Lemont's mother face first to the deck and put a knee between her shoulder blades. Hadfield helped Desmond handcuff the woman and heard Lyle Thigman.

"Busby you said you'd never been in a fight. At least you know how it feels to lose one."

Busby vomited up coffee and donuts.

Melvin Simpson missed the ruckus. He'd sit it out with the barrel of Griffin's partner's revolver stuck in his mouth.

Theodis Cleckler picked Melvin Simpson up at the detective's office. Lemont's mother approved his release to the Reverend from jail. As usual the punks made it home before the cops finished the reports. Both gang bangers got a decent lunch out of the deal.

Busby was in his office with the door closed. His pants were open. He'd placed a plastic bag full of ice inside his skivvies to ease the pain and swelling. The office door opened. Before he could speak. Havelee Harris and another agent stepped inside.

"Alan Busby we have a warrant for your arrest. You are charged with Interstate Trafficking of Child Porn-ography with Intent to Distribute."

With no wasted motion the two agents handcuffed his hands behind his back. It was a memorable perp walk down a hallway he once lorded over. Busby walking spread legged between two raid jacket wearing FBI agents. Holding his pants up from the rear the front of them open exposing his plastic bag swollen briefs. Rumor said they'd caught him jacking off.

Bernard DePiano was being led out of Federal Court by US Marshals. After giving his wife the crabs, getting thrown out of his house and sued for divorce. The Big Dago went for one last hurrah with Maureen Peterson. He'd beat her bad enough to warrant an emergency room visit. Which generated a domestic violence call to the sheriff's department. DePiano was still feeling froggy when two deputies arrived. They both preferred lead weighted flat saps. The first cousin to Lyle Thigman's blackjack. The former vain Italian dandy was still showing effects of that evening when he plead guilty to the Federal charges against him. The domestic violence charges would wait four years until he got back.

All the acting designations were gone. Provisional Captain Jolene Hadfield was presented her new badge by Deputy Chief Thigman. The provisional would go away on January first.

Captain Don Smith recommended officers for promotion to lieutenant and sergeant in his division. The Deputy Chief approved them without comment.

"We have one more slot left. Hildibrand you are now the detective lieutenant in Captain Hadfield's division.

We have a sergeant's opening in the detectives. Who is on the promotional list you like for the job?" Thigman asked Hadfield and Hildibrand.

"Desmond Taylor is at the top of it. I recommend him." Jolene answered.

"I like that guy." Mark said.

Thigman nodded and picked up his phone. He told dispatch to have Taylor report to his office. He was not in the building. It was twenty minutes before he arrived.

Desmond had a look of trepidation when he entered the office and saw who was there. Lyle Thigman didn't help his feelings when he said. "Come in and close the door Taylor."

"You did a good job handing that woman today Taylor." Thigman said.

"Thank you sir. I was beginning to hope you had your blackjack."

Thigman smiled. "Well you let go at the right time. I like a man who follows orders."

"Yes Sir," Taylor said smiling sheepishly.

"Taylor as you might imagine there have been some personnel changes around here today. Captain Hadfield is now over the Detective and Administrative Division. Lieutenant Hildibrand is over the Detective unit."

Taylor's eyes lit up when he smiled. "Congratulations Captain Hadfield."

"Thank you Desmond. If I may Chief?"

"Please do."

"Desmond you've done a good job in the detective unit. And you had a good record in patrol before we got you. This is your new badge Sergeant Taylor." Jolene stood and handed the detective the gold shield. He stood speechless looking at the badge.

"It's ok to say something Desmond." Mark added.

"Uh Ma'am Chief Lieutenant. Thank you. I'll do my best."

The knife was perfect. The best he'd ever made. Its seventeen-inch blade was forged out of rifle barrel steel. The pieces left over from rebuilds were melted and cast in a mold. The result was a piece of steel that he heated red hot and hammered until it was twice its length. He folded back over its self, heated it again and hammered it to length once more. He repeated the process. It was a technique used by the ancient sword makers of Japan. Finished it was three eighths of an inch thick and two and three quarters of an inch wide. On top of the thick blade at exactly ten inches from the handle a razor sharp edge began a seven-inch reverse curve. The bottom edge began a gentle curve increasing in radius until both curves blended into a needle sharp point. The coffin shaped handle was craved from ebony and polished to a glistening black luster. A heavy hilt of nickel silver bent slightly forward toward the point separated the handle from the blade.

Andy finished acid-etching two words across the girth of the blade in front of the hilt: 'Burns Made' He picked up a cotton cloth and began polishing the knife wondering what the ancient sword makers and Jim Bowie would have thought of it? The ancient ones would likely give nods of approval for craftsmanship. The design would be another matter. The real Bowie would probably have gotten drunk and skewered somebody with it.

He held the knife at arm length examining the blade in the sunlight from a nearby window. The phone rang. Bob Rabun was on the line.

"My professional organization, the Gulf Coast Crime Scene Technicians Association, has hit a snag on our fall meeting place. Can we hold a barbecue at your lake on the second Saturday in October? We will clean up and provide everything we need. There'll be about fifty officers."

Andy turned to his appointment book and laid the knife down as he flipped the pages to the date in question. He drew a line across the page and wrote Rabun's association on the line.

"I don't have a problem with that. And if you need to come out the day before and set things that will be fine. If alcohol is served the range is closed and guns go in cars. No exceptions."

"Thanks Andy, I really appreciate this."

"Not a worry," Andy answered. He thought about the lake crime scene and Jolene Hadfield. She was the only thing pleasant about that situation. The phone rang again. Theodis Cleckler was on the caller ID.

"Andy I had to pick up Melvin Simpson at the police station yesterday. They said he was involved in a house burglary."

"Is that one of those gang bangers you brought over here?"

"Yes"

"Theo, I know you're trying to do the right thing. But that kid is bad news. Short of a miracle, he won't change. And I'm not sure that would work. You don't need him around."

"Andy I can't put this child out on the street. I'm his court-appointed guardian. I'm worried about him. I pray for him every day. He had over five hundred dollars hid in a drawer in his room. And he beat up my youngest boy for telling me about it."

"Theo, ask yourself where in hell a fifteen-year-old kid gets that kind of cash. He's selling drugs or doing something illegal. He sure as hell ain't cutting grass. Go back to court and tell them you can't handle him."

"Andy I got to do something. I've been invited to preach a revival in Corinth Mississippi the last part of October. My family is going but I'm afraid to take him and I'm afraid to leave him here."

"Theo, go back to court that kid needs to be someplace else."

"Andy I don't want to give up on him."

"Have you missed anything valuable since he's been at your house?"

There was a pause and Theodis exhaled.

"What's missing, Theo?" Burns asked in a softer tone,

"My pistol and some church offering money."

"You need to report that pistol stolen right now. Call the police when you hang up and make a report. You can't afford for that gun to be used in a crime and it connected to you. You just think there was trouble over those knives. Report the gun stolen Theo and don't drag ass around doing it!"

"I know Andy. They came talked to me about finding another knife. Fortunately I was cleared on that. I'm worried there's one more knife out there. Thanks for your help Andy."

"Sure thing. Report the gun stolen and go back to court on that kid."

The project playground was no man's land. Located next to a four-lane road that gave those who wanted to see how the poor lived in government-subsidized housing a comfortable but not safe route to cruise. The major intersections were well lit at night and frequently patrolled by police. More than one project tourist had been carjacked while waiting on a light to change. The tourists were safe tonight. The carjacking providers were on the playground. A few were shooting hoops one-on-one in the light of a single mercury vapor lamp. The playground was a landmark for drug customers. The group was a racial mix of Asians and Blacks. They were lookouts.

Lemont Jones drew himself up to his full height. He hoped the bandage on his forehead would make him look as bad as the Vietnamese man in front of him. The thin Asian had close cropped black hair that contrasted nicely with the Fu Manchu mustache for a menacing appearance. The real image kicker was the large tattoo of a dragon on his neck. Chuck the Dragon was one bad ass gook. Contacting the Asian gang and cutting them in on hitting Burns' place was Lemont's idea. The Asians specialized in home invasion robberies. Melvin Simpson was strutting his bravo trying to convince the Dragon a hit on Burns would be worthwhile. Lemont knew Melvin was lying about the house being full of jewels cash and guns. What Lemont did know was the dogs and their owner were bad news, but there were only two dogs and one man. Their AK 47's equalized that situation. And no red neck was as bad as these gooks.

"One more time," Chuck the Dragon's voice was as cold as the look he gave Lemont. "Where is this house?"

Lemont recited the directions to Andy Burns' place. For insurance, he substituted a right turn for a left. Lemont could always argue the gooks got it wrong. He expected the Vietnamese to double cross them. Melvin said to tell it straight let the gooks kill the honkey. Lemont wanted revenge.

"OK," Chuck the Dragon said. "We will meet at the Chevron off I-10 across Mobile Bay. We do it in two weeks no sooner. We have to plan. If you have told us wrong." He pointed at Lemont. "You will die first." The tattooed hand and finger swung toward Melvin. "You die second."

The Vietnamese gangsters left the playground disappearing like ghosts. Lemont and Melvin started to leave when a deep gravely sounding voice spoke from the shadows. It was Earl, known on the street as Duke of Earl. The six- foot five-inch tall three hundred and twenty five pound black boss of the Biloxi Crips. The two punks turned to Earl and the big man stepped in front and between them. In each massive hand he grabbed their crotches, taking up the slack in their baggy pants until he had Melvin's balls in one hand and Lemont's in the other.

"Yo little niggers hear dis. If yo lied to da gooks. Or if yo fuck dis up. I'ms gonna yank dese off and den give yo to da dragon." The Duke of Earl squeezed and yanked punctuating his edict. The last thing Earl wanted was the Asians pissed at him.

Lemont and Melvin adjusted themselves and left the playground with as much dignity as they could muster hoping no one had witnessed Earl's chastisement. Two blocks away Melvin stopped and said he had work to do.

"That big nigger will be dead when I'm done and them gooks ain't gonna fuck wid us."

"What you jiving about man?" Lemont replied.

"My main man's paying five big ones tonight. We gonna do somebody. He says when this one is done. He'll do Earl so I can be the main man."

"Nigger, you full of shit."

"Where'd you thing the bread came from fo dem guns we gonna do that red neck dog honkey wid."

Lemont didn't say anything. Melvin always had a lot of cash. Cash that Melvin said came from the white hit man. Melvin crossed the four lanes and walked down a side street. Lemont watched. He couldn't see well enough to tell where Melvin went. A moment later a dark SUV turned on to the four lane.

CHAPTER THIRTEEN

IT was Jolene's first week on call as command staff member. This chore was rotated between the Chief, Deputy Chief and the two Captains. Mostly this duty entailed answering cover your ass calls from lieutenants and detectives. She finished in the top three of the last qualifying tournament for next year's women's pro tour. Tucker Lee Harrellson offered to buy dinner at this Saturday night at Saturday night at Caesar's Grill in the Gulf Palace Casino. Jolene accepted his invitation to dinner with the understanding she would drive her city car and meet him there.

Harrellson was waiting on her in the lobby. "Jolene I'm sorry even with reservations it is at a least forty five minutes wait. The food had better be worth the trouble."

"I've heard it's always busy. Let's look around I haven't spent much time in this place.""Sure," he answered with a patronizing smile.

Soon they were surrounded by the jangling noise and gaudy lights of row upon row of slot machines. The electronic gambling devices take up the majority of gaming space in a modern casino. The promised payoffs do, on occasions, make millionaires out of retirees or waitresses. Usually after those retirees and waitresses have collectively lost millions to the same machines. Table games, roulette, blackjack, and craps occupy much less floor space.

The action was at the slots this night. Over half the table games were closed. Four blackjack tables were busy and one roulette wheel was turning. A crap table crew chatted with each other while the table behind it only had three players. These were all twenty five dollar minimum bet tables. Jolene wondering where the five dollar minimum tables were when the action on the closest crap table caught her eye.

The shooter rolling the dice was trying to make a point of nine before the two cubes turned up seven. Craps is the fastest game in a casino. Savvy bones rollers can make big money quick at craps. The action is fast when the dice are hot and the bets are down.

Jolene saw the dice were making numbers. Tonight she had money to gamble. She dropped five one hundred-dollar bills on the table between rolls.

"Chips, twenty five on come, place the six and the eight," she said. The dealer quickly shoved the bills to the box man, who deftly inserted them into the bank box and watched the dealer lay Jolene's bets. The box man is the table boss overseeing two dealers and a stickman. He or she watches the game, the dice, the players, and the dealers. Political correctness does not extend to the job titles on a table crew. These jobs are the most skilled in the casino. Dealers must figure odds rapidly in their heads plus remember whose bet is where on the table. The box man has to keep up with it all.

The shooter rolled the dice. The cubes bounced down the table stopping with a pair of twos pointed up. The stickman intoned, "FOUR!"

Jolene watched as her twenty five-dollar chip was placed on the number four box. She dropped another twenty-five dollar chip on the come line.

The shooter rolled.

"TEN, NUMBER TEN IT IS!"

The dealer took Jolene's second twenty-five dollar bet and placed it on the number ten box. She now had the four, ten, six and eight covered.

"DICE ARE OUT ITS AN EIGHTER FROM DECATUR," the stickman announced in table lingo. The shooter had rolled an eight. Jolene's bet on the eight was paid and she doubled her bet on the number eight.

"DICE ARE OUT, SIX NUMBER SIX."

Jolene was paid on the six. She doubled that bet.

The shooter rolled a four. Jolene's number won. She took the even money pay out and placed two twenty-five-dollar chips on the come line. The shooter rolled another four. Jolene took the pay off and placed three twenty-five-dollar chips on the line. The next two numbers rolled were eight's. Ten minutes into the action all of Jolene's bets had won

The number seven had not appeared. Another player joined the table. And the pit boss stepped over to watch the action. After four more rolls and a craps roll on the number two and boxcars on the number twelve. The pit boss summoned the floor boss and confirmed a security supervisor was watching the camera focused on the players and the crew. There were too many large denomination chips in play.

The supervisor recognized Hadfield. He watched Harrellson whisper in her ear and her acknowledge with a nod. A zoom in showed Harrellson handing Jolene the restaurant beeper while he held a cell phone. Tucker Harrellson made his way to the casino lobby his progress observed and recorded by cameras.

Jolene pocketed five one hundred-dollar chips in her pants pocket. She put at least ten more one hundred dollar chips and a couple five hundred dollar ones in her blazer pocket. There were at least forty more chips in different denominations in the rail rack in front of her. The dealer paid her even money for a five hundred dollar bet on the number four.

Jolene inhaled, she now had a thousand bucks on the four, six hundred on the come line, eight hundred on the ten, one thousand on the six and fourteen hundred on the eight. And her heart was racing like she'd set the record on the department's physical fitness test. The run on this crap table caused the casino manager and the chief of security to be notified.

The shooter rolled an eight. Jolene couldn't remember what Tommy Hadfield would do in this situation. And she numbly told the dealer to press her bet on the winning number. She now had twenty eight hundred bucks riding on the eight.

The shooter rolled a five. Her come line bet went on the number five.

"DICE ARE OUT! AN EIGHTER FROM DECATUR!"

The twenty-eight hundred-dollar bet on the eight won. The only thing Jolene could think to do was press the bet again. The dealer doubled her chips to fifty six hundred on the number eight. She wondered if the other players could hear her heart beating. The shooter rolled a twelve, boxcars.

"DICE ARE OUT, SNAKE EYES CRAPS!"

No bets affected and the stickman slid the dice to the shooter. Security identified him as Malon Wilson, a regular high roller from Jackson Mississippi, the type of gambler they liked. Malon was a regular high loser. He blew into his hands cupping the dice and shouted. "Buy baby some shoes!" The bones rolled.

"FIVE"

Jolene was paid on her fifteen-hundred-dollar bet. The dealer slid three thousand in chips across the table. Momentarily her mind went blank.

"DICE ARE OUT! EIGHT THE HARD WAY!"

The two cubes landed in front of Jolene, two up and a six up. The dealer motioned to the box man, who drew ten one-thousand-dollar chips and twelve one-hundred-dollar ones out of his bank. These went to Jolene. The other dealer had to pay out over thirty thousand. And another twenty grand in chips left the box man's bank. The stickman swung his stick to the dice. On a signal from the box man he shoved the dice to center of the table. The box man picked up the cubes to exchange them. Malon yelled.

"PUT THEM FUCKING BONES BACK ON THE TABLE, ASS HOLE!"

Three uniformed security men started toward Malon. And the box man started to speak.

"Sir we can change the dice. Please watch your ....."

"SHUT THE FUCK UP DICK HEAD! I LOOSE A QUARTER A MILLION A YEAR IN THIS SHIT HOLE! PUT THOSE FUCKING BONES BACK ON THE TABLE OR GET THE BIG BOSS DOWN HERE!"

Twenty grand in winnings had just been slid to Malon when a young cop wannabe security guard grabbed his arm. The former Ole Miss linebacker slammed an elbow into the guard's gut. The other guards had second thoughts about reaching for the angry gambler. The floor boss stopped the dice change and replaced the box man. Jolene forgot to place a bet on the next roll. Malon slid the twenty thousand he had won back out to the come line.

"DICE ARE OUT," yelled the stick man as Malon rolled the bones. And the sudden angry vibration from her jacket pocket scared the hell out of Jolene. She slapped at her pocket and realized it was the restaurant pager Tucker Harrellson had handed her. Its noise distracted the closest player as it vibrated among the chips in her pocket.

"SEVEN OUT" shouted the stickman. And Jolene watched all her bets being swept from the table. She lost. And it was time to go. She scooped all the chips up from the rail in front of her, over fifteen thousand dollars. The pit boss and a security man appeared next to her each holding empty chip trays.

The floor boss called the restaurant and advised they hold the table for Harrellson. And the guard accompanied Jolene to the cashier's window. It had not been a bad fifty-six minutes, after taxes, Jolene netted $28,000.00. Her heart was still beating when an out-of-breath Tucker Harrellson walked up. Jolene folded up the check and put it in her ID wallet.

"We just got paged to dinner, and they are holding the table." she said.

Harrellson was pale. He apologized for taking so long saying there had been a problem at one of the power stations.

"Don't worry, Tucker, dinner's on me and I'm starved."

Jolene pushed her chair back from the elegantly set table, as the staff cleared away the plates. She removed the linen napkin from her lap. Within moments, the waiter set a steaming cup of coffee in front of her. She politely turned down an offer of desert or wine. She was giddy with the thought of the check she carried, and smart enough to quit when she was ahead.

"Tucker it has been a wonderful evening. This was absolutely the best meal I've ever eaten. Thank you asking me out tonight."

"You are welcome. I'm sorry the problem came up at the plant. I would have loved to watched you play craps." He smiled and held up his hand. "Wait a minute, I didn't get that right, you shoot craps don't you?"

"I think either one works. At the table you are a player, when you roll the dice, you are the shooter."

"That game is much too fast for me. I can't think that quick. Besides, I'm not going to give my money to one of the these places for the experience. However, paying the restaurant check is an entirely different matter. This meal was excellent."

Jolene smiled again and laughed softly. She started to speak when her cell phone vibrated. The caller ID showed the communications room number followed by 911.

"Excuse me Tucker, I've got to call the office." She took the cell phone from her purse and punched the speed dial. Jolene listened to what the dispatcher told her.

"I'm at the Gulf Palace now. Tell Sergeant Taylor and Lieutenant Hildibrand I'll meet them at the concierge desk in the main lobby."

She quickly finished off the cup of coffee. It would be the last one for a while and it was good. As she got up from the table and shouldered her leather purse her expression was all business.

"Tucker, I'm sorry. I've got to go. This has been a wonderful night. Thank you"

"It's OK, I understand when duty calls." He rose and kissed her chastely on the cheek.

The dignified, tuxedo-attired server appeared. "Sir, the lady is a big winner this evening. Your meal is on the house."

A thin athletic built man with light red hair and beard greeted Jolene when she arrived at the marble concierge counter in the main lobby. He was casually dressed, jeans, sport shirt, a tan jacket five eight maybe five nine mid-forties. Adam Hall didn't fit the stereotype of a person in his line of work. He looked more like a preppy dressed pirate.

"Captain Hadfield, I'm Adam Hall." He handed her a gold embossed business card. "I hope you had time to enjoy the grill and congratulations on your winnings."

Jolene wondered how he was so well informed. The card identified him as Director of Security Gulf Enterprises and listed the Gulf Palace Casinos in Las Vegas, Reno, Atlantic City, Biloxi, and the Bahamas. Apparently Adam Hall was the security boss for all of them. She had never heard of him.

"I had beginners luck Mr. Hall."

"Hardly Captain,' he smiled knowingly. 'You placed your bets too skillfully for that to be believable. And don't make me older than I am. Please call me Adam."

"Adam, how do you know so much about my crap shooting skills?"

"I was notified when a high roller customer complained that our box man switched dice on him. I'm sure you remember the rather vocal gentleman who was at the table with you."

That answered her question. He had reviewed the security camera tapes. And he could have been at the table for all she knew. She was too engrossed in the game and still in shock over her winnings

"OK Adam, my dispatchers tell me your CEO hasn't made it home. Our track record on missing casino execs isn't great. Two of my detectives are on their way here from his house. Why is head of security for every casino Gulf Enterprises owns at work in Biloxi, Mississippi on a Saturday night?"

Hall smiled again. "Captain I am here because our local CEO who is also a corporate vice president has chosen to ignore the precautions I've put in place since the Hoffman and Austin homicides. Unfortunately Big Jake Serrano is headstrong and doesn't think he needs any help protecting himself

"Jake works seven days a week, sometimes ten to twelve hours a day. And he travels to and from home by the same route every day. Mrs. Serrano lets him get away with his workaholic ways provided he comes home for dinner every night. Unfortunately she shares Big Jake's tendency to ignore precautions. I've asked him to call if he were more than five minutes delayed traveling to and from home. Tonight he called Mrs. S. and said he was stopping by Wal-Mart. He has been out of the nest so to speak in excess of three hours. Mrs. S. called me and I asked her to file the report. My local security chief is with her now.

"I'd ordered a bodyguard team to follow Big Jake. He raised hell then all I could get was random following." Hall drew a breath and rolled his eyes. "And he let the team off tonight. He figured the tracking transmitter we put in his car was enough."

"Tracking transmitter?" Jolene asked.

"A satellite tracking unit broadcasts the location of his car at all times. Unfortunately the system picked tonight to go down for maintenance. Something they have to do every six months. It won't be back on line for another two hours. I've got teams out trying to pick up the signal now. They are working a one hundred-mile radius and all of Baldwin County, Alabama."

Jolene was impressed at Adam Hall's thoroughness. He had a good plan considering how far away the vehicles of

Austin and Hoffman had turned up. Hall was obviously very well informed about the two cases.

"Do you have any videotapes of the parking area where Mr. Serrano parks his car?"

"Yes, all security tapes since noon are in lock up. And the one you are asking about is cued up in the security office."

During their walk to the office Jolene learned that Adam Hall had arrived that afternoon on a corporate jet. His mission was to convince Big Jake Serrano to follow the rules. Now he feared the worst. Hall was a former FBI agent with over ten years in the Las Vegas office.

While viewing the tape they noticed a young black male near the parking area. Hall froze the tape and zoomed in on the subject enlarging the image on the monitor screen. Jolene recognized Melvin Simpson. She called dispatch and issued a pickup order for him. The dispatcher told her the juvenile court system already had a pickup order in place. Reverend Cleckler had relinquished custody to the court and Melvin hadn't been seen in for six days.

Henderson and Scott found Serrano's gray Mercedes three blocks from Theodis Cleckler's home. They radioed in the code for homicide and requested supervisors and crime scene units. Hildibrand and Taylor radioed they were in route to that scene.

Hadfield switched off the cell phone and looked at Adam Hall. "One of our patrol units has located Mr. Serrano's car. They have reported a homicide and asked for crime scene technicians and detectives. You are welcome to ride with me. I may not be able to bring you back anytime soon. I can always get you a ride."

Adam Hall sighed with a look of resignation about him. "I'll take you up on that." He picked up a thin attaché case and followed Hadfield.

Henderson and Scott had made good use of the POLICE LINE DO NOT CROSS-barricade tape. The entire block where the Mercedes sat was roped off with the yellow tape. Flashing lights of police cruisers and officers with brightly-lit red traffic wands turned cars and pedestrians away from the area. Jolene arrived at the same time the evidence technicians did. Taylor and Hildibrand were already there. The senior tech carefully walked into the scene following Taylor. After Hadfield's introduction Adam Hall was accepted into the crime scene. After a preliminary inspection the tech returned.

"Captain would you and Mister Hall follow me into the scene. Please step where I step."

Once they reached the vehicle the tech illuminated the interior with a powerful spotlight.The carnage caused Jolene to catch her breath. The tan leather interior resembled an abattoir. Everything was covered in wet dark red blood. A single drop fell from the rear view mirror. The corpse of a large man wearing a black suit was slumped across the front seats. His shirt was blood colored. His jugular had been slashed. The left sleeve of his suit coat was cut open from the shoulder and his left hand was almost cleaved in half between the thumb and forefinger. Jolene's gaze followed the spotlight beam, as the technician swept the interior. Three severed fingers lay in the right front floorboard. They must have come from the right hand, which was clutching the handle of a distinctive knife protruding from the man's chest. The third Cleckler Bowie had been found.

"That is Jake Serrano," Adam Hall said solemnly.

The technician looked at his watch and radioed his partner to log official identification of the deceased and the time. Jolene hadn't spoken since they entered the crime scene. One thing was for sure, Big Jake Serrano hadn't accepted death complacently. Unlike Austin, Serrano had fought hard. And the trail to his killer was still warm.

"Captain Hadfield, "the technician said respectively, "I need you and Mister Hall to follow me out of the scene and remain outside the tape."

Deputy Chief Thigman was waiting when they reached the barricade tape. She introduced Adam Hall.

"Captain Hadfield, the media already has this. I'm here in case the mayor decides to make this a campaign stop. I'll get rid of him for you." Thigman said formally. Desmond Taylor and Mark Hildibrand approached the group.

"Go ahead Desmond. You're up to speed on this." Hildibrand said.

"Captain, Officer Reardon, the evidence tech wants backup from the state lab in Jackson. You remember Doctor David Higgins offered all assistance on any of these cases. I want to secure the scene and call him."

"I like that idea, but it will take at least four maybe five hours and even more to get him down here. That is if you can find him."

"I have his home number, Captain. And we've got a warm trail here, we can't afford not to try."

"Call him." Hadfield said noticing Hall was dialing a number on his cell phone.

"This is Adam Hall. Send the Citation to Jackson, Mississippi immediately. They will pick up a Doctor David Higgins and bring him back here. Advise their ETA Jackson and arrival ramp ASAP. The captain will notify me on my cell phone when he is airborne."

Hall clicked off his phone and looked at Hadfield and Thigman. Jolene was impressed, she had never seen anybody cut red tape and issue orders like that. Thigman asked a question.

"Mr. Hall, what is a Citation?"

"That is our corporate jet Captain. The crew has been on flight line standby since Big Jake disappeared."

They heard Desmond Taylor talking into his phone. "Thank you, Doctor. I'll pass that on." He looked at Adam Hall. "Mister Hall, Doctor Higgins says there is only one private jet operation at Jackson, he and his team will be there in thirty minutes..."

Hall's cell phone rang and he held up his hand in a standby gesture. "Hall." He answered and listened briefly. "Thanks John, your passengers will be there in a half an hour or less. Put the power on it and get back here. There will be a cruiser waiting for you on the Gulfport ramp."

Adam Hall clicked off the line and looked at Taylor. "Tell Doctor Higgins, Cessna Citation November Seven-One-One-Golf-Echo will be waiting for him when he gets to the airport."

"That's quick Hall, that's quick as hell." Thigman said.

"Chief, you get what you pay for. And we pay for the best. All of Gulf Enterprises resources are available to your Department for the asking. I need a ride to the Serrano residence. Can you accommodate me?"

The street cops had not forgotten the pickup order on Melvin Simpson. Officers Gresham and Graham eased their cruiser into the project playground. A scream caused them to turn the spotlights toward the sound. A gang banger was screaming and running toward the police car. Usually they screamed and ran the other way. Gresham riding in the passenger seat jacked a round into the chamber of the twelve gauge Remington he was holding.

"Could be a banzi charge," he said. Graham nodded drawing his Glock. Both cops exited the cruiser and commanded the screaming gangster to freeze. Which he did by hitting the ground spread eagle, yelling.

"OJ BACK DERE DAID!! HE GOT A UZI STUCK UP HIS ASS!!"

The teenager continued yelling while Graham searched and cuffed him. The officer lifted him up and asked him to show them whatever he was screaming about. The gang banger's legs went limp in refusal to comply. He went from yelling intelligible words to a keening moan. Graham put him in the back seat of the cruiser. After shutting down the spotlights the cops radioed for back up. Then cautiously moved with weapons ready in the direction the punk ran from.

They walked toward a large trash holding area. The cops carefully surveyed the offset alley from the cover of a brick wall. Something in front of the dumpster caught their attention. Gresham leveled his shotgun and whispered to Graham. "Light it up."

The high powered flashlight cast a bright beam over the area. They simultaneously said, "SHIT!"

A body was posed on its knees face down. The victim's pants and drawers were around his ankles with his bare ass elevated.

Protruding from between the buttocks was the receiver of a Tec Nine assault pistol. Graham focused the light on the gun. Gresham said. "Somebody must have stuck it up his ass and pulled the trigger! The thing has got a stovepipe jam! A fucking piece of brass is sticking out the ejection port!"

Graham swung the light around the area near the body. The blood was starting to congeal. Two empty brass cartridge cases off to the right of the body reflected in the light. Graham calmly said, "It looks like somebody pulled the trigger more than once. That's a hell of a substitute for Preparation H."

For the second time that night the homicide code was broadcast. And the pickup order for Melvin Simpson was canceled.

CHAPTER FOURTEEN

IT was after midnight when Citation November-Seven-One-One-Golf-Echo delivered Dr. David Higgins and his lab team. In the darkness Higgins quickly examined both crime scenes. He suggested the Biloxi PD techs work the Simpson scene and move the body before daylight. The evidence collection effort for the Serrano scene would be done in the daylight. Higgins ordered tarps hung to block the Mercedes from the view of long lens press cameras. Like Thigman predicted the Mayor showed up at first light with the Chief in tow.

The Mayor's first demand was for immediate removal of the corpse. He waxed eloquently about respect for the families and their privacy. The Chief stood by shaking his head and issuing orders that would have ended the evidence collection.

Adam Hall and Lyle Thigman watched the Mayor's media show from the command post. Hall opened his briefcase and removed two file folders. He walked over to the Mayor and the Chief. After identifying himself, Hall politely asked if he could speak with them privately for a moment.

"Hall," the Chief opened in an intimidating tone calculated to impress the Mayor. "Your interest here is understandable, and whatever help you have given is appreciated. The Biloxi Police Department is quite capable of handling this matter without any help or interference from Gulf Palace Casino security."

"Gentlemen, please examine the pictures in each folder. And go do whatever you normally do on Sunday mornings." Adam Hall handed each man a folder then returned to where Thigman stood. The Mayor promptly informed the press that any follow up information would come from Deputy Chief Thigman. The Police Chief was gone before the Mayor finished speaking.

"How did you do that Hall?" Thigman asked.

Adam Hall smiled like a pirate that had just seized a chest of gold. "We have pictures of every known prostitute that works our hotel. We get pictures of their johns whenever possible. I hope those two don't find out they're screwing the same woman."

"What do you have on me?" Thigman asked.

Hall smiled his red hair rippled in the morning breeze. "You consort with the lowest sleaziest FBI agents and Federal Prosecutors on the Gulf Coast. And there are no photographs."

Thigman noted the seriousness of Hall's words. He answered. "Thank you."

The morning light revealed a blood trail to the crime scene techs. It was easily followed for the first block and a half from the Serrano scene. A sharp eyed cop pulling scene security spotted a dried drop of blood. The officer was a veteran deer hunter and a blood trail on concrete was easy. Higgins pressed him into service. Where the trail ended almost sparked a riot.

"POLICE AIN'T GOT NO BIDNESS IN PREACHER CLECKLERS YARD YOU GIT OTTA THERE." A large woman screamed from her porch.

"Biloxi Police! We're searching for evidence! This is official business!" The blood tracking officer responded.

"I DONE TOLT YOU BOY THERE AIN'T NO POLICE BIDNESS IN PREACHER CLECKERS YARD. YOU BETTER GIT I GOTS MY SHOTGUN!"

"She's got a double barrel sitting right next to her chair. Just ease on back to the street. We'll handle this another way." Higgins told the cop.

A Biloxi crime scene tech tried her hand a calming the situation. Neighbors were coming out to see what was going on. "Miz Gertie! We just trying to find some evidence! There's been a bad crime a few blocks away!"

"YOU AIN'T FINDIN IT HERES! PREACHER CLECKLER AIN'T BEEN HOME IN A WEEK! ONE A DEM GANGSTERS BEENS SNEAKING AROUND OVER THERE. I DONE SHOT AT EM ONCET! Y'ALL GIT!"

Police cars were beginning to arrive on the street. Several unmarked units arrived. Captain Hadfield got out of her car with Hildibrand and Taylor close behind. Lyle Thigman and Adam Hall had to park a half a block away. The Deputy Chief told a couple of officers to keep the media off the street. That didn't work a cagy TV cameraman was already filming. It wasn't the arriving cops that commanded everyone's attention.

A phalanx of dignified men all dressed in suits complete with matching white lapel flowers marched down the street and took up station in front of Theodis Cleckler's house.

David Higgins ever mindful of evidence was eyeing a pristine footprint in the oily driveway surface. He spoke to the leading gentleman. "Sir be careful stepping in that oil. It might ruin the shine on your shoes."

The lead man avoided the oil. "Why thank you sir. I am Emmond Mason, Head Deacon in Reverend Cleckler's church and you are." Mason extended his hand.

"I'm Doctor David Higgins, Mississippi Department of Forensic Science. Pleased to make your acquaintance Deacon Mason." Higgins accepted the proffered hand.

"Are you a doctor of medicine or of science Doctor Higgins?"

"Science sir."

"I see. May I ask what brings you to our pastor's house this fine Lord's Day?"

Higgins was joined by Thigman Hadfield and Taylor. "My agency is assisting your police department with a crime scene investigation a few blocks from here. We were following a blood trail."

"A blood trail like tracking a wounded animal?"

"Yes sir pretty much the same thing. The officer standing over there is a deer hunter experienced in following blood trails. We also sample the blood dripped on the ground." Higgins showed the Head Deacon the test tubes and how this was done.

Emmond Mason ponder this for a few seconds. "Then this blood trail led you to here Reverend Cleckler's driveway?"

"Yes and that lady next door with the shotgun stopped us."

This caused Mason to jerk his head toward Gertie who was sitting in her rocker with the shotgun nearby. He turned to the closest deacon. "Deacon Houser would you please go take Miz Gertie's shotgun in her house. And make sure it is unloaded." This deacon nodded his ascent and went to Gertie's porch mindful not to step in oil or blood.

As the shotgun was removed Gertie yelled out. "DAT BLACKJACK THIGMAN OUT DARE?"

"Yes Miz Gertie I'm here!" Thigman answered smiling.

"YOU MEMBER WHUPPING MY DAID HUSBAND WHEN HE BEAT ME UP?"

"He wasn't dead when he beat you Miz Gertie! You killed him a couple of years after that!"

"I MEMBER YOU WAS SOMEPLACE ELSE AND HE NEEDED KILLIN!"

"The judge thought so too Miz Gertie!"

"I GOTS TO GET READY FOR CHURCH! YOU WHUP THAT POLICE DAT TRIED TO GET IN PREACHER CLECKLERS YARD!"

"I will Miz Gertie!" Thigman said, smiling as he shook his finger at the deer hunting cop.

"The Lord has granted that dear soul a long life. But I believe He has taken some of her facilities. Mrs. Cleckler looks after her a good bit." Mason said. "Doctor Higgins do you believe Reverend Cleckler is a suspect in this heinous crime we learned of on last night's news?"

"Deacon Mason that is not for me to decide. I am a scientist. I follow the evidence. And the evidence has led me to this driveway. My task is to collect it and examine it in the lab. I present my findings to the police department and the district attorney. You asked if I believe he is a suspect. I don't. But I must examine the evidence that leads to his doorstep."

"Doctor Higgins you appear to be an honest professional man. Unfortunately Reverend Cleckler has born the burden of being falsely accused by the Biloxi Police Department. He is away doing the Lord's work in Corinth Mississippi. He has been gone all week. We cannot permit you to trespass on his property without his approval."

"Deacon Mason," Chief Thigman said. "Those who accused Reverend Cleckler are no longer with our department. That person is serving time in Federal Prison. The evidence we seek could help us catch a serial killer."

"Excuse me Chief," Jolene Hadfield spoke. "Deacon Mason when will Reverend Cleckler return?"

"We expect him this evening ma'am. Are you the lady who was falsely accused with Reverend Cleckler?"

Jolene's cheeks colored slightly. "I am. Would you object if we left a police car and an officer here on the street blocking Reverend Cleckler's driveway? The officer can protect the evidence until the Reverend returns. Then we can ask his permission to retrieve it."

Emmond Mason considered this for a moment. Deacon Houser whispered something to him. "Captain Hadfield, if you assign Sergeant Desmond Taylor to that duty and Deacon Houser assumes that duty with Sergeant Taylor we will go to the Lord's house and worship His name. You all are invited."

The cops dispersed and the deacons marched to the church. Everyone breathed a collective sigh of relief. Adam

Hall addressed Thigman as they drove off. "That sort of thing makes me glad I was with the FBI."

Eighty-five officers from police departments between Apalachicola Florida and New Orleans Louisiana attended the meeting of the Gulf Coast Crime Scene Technicians Association at Andy Burns' place. Bob Rabun and a couple of other members spent the night before barbecuing meat. Most of the programs were informal discussions and presentations of unusual crime scenes the members had worked. The greatest interest was in the casino CEO homicides. Everyone listened as David Higgins summed up the cases.

"We have identified the same tire treads at all three scenes. They are Michelin all terrain radials. We can positively identify these tires. You have photos of these treads in your handout materials. We have identified the same two pair of shoes at every scene. A pair of Gokey hiking boots and a pair of Reeboks. The Reeboks were worn by the late Melvin Simpson whose body was found the same night Jake Serrano was found. We found some of Simpson's DNA at the Serrano scene and the Austin scene. He was an active participant in these crimes. And Gokey boot prints were found near Simpson's body.

"The Gokey boots and shoes are made by an old time shoe maker. They are very expensive and distinctive be- cause the word Gokey appears on the soles. Find those boots and you have the CEO killer. Pictures of those soles are in your handout material as well. Any questions?"

"Doctor Higgins, you said these shoe prints were found outside the Cleckler residence along with bloody coveralls in his garbage. And you've told us he is not linked to any of these crimes other than making the murder weapon. Do you have any thoughts on why that evidence was on his property?"

"We know that Melvin Simpson lived in the Cleckler household for several months. Starting after the Hoffman homicide and ending before Serrano. Reverend Cleckler petitioned juvenile court to give up guardianship of Simpson. I expect the Reverend couldn't handle him."

An 'amen from the crowd drew a round of laughter. Higgins continued.

"We found prints from both shoes going to and from the garbage can. There were many garbage cans and dumpsters between the Serrano scene and Cleckler's house where bloody evidence could have been disposed of. I hate using the crime drama cliché word framed. But it is possible in this case. I understand Cleckler's boys say the same man purchased three of the Bowie knives from them. The boys can't agree enough on what he looks like for a composite. And Reverend Cleckler will not let us try to make another one. He has cooperated in everything but that. He let us look at all the shoes in his house and even gave a DNA sample. His lawyer has had him polygraphed after each homicide and he's passed all of them.

"In closing, if any of you find any tire treads or Gokey boot soles. Contact my office immediately. I don't care what jurisdiction you are from. We will serve as the clearing house for this evidence. That's all I have. Thank you for listening to me. I'll be here at least until the beer runs out if any of you want to chat."

Burns sat at his workbench examining a rifle action with a lighted magnifying glass. He looked at his watch. It was after ten p.m. This project could wait until tomorrow. The day was good. He enjoyed the easy camaraderie with the cops attending the conference. Most of them took the time to thank him for hosting the conference. The phone rang. He answered before the second ring.

"Mr. Burns, this is Deputy Ted Turner, Escambia County Sheriff's Department. You put night sights on my Glock three months ago."

"Yes Ted what can I do for you?"

"We had an attempted home invasion up here. The intended victim is a former Navy Seal with his own M-16. He won. The bad guys were members of an Oriental gang out of Biloxi. One of them a mean looking gook with a dragon tattooed on his neck said something you ought to know."

"What's that Ted?"

"He said, niggers lied, not Burns, no lake, no dogs. I asked who he was talking about, and he said, 'Yardman and OJ.' Then he died. You've got a lake and dogs. This bunch was heavily armed, and I think these guys may have been looking for you and went north off I-10 instead of south. I just wanted to give you a heads up."

Andy thanked Turner and was speculating on the possibilities when the gate alarm sounded. The dogs began growling. He looked at the screen and saw the green images of six males climbing over the gate. All were carrying weapons. Burns entered a key stroke turning off all the automatic light sensors. He watched one of the gate climbers drop his gun. It fired. The intruder clutched himself and fell off the gate onto the hood of their car.

One down five to go, mused Burns. He watched them argue amongst themselves. One kept pointing a Tec Nine pistol at the other four. They started moving down the drive. Their movements overly cautious as they jerked their weapons around. Andy thought they were afraid of the dark. 'They should have stuck to the projects' he said to himself as he removed a pair of night vision goggles from a cabinet. Realizing he didn't have a pistol in the shop he chose the $85,000.00 English double barrel shotgun that hung above the shop door. The bespoke John Dickson piece was a Charlie Raifield purchase that Andy enjoyed shooting.

The gangsters made it to the cannon garages. Andy flipped the switches that raised the doors and turned on the lights inside. It didn't have the effect he wanted. All five started shooting gunning down three of their number. After empting his magazine one AK 47 equipped gang banger threw down the rifle and ran for the gate. The razor wire concealed in the grass stopped him.

Lemont Jones ran through the darkness shooting the Tec Nine until it jammed. Yardman was slapping at it with his free hand when Andy Burns aimed the Dickson twelve bore. He fired the tightest choked barrel sending a pattern of seven and half shot into the crotch of Lemont's low rider pants.

The teenager dropped his weapon and grabbed himself hoping his vitals were still there. At that instant the dogs got him.

Burns walked over to the screaming gangbanger. After commanding the dogs to watch he shoved the shotgun barrels in Lemont's mouth.

"Shut up or I let the dogs finish you! And I'll throw what's left of your sorry ass on the other side of the lake with the snakes and alligators! You will never be seen again! YOU UNDERSTAND ME BOY?" He jabbed the barrel further into Yardman's throat. The wide eyed punk gagged and shook his head yes.

"When I remove the gun you start telling me about Melvin Simpson and killing people. You say anything else or stop before I say stop and the dogs get you!"

"OJ DAT BE MELVIN," Lemont blurted out. "OJ HE BE WERK FOR A RICH WHITE DUDE. DAT DUDE PAID HIM TO JACK THE GAMBLING PLACE DUDES AND MAKE EM DRIBE TO WHERE HE TELL EM. THEN THE WHITE DUDE HE KILL WITH A BIC BLADE! OJ SAY UNCLE TOM NIGGER CLECKLER BE MAKE DEM BLADES! THE WHITES DUDE HE BUYED THEM FROM CLECKLER'S KIDS! OJ SAY DE WHITE DUDE BE BIG AND HE BE QUEER! ALL HE BE WANTIN IS OJ TO SHOW EM HIS DICK! DRIVE SUM BIG ASS FANCY JEEP LIKE THING. BLACK MAYBE. DATS ALLS I KNOWS MAN. YOU GOTS TO HELP ME!"

Burns watched Yardman writhe and squirm moaning in pain while he held what remained of his package. He heard the one caught in the razor wire screaming. Andy left the dogs guarding Lemont and walked back to his shop. He dialed 911. And then started cleaning his shotgun, carefully wiping down the muzzles with an oily rag.

The gray light of dawn begin to show itself when Bob Rabun finally left Burns' place. The death toll was only two with the same number critical. One of these was Lemont, he was only minutes from bleeding to death when medics reached him. One fratricide victim would fully recover. The baggy oversized clothes worn by the razor wire victim saved him from debilitating injury.

Biloxi PD dispatchers would not disturb Captain Hadfield over a home invasion in Alabama. When he mentioned it involved the CEO homicides Desmond Taylor called him back.

Burns answered the phone. "Thanks for calling me back so early in the morning Sergeant Taylor. Congratulations on the promotion. Your local gangbanger Yardman turned up here with a few friends last night. Before the medics hauled him off he told an interesting story about Melvin Simpson."

When he finished relating Lemont's story and answering Taylor's questions. Desmond told him about all the promotions. "Desmond they promoted good people that deserved the promotions. I think your department will be better for it. Please pass on my congratulations to them." Burns said.

"Mister Andy, you ought to call Captain Jo and tell her yourself."

"Desmond I doubt I could get her on the phone. Thanks for calling me back and hope what I told you helps." Burns hung up the phone and saw the sun the rising. It was time to ride.

He walked to the barn. Too much adrenaline remained in his system for him to feel the effects of the sleepless night. He noticed Major was not at his usual place. The dogs started barking and ran toward the paddock. Andy broke into a run when he saw the horse lying on its side trying to lift its head.

Andy's foot only touched one rail as he vaulted the fence. He saw the buckskin painfully raise its head its eyes filled with agony. Major's hide was matted with blood on one side and ground beneath him was soaked. Andy had seen enough gunshot wounds to know that the horse would not survive. Major's time was down to minutes or less.

Andy fell to his knees. The buckskin relaxed and laid his head in Andy's lap. Major looked up at him and nickered softly saying goodbye. As he looked at his friend and soul mate Burns' eyes filled with tears. He cradled Major's head in his arms sobs racking his body as he hugged the horse.

It was midday when he felt the suns heat. He looked around and saw the dogs lying nearby. He got up and went into the barn. In a few minutes he came out carrying a pick and shovel. The Pudelpointers followed him as he walked to the center of the meadow.

Chapter Fifteen

THE deadly home invasion attempts in Alabama moved the CEO murders and articles about the knife making preacher below the fold or to the second segment on broadcast news. The following Monday was almost routine for the detective division. The afternoon was half gone when Desmond Taylor sat down with his bosses and recounted his trip to visit Lemont Jones in the jail ward of a Mobile Alabama hospital.

"For all the dope he had on board he was amazingly lucid. He told me all about his relationship with Melvin Simpson and how they planned to travel to Alabama and kill Andy Burns his dogs and his horse. After they looted the house they were going to burn it down. Lemont even admitted it was his idea to recruit the Asians and then gave them bad directions." Taylor said.

"And he remembered how to get to Burns place after riding over there in Cleckler's church van for a fishing trip? And then found it at night?" Jolene asked.

"Yes, you've seen all the camera video. He found it alright."

"I can imagine Andy Burns thinking they needed firearms safety lessons after seeing that one drop his gun and shoot himself." Hildibrand commented.

"What all did he have to say about Melvin's relationship with this white guy?" Hadfield asked.

"He was adamant about having never seen him. And he said Melvin always had a lot of cash and used some of it to buy the guns they used Saturday night. He kept saying Melvin called him a muscle man. And Melvin apparently thought the guy was gay. Lemont said he called him queer many times. The guy may be a body builder." Taylor replied.

"There are some gay body builders at the gym I go to. They don't seem like the sort to stab people with knives. I can see them carving each other up in a domestic fight. But not out and out cold blooded stabbing someone. Tucker Harrellson fits the rich part and he drives a Land Rover. I really don't think he's gay. I've gone fishing with him several times. We've gone to lunch and dinner. He's always a gentleman. He's never made any suggestive remarks or tried to put the move on me. Going out with gay guys would probably be livelier. All he talks about is fishing and the environment. Listening to a dissertation about stress factors in a concrete mix will bore you to death. I find it hard to call going out with Tucker Harrellson a date." Hadfield commented.

"Deputy Rabun over in Baldwin County made sure I left with photos of the tire treads and Gokey boot soles. He said they were at every scene. Maybe we could look around the gyms." Taylor said.

"Our Captain could distract Harrellson in the gym while we check his tires and boots." Hildibrand said smiling.

"Come to think of it. I've never seen him wear boots." Jolene said.

It had been five days since he buried Major in the meadow. He spent most of the days sitting in the pasture next to the grave. Work was not done. He went to the shop once and stood in the doorway looking at the hitching rail. His dogs guarded him faithfully. Once he realized they might be hungry. He was relieved their feeder still held food. He refilled the feeder and realized how dirty he was. After showering he put on clean clothes and went back to the pasture.

The dogs growled a warning. Andy turned and saw Theodis Cleckler walking in from the gate. He was the only person other than Burns lawyer accountant that had the gate code. Andy realized he hadn't received any phone calls. Or maybe he hadn't answered any. The dogs started growling aggressively as Theodis approached. Andy spoke to them. They lay down and stayed quiet. Theodis was now close enough to speak.

"Andy I've been calling since I heard about the tragedy here last weekend. All I got was your answering machine. It doesn't have room for any more messages. I called just before I left. I was worried something had happened to you. Your house and shop are unlocked. What is wrong?"

Burns didn't answer, he just looked at the fresh mount of dirt.

"Andy I don't see your horse. Has something happened to Major?"

Tears began to flow once more. Theo sat down next to him and put his hand on his shoulder. "I'm here with you my friend. I would have come sooner had I known."

Neither man spoke. After a time Theo excused himself and walked a respectful distance away. He pulled his cell phone and called his wife. He told her what was going on and that he would be late. When he sat back down Andy began to talk.

"I might understand my feelings better if I were grieving for a human being instead of a horse. The best damn horse I will ever own. He didn't have a mean bone in him. And he would do anything I asked. Why was he taken from me? I would watch him run and play out here in this pasture and give thanks to the Lord for bringing such a magnificent animal into my life. At the same time I would cry and grieve for a woman I loved too much."

Andy paused and sighed as he looked around the pasture. "Theo I should have got the rifle out and shot those little bastards when they climbed my gate. But I had to try and scare them off. Look what it got me. Do the right thing and you lose."

"It really frightened me when you roughed up Melvin and Lemont that day. And I hope the Lord forgives me for saying this. Now I don't think you roughed them up enough. I have accepted the fact that both of them were pure evil. I understand Lemont will likely spend the rest of his life in prison. Your soul is safe Andrew Burns because you did the right thing. When you could have taken lives with the blessing of the law you gave them a chance to live.

"You've come a long way since you came back here from Arizona. I believe the Lord gave you that horse to heal all the hurt you'd suffered. Now I believe He is telling you it is time to move on. There are lessons to learn from this. He knows what they are. We mere mortals have to figure them out. You are truly a blessed man Andrew. You have used this magnificent blessing from Mister Raifield to do good things. The Lord blesses that. One day He will bless you with a horse more magnificent than the one you mourn. And you will honor Major's memory with that animal."

Andy stood up and gave a hand to Theo pulling him up right. "I hope you're right my friend. Thank you for being here. Let's go see what we can find to eat."

Over sandwiches Theo asked a favor. "I've decided not to make any more knives. I'm going to sell all that's left at the gun show this weekend. My boys will have to do the selling because I've been called to preach a weekend revival in New Orleans. Would you go to the show with them for me?"

"Be glad to, would you mind if I put a knife on the table?"

"Be my guest. Are you selling the knife made out gun barrels?"

"Yeah, it's time for that one to go. I've got a question for you Theo. At any time in your life have you ever had any cross words or dealings with a homosexual who might hold a grudge?"

"No Andy I've never had any dealings with a gay person that I am aware of. I don't condone that lifestyle but I will not turn those people away from the Lord or my church. Why would you ask something like that anyway?"

"Humor me for a few minutes Theo. How about a rich white guy that you may have had a conflict with. It doesn't have to be recent. It could even be years ago. Perhaps someone that had a conflict with your family."

"The only rich white person I've ever known was Mister Raifield. Conflicts I don't know. The Harrellson family wanted the church property. But I never met a Harrellson during that ordeal. I only spoke with bankers and lawyers."

"You and your family have lived on the coast since you were a child. As I recall you moved there from someplace inland. Any conflicts growing up."

"We moved to Gulfport from Poplarville when I was in grade school. My daddy found work in the shipyards. It was after I got out of the Marines that he was blessed with the shrimp boat." Theodis sat quietly for a few minutes. "There is one thing I recall. My older brother Cedric got into some serious trouble as a young man and it involved a white child from a rich family. That is all I know. It was the first time I ever heard the word rape. I didn't know what it meant. My daddy caught me listening at the door and gave me a whipping I remember well. Whatever the trouble was it wasn't spoken of again. My parents carried it to the grave. Of course Cedric gave them so much heartache. He was a terrible cross for them to bear. He was on death row for five years. That just about killed my mamma. She learned his sentence was commuted to life without parole just before she died. Now are you going to tell me why are asking this?"

"I think someone is deliberately trying to point the finger at you for these CEO murders."

"You mean frame me?"

"Yes. How much trouble is it to visit Cedric?"

"I haven't seen him in three years. I got tired of driving up to the prison and not being able to see him. Because he couldn't have visitors for disciplinary reasons. Twice I called and they said he could have visitors. I got there the next day and found out he had gotten into trouble the night before. The past three times I've called he's been locked down."

"Would you mind if I went to see him?"

"No. But you will probably waste your time. I really don't see how he could help. And they have strict visiting hours and days you can visit. It will be more trouble than you think."

The fall gun show attracted many visitors. Most hunting seasons were beginning to open throughout southern Mississippi and Alabama. This show was always good for sellers. Andy kept an eye on two tables manned by Theo J and Jerry. The youngsters frequently admired the gun barrel steel Bowie that Burns put out for sale. The thirteen hundred dollar price astounded them. They were even more dumbfounded when Burns told them to triple the price on every knife Theodis had for sale. The knives were selling briskly. Publicity about the knife making preacher drove the demand.

B. Johnson Hassinger dropped by and asked Andy to join him for a cup of coffee.

"Nice show, Andy, how are Theo's boys doing?"

"At the rate they are going, they will sell all his knives before the end of the day."

"That's good. Will you take nine fifty for the Bowie?"

"No, melting down rifle barrel pieces to make a knife blade wasn't the brightest idea I've had."

Hassinger got down to business. "All Cedric Cleckler juvenile records have been destroyed. He is in disciplinary lock down at the prison. He cannot have any visitors even family. However, investigators are not included. You can see him Monday morning at ten thirty." Hassenger reached into the inside pocket of his sport coat and removed some documents. "Here are your credentials, a letter to the warden, an order from a judge to interview the inmate so on so forth and your business cards. I pulled some strings inside the prison system to make this happen."

Andy looked at the business cards. He was identified as an investigator for the law firm Hassenger & Brown. "Nice cards, when do I get my pay check and vacation?"

Hassenger laughed. "I suppose you want to know about health insurance too?"

Andy smiled slightly, "I hope this points us in the direction of the real killer."

"I don't understand why you're going to the trouble. You don't have a dog in the hunt so to speak. Let the police solve it. Or are you trying to curry favor with a certain Biloxi Captain?"

"It really pisses me off about that somebody would go to so much trouble to dump a body in my lake. It looks like someone is trying to frame my friend. I have the time and money to play private eye. So I'm going to. The airport operator told me he has a loaner car. The weather looks good for Monday I'm flying up. I appreciate your helping me get in there."

Andy browsed the show on his way back to the knife tables. He stopped to examine an English double-barrel shotgun for sale. After having been gone the better part of an hour he got back to the Cleckler tables. Theo J was off roaming and Jerry was grinning. Both tables were empty and Andy noticed his Bowie was missing.

"Mr. Andy we've sold out! And I sold your knife! The man gave me thirteen one hundred-dollar bills! I never had so much money in my pocket! Theo J has all daddy's money!" The boy reached in his pocket and pulled out the crumpled bills. "And Mister Andy he was the same man who bought Daddy's three Bowie knifes!"

"How long ago did he buy the knife Jerry?"

"We sold the last of Daddies knives after you left. Theo J left about thirty minutes ago to pay our table rent. He was going to look around some. I sold it right after he left."

"Let's walk around the show some Jerry. If you see the guy point him out to me."

Burns realized after a half an hour it was a lost cause. They found Theo J and made their way back to their tables. The boys rolled up the table covers and carried some boxes to the trash. As Andy drove them home Jerry asked an unsettling question.

"Mr. Andy is that man going to kill another casino boss with your knife?"

He didn't answer right way. When they got home Theo J disappeared into the house. Jerry hung around Andy for a few minutes. "Jerry did Theo J help you sell my knife?"

"No Mr. Andy I did it all by myself."

Burns pulled out a hundred dollar bill and gave it to the boy. "This is your commission for selling my knife. You make sure this goes into your savings account. You understand?"

"Yes sir. Do I really have to? Daddy and Momma will make me put ten percent of it in the church offering if they know I got it."

Andy smiled and patted the young man on the shoulder. "Yes you have to. And it is a good idea to give Jesus what is his."

"OK Mr. Andy. But is a commission like you earned money. You only have to give ten percent on what you earn."

That got a laugh out of Burns. "Yes a commission is what you're paid for selling something. If you don't sell it you don't get paid. So you earned it. Go tell your momma and cough up the Lords part tomorrow morning at church."

"Yes Sir. You didn't tell me if that man is going to kill somebody with your knife?"

Andy drew a deep breath. "I don't know Jerry. I hope not I really hope not."

Before he started back to Alabama Burns called Desmond Taylor. He left a voicemail message about the Bowie knife purchase.

Landing the Cessna floatplane at the small airport near the prison caused the usual flurry of interest. Burns had not decided what approach to take with Cedric Cleckler and wondered if he were wasting his time. He arrived at the prison early and was greeted with unfriendly efficiency. The guards ordered him to remove everything in his pockets and his wrist watch. They searched him and thoroughly inspected his small tape recorder. A guard captain told him how the interview would be conducted.

"Mr. Burns you and inmate Cleckler will be in an eight by ten foot interview room. All the furniture is bolted down. Inmate Cleckler will be shackled hand and foot. His shackles will be locked to the chair he sets in. You will not touch him. Both of you will be observed via a camera recording the interview and through a two way mirror. The door to the interview room does not lock and a team of guards will be outside the door. Should Cleckler become unruly you move to a corner near the door. Exit as soon as the guards enter. Remain in the hallway until a guard escorts you out. This interview will last thirty minutes."

Cedric Cleckler was led in and shoved bodily into a straight back chair across the metal table from Burns. The two burly guards escorting Cleckler secured his manacles to the chair and informed him cooperation would to his advantage.

The only difference between brothers Theodis and Cedric was expressions. Theodis' countenance radiated warmth and peace. Cedric's face was graced with a scowl and projected pure hate. Even with ten years difference in their ages, the two men could be twins. Looking at the rippling muscles Cedric flexed to intimidate him Burns was glad the man was chained. Were the attempts to frame Theodis the result of something Cedric had done years ago? They stared at each other after the guards left. About thirty tense seconds passed when Cedric snarled.

"What the fuck you want?"

"Theodis is being framed for three murders."

"Well that I believe. Cause brother preacher ain't got the balls to kill nobody."

"I believe you're right."

"Maybe youse ain't is dumb as you look white boy. What's brother preacher being framed gots to do wid me?"

"The family of the rich white girl you raped back in the sixties is probably doing it. They may think Theo is you."

"Shiiit, you dumber hell white boy! If'n I'd raped any white girl I'd been hung from a tree and be dirt in graveyard by now. If'n it'd been a rich un I'd been hung quicker. Sides I's only fucked one white woman in my life an killin her boyfriend what got me in here. Dat honky muther didn't like eatin pussy after no nigger dick been in it."

"Whatever you did got your brother whipped for listening to your parents talking about it. He remembers the word rape and a rich person involved and the whipping. What do you remember?"

"You dumb ass you think I'm some genius nigger or sometum? That shit was over forty years ago and you expect me to 'member it? Man you got it wrong."

"Let me tell you what I expect Cedric. I expect a lot more than your convict bullshit. I expect you know how hard it is to get see you when it's not visiting day and you're locked down no with visitors allowed. And I didn't come to waste my time. Help me and you might be better off. That is might be. The only promise I'll make you is things here will be the same or worse. You choose." Burns said still wondering if he were wasting time.

"Why don't you tell me what I've got wrong?" Andy said watching Cedric. The convict's mind was working. "Talk to me Cedric, I haven't got all day and you don't either."

"Why don't they come see me no more 'n dey do? My brother and my sister

"You stay on punishment status too much. They've been up here and weren't allowed to see you. That is not their fault."

Cedric sighed and looked down. A full minute passed before he said anything. "They don't send me money."

"What do you need money for Cedric? They won't let you keep it on you?"

"They gotta canteen, a store for inmates. We can keep money in the inmate bank. We can get candy and cigarettes and model ship kits, craft stuff in the canteen. Ah ain't got no money in da inmate bank."

Andy noticed the convict's expression changed from hate and defiance to shame. It was probably a con, inmates were master cons. Still it was an opening.

"I'll check your prison bank records before I leave. If you are telling me the truth I will put money in your account. If what you tell me helps catch a killer. I'll see to it that you have money every month."

"Why you a white guy doin this for a nigger convict? How much money you talking?"

"Your brother is my friend. Help me and you will get spending money."

"Shit man, how much?"

"None until you tell me who the rich people were. Cut the con and talk."

Cedric laughed and shook his head. "Man I ain't thought of that shit in years. Dey was dis little white kid on his Honda motorbike would come in the quarter trying to score marijuana. We'd steal his money more times than we'd get'm dope. He came one afternoon an I took his motorbike away from 'm. He said we could have it if we could get him some pussy. Man that little asshole wouldn't a knowed what to do wid pussy if he'd had any. I axed 'em if he had enough dick to do a woman any good. He said he did. So's me an some others made 'm drop his pants an show us." Cedric laughed again, his eyes began to tear as he laughed louder. "Man that little white boy didn't have no dick. He mighta had an inch hard if dat. He couldn't a peed standing wid out peeing on his pants. An he had a butt like a girl. A little white round butt."

A broad toothless grin came on Cedric's face. So much for prison dentistry, Andy thought. He had an idea of where the story was going and didn't want to ask. Cedric still grinned and giggled. Andy sighed. "What happened then, Cedric?"

"Man we butt fucked that white boy. Four of us, an you know what. He came twice. Squirted jizz rite outta the end of his little dick."

Andy Burns wanted to leave the giggling convict. If this story were true, the kid would be grown now. And he might not remember full names, but he remembered faces, and Theodis looked just like his convict brother.

"All right Cedric, who was this kid?"

"Man, I don't member his name. Do member dat if I hadn't ah kept that Honda motorbike I wouldn't na got caught. I got sent to the boy's reformatory for dat. Had ta be wat brother preacher talkin bout. Cause I member da ole man sayin he'd beat his ass."

Burns heard enough. He got up and knocked on the door. The guards unlocked Cedric and led him out of the room. A minute later an escort officer arrived and led Andy back to the administrative area. After the guard captain gave him his watch wallet and other belongings back Burns asked a question.

"Tell me about the inmate bank and store. I can see some advantage to Cleckler having money to spend. But I was also hearing a convict conning me. Do you think it would make his time any easier?"

"Mr. Burns, Cleckler doesn't have any money. He has gotten ten dollars at Christmas for the past five years from a family member. That doesn't last too long here. He is not the classification of inmate we allow to work in prison industries. I think he might be less trouble if he had some spending money. He does alright when he has something to occupy his time. I've been here 17 years. I've seen him build some fine looking models from match sticks and pop sickle sticks. I purchased him a boat kit to build for me a couple of years ago. It is at home on the wall. He did a good job with it, better than most that comes out of here. The rules won't let us do that anymore."

"Can I deposit money in his account?"

"Yes and we will give you a receipt. Cleckler will be told who put it there. If you leave him something today he can't use it until Christmas. He is in disciplinary isolation."

Andy opened his wallet and removed a hundred dollar bill. "Can I leave the money with you?"

The captain's eyebrows raised at the amount. Then he looked carefully at Burns for a moment before calling a clerk and directing him to give Burns a receipt for the deposit in Cleckler's account.

"I didn't say this Mr. Burns. It took some serious clout for you to get in here and see an inmate that is disciplinary isolation. Use some more of it and inmate Cleckler might can build somebody a boat for Christmas."

"Thank you." Burns said.

After paying his fuel bill at the airport and tipping the owner of the borrowed car. Burns saw several aviation buffs perusing his floatplane. He knew he would be subjected to the usual questions so he took a few minutes to make some phone calls. He was aggravated to find that both Desmond Taylor and Mark Hildibrand were at an FBI school for the whole week. He had to settle for leaving a message on Jolene Hadfield's voice mail about the purchaser of his Bowie knife. B.J. Hassinger's response was more to Andy's liking. 'Will do. I'll let you know.'

"This is what will happen with Cedric Cleckler. He will have to remain in isolation until this disciplinary time is done. Then he will be moved to a segregation unit. He is never going to be allowed back in general population. However, they will let him have access to his money and canteen privileges. So if he wants to buy a craft project he can have it in isolation. And they will let him have family visits on visiting day. Hope he gave you something you can use." The message from Hassinger clicked off. Burns walked out to the meadow fence and leaned on the gate.

He didn't really have anything he could use. If the boy Cedric and company raped grew into adulthood and harbored a grudge or mental anguish. Then it might be the answer to why Theo's knives were used. Whoever this kid was might never be known. Likely the only thing he'd accomplished was doing a good turn for Cedric Cleckler. Maybe it was time the guy got one. Andy closed his eyes and imagined hoofs thundering across the pasture.

Chapter Sixteen

"THIS is Captain Hadfield." Jolene said answering her desk phone.

"Jolene, Tucker Harrellson here. Are you free for dinner at my place Friday night? I'm cooking, casual dress affair. I expect a couple of my colleagues and their wives."

She looked at her desk calendar more of habit than necessity. "I don't see why not. I start my week on call that evening. So I will have to drive my city car. What time."

"Six o'clock. That will give you time to see the house and we can visit a bit before everyone shows up at seven."

"I can make that. I'll see you then." Jolene hung up the phone and looked once again at the work on her desk. With Hildibrand away at school she was covering for him as well as her duties. The job was fun when she was filling in for Thigman. Now it was demanding. They were in the middle of budget preparation and the city elections were in one week. Don Smith was facing the same challenges. They conferred often and Deputy Chief Thigman was always available to answer questions. What would they do when he retired?

She hadn't thought about Harrellson since the conversation with Hildibrand and Taylor the week before. Was it possible Harrellson was involved? Her gut feeling was no. Being invited to his house would be an excellent opportunity to snoop around. She remembered the voice mail message from Andrew Burns about the Bowie knife purchase. If Harrellson had a Burns Bowie knife on his coffee table things would get interesting.

Andrew Burns was thinking about Harrellson and his Bowie knife too. Jerry Cleckler had called and told him there was a picture of the man who bought the knives in the local newspaper. Andy procured a copy and was looking at a picture of a hard hat wearing Tucker Lee Harrellson. He was standing with three other hard hat wearers at a power plant construction project. With Bob Rabun's help Burns learned a lot about Harrellson. He owned a Land Rover and could afford Gokey boots. The phone ringing interrupted his thoughts.

Bob Rabun's voice was cheerful. "Andy, we struck gold. One of our patrol deputies, Mike Glass, arrested a stalker last night."

"And it was Tucker Harrellson driving his Land Rover wearing Gokey boots and carrying my Bowie knife." Burns replied.

"Uh no. Mike has been watching a place outside of Summerdale for a couple months. The lady that lives there reported a prowler several times. Her house was burglarized but there was not much evidence because there was no forcible entry. Well Mike caught the guy last night. Turns out he is sleaze bag private eye out of Gulfport Mississippi named Simon Duke."

"So where is the gold mine?" Andy asked.

"Duke wanted to make a deal to get out of felony stalking charges. And he offered information about the Hoffman murder."

"What kind of information?"

"Duke told our detectives this morning that Tucker Harrellson hired him to get information on Theodis Cleckler. Duke followed Cleckler for over six months. He even purchased a Bowie knife Cleckler made at a gun show in Hattiesburg, Mississippi. He also followed Cleckler to your place and conducted a reconnaissance of your property. He claims he mapped the dirt roads and located your rear fence line on the map for Harrellson."

Who had Jerry Cleckler identified? Andy wondered. The private detective's story would discredit that identification. Rabun continued.

"Duke was driving a Chevy Blazer. It has Michelin tires on it. I've taken prints and photos of the tread. I will send them to David Higgins in Jackson. Our detective has contacted Gulfport PD. They are helping us get warrants for Duke's office and home. I'll be going on the warrant service. So I'll keep my eye out for anything that connects all the dots in these cases."

"Bob is there any resemblance between this Duke and Harrellson?"

"I got a copy of Harrellson's last driver's license picture this morning from Mississippi DPS. Duke and Harrellson are the same age and there is a resemblance. They could be mistaken for each other if they were wearing hats. Duke has a receding hair line, and Harrellson has a full head of hair. Do you think Reverend Cleckler would let his boys look at these pictures while I'm over there?"

"I'll ask him for you."

If Duke has the Bowie knife in his house or office. And his tire treads and boot soles match. Harrellson would be off the hook Burns thought. He turned to his CNC lathe and watched it run for a few minutes. Andy had accepted a rifle building project from a politician running for mayor in Biloxi. The guy really expected to win. Win or lose, he would still have an heirloom quality hunting rifle. Keeping his mind occupied doing things was good. Burns walked into the knife shop. He picked up a left over piece of the steel plate he'd molded from gun barrel scrap. After contemplating the material. Andy lit the forge and donned his leather gloves.

A few miles west in Pass Christian, Mississippi love was about to play a part in solving the casino CEO murders.

Officer Mike Leigh of the Pass Christian Mississippi PD was helplessly in love with Stella Hicks. A mixed race African-American Vietnamese woman. Her hair was a silken coal black mane that stretched to her narrow waist. In Leigh's eyes the contrast of hair color to her unblemished golden skin was nothing short of perfection. And at the moment that perfection was damaged.

Stella's hair was full of wet concrete. Her pert breasts strained at her mud and concrete covered shirt and the messy gray matter accented the molded-on fit of her jeans. She was used to getting wet concrete on her, but not this much. Her job was to ascertain the concrete being poured met design specifications. As each mixer truck arrived she would draw a wheelbarrow sample and test it.

The problem started when Stella rejected a truckload because its contents were too wet and stopped the pour. This led to a confrontation with a Gulf Power & Light engineer who was making a progress inspection.

The conflict might have gone unnoticed except the engineer yelled, "No half nigger bitch with a high school education is going to tell me my concrete specifications! I'm a registered professional engineer, and I designed this fucking place!"

The area foreman immediately radioed for the contractor's project engineer and the union steward when the exchange started. The situation might have been resolved had Stella not told the registered professional engineer he was wrong.

He struck Stella with a vicious backhand knocking her into the concrete pour. After kicking over her equipment and upending the wheelbarrow sample. He got in his fancy four by four and drove through the wet concrete.

Stella's injuries were restricted to a rapidly swelling black eye, lacerations, contusions and considerably damaged pride.

When Officer Leigh arrived on the scene two arrogant members of the plant's security division met him. The brouhaha at the concrete pour could shut the project down.

The union steward demanded the engineer be arrested. The contractor's engineer demanded that work resume. And Stella demanded the concrete be removed.

The problem escalated when the security men told Leigh he was on private property and he could leave or be removed. Stella saw Leigh's cruiser and screamed at the same instant one of the security goons reached to restrain him.

Leigh radioed the code for officer needing help. He pulled a can of pepper spray from his gun belt and split the contents between the security thugs. After applying a few whacks with his baton. Leigh cuffed the company heavies and informed them they were under arrest.

A tidal wave of police cars with blue and red lights flashing accompanied by sirens engulfed the construction project. As the cops arrived with the subtlety of an air strike, workers with warrants for their arrest fled in opposite directions.

All the participants at the concrete pour except Stella were spread eagle on the ground covered at gunpoint by Leigh. They weren't complaining because she was using the water hose on the mixer truck to remove the concrete mess on her clothes and hair. Her unbuttoned wet shirt providing them a memorable show.

A police sergeant began sorting out the problem. Stella cried while describing the engineer and his vehicle. A deputy sheriff and evidence technician named Buddy Wade heard the description. He'd attended the conference at Burns' place. Wade immediately looked where she pointed.

The ground was covered with wet concrete that was beginning to dry. Its consistency was perfect enough that several shoe prints and tire tracks were setting up nicely. Buddy declared the area a crime scene and cordoned it off with yellow tape. He could recover the actual tracks when the concrete solidified.

David Higgins detested paperwork. When his secretary called him saying a deputy from southern Mississippi was on the phone he welcomed the interruption.

"Doctor Higgins, this is Buddy Wade, I'm a deputy sheriff in Hancock County, down here on the coast. I'm an evidence technician and I was at the conference in Alabama a couple of weeks ago."

"Yes Buddy, I remember talking with you. How can I be of assistance?"

"Doc I've got some tire tread and shoe print evidence. You said you wanted to see anything we came across like that."

"Buddy do you have a suspect with this evidence?"

"We sure do Doc we know whose car it is."

"What kind of case is it Buddy?"

"A misdemeanor assault, an engineer on this power plant construction job decked a female technician and left the scene. Witnesses say he threw a temper tantrum because the woman said the concrete was too wet to pour. He's some rich guy with plenty of clout. 'Cause power company security people tried to keep the police off the site. Pass Christian PD officers are going to get a warrant signed on the guy."

"What kind of car were the tire prints from?" Higgins asked.

"A Land Rover, that's what made me remember what you said. Expensive four by fours would have those tires. And I don't know about the shoe print. It has got the word Gokey in the middle of it. I thought you said something about corky."

Higgins just about bit the stem off his pipe. "Buddy give me your phone number and stay right where you are. I will call you back ASAP."

Ten minutes later Wade received a set of instructions that defied his imagination. He went to his supervisor who listened to the story and said, "Wade this had better not be any bullshit."

One hour later a Hancock County Sheriff's car pulled into the general aviation ramp at Gulfport Biloxi Regional Airport. Buddy Wade saw the red-headed man waving to him.

"Doctor Higgins said I should look for a guy with a red beard who looks like pirate without an eye patch." Wade said.

Adam Hall laughed and shook hands with Wade. The concrete impressions were carefully packed into a cardboard box. Buddy carried the box to the waiting jet and refused to relinquish it to the copilot as he cautiously climbed the short stairway into the citation's cabin. Wade kept the box in reach while he settled into a seat and buckled his seatbelt. He picked up the box and held it tightly in his lap. Adam sat next to the deputy. When the copilot closed the cabin door Wade turned pale. Hall noticed the reaction and asked casually. "Have you ever ridden in a private jet, Buddy?"

"No," croaked Wade. He had never flown in his life.

Stella Hicks was nursing a serious shiner and few bruises. Mike Leigh wanted justice for Stella.

"Honey call in sick tomorrow and we'll go to the magistrate and you can swear out a warrant for that asshole." Leigh pleaded.

"He'll just pay a fine and that'll be all. I lose time off work doing that. Next time he comes around I'll kick the buffed up bastard in the balls."

"And then he'll take a warrant out on you. And you'll lose your job. Take a warrant out on him now. He'll get convicted and pay a fine. But then you can sue him and the power company. And they'll pay up quick cause they don't want the publicity of their engineers beating up women on the job. And that rich prick will have to pay too. Look, we could have a paid for house out of this if we do it right."

The possibility of a paid for American dream was enough for Stella. She agreed to go with Leigh to the magistrate's office the next morning.

Friday was busy. Deputy Chief Thigman was in charge. The Chief of Police was off to the annual International Association of Chiefs of Police conference. Depending on your point of view the yearly IACP bash was either a training session or a party. Thigman had never been to one.

Today he and Captains Hadfield and Smith were in a budget meeting with all the councilors and those who were running against them in next week's election. The mayor and all those seeking that job were also in attendance. This daylong meeting caused Jolene to wonder about the wisdom of being a captain.

During a break Smith confided in her. "Being the SWAT lieutenant was the best job I in this department even with DePiano as boss."

"I wasn't a lieutenant long enough to learn how to spell it much less enjoy it." Hadfield answered rolling her eyes. She'd never interacted with politicians enough to realize they suffered from overly inflated egos. Her father always told her, the higher you got in a police department the worse the job. Working the street was the best cop job in the world.

Friday was a good day for Stella Hicks and Mike Leigh. Stella signed the warrant and Leigh would get to serve it that afternoon. They spent midday in bed.

Bob Rabun and the Baldwin County Sheriff's Detectives served search warrants on Simon Duke's home and office. A Gulfport officer who accompanied them on the search commented that sleazy wasn't bad enough to describe Duke's private eye activities. Photography via bedroom windows was the man's forte. As was collecting semen stained women's underwear. Need to prove infidelity, Simon Duke was your man.

Theodis Cleckler agreed to let his boys look at Rabun's photo lineup. The meeting took place after school in the church office. Theo J and Jerry had met Deputy Sundae before and liked him. They identified both Simon Duke and Tucker Lee Harrellson as the Bowie knife purchasers. Jerry was insistent that Harrellson himself had purchased the Burns knife. Rabun dutifully left this information on the voice mails of Hadfield, Taylor and Hildibrand. It would be next week before any of them heard the messages.

Higgins conferred with his senior tool mark examiner. "Ralph, I concur with your findings. The tire treads and boot soles are identical for all three crime scenes. I will pass these findings on to MBI."

A few minutes later Higgins was on the phone with Major J.C. Pickens at Mississippi Bureau of Investigation. The call from Higgins was good news. She asked her sergeant to run a criminal history on the name Higgins provided. Five minutes later she was looking at the computer printout. Tucker Lee Harrellson's family money had gotten him out of everything. The only records were traffic infractions and a not guilty verdict for every charge. Including a ticket she had written him when she was a uniformed highway patrol trooper. Pickens picked up her phone.

"Charlene how in the world are you?" Richmond's voice boomed over the line.

"If I were any better there'd be two of me."

"And we couldn't stand it." Judge Richmond laughed as he completed the greeting. "If you're calling to say you're coming to the coast this weekend. Margie and I would love to have you over for dinner."

"No Emory, but I will take a rain check. I need a search warrant."

"It's not my month to do warrants. But you are the exception to the rule. What have you got?"

"A suspect in the casino CEO cases. We have good direct evidence. We need a warrant for vehicles, shoes & boots, DNA and knives. The suspect is Tucker Lee Harrellson."

"You will have the warrant. What time you do you need it."

"I've got a team assembling now. We will want to go this evening. Doctor Higgins at forensic science has got a jet on call."

"Your warrant will be ready by three. And I don't want to know what the mad scientist is doing with an on call jet."

"Leigh listen to me." The Pass Christian PD Sergeant said. "You will not go to Biloxi and attempt to serve this warrant by yourself." The sergeant held up the document Leigh presented to him. "Myerson will go with you. The two of you will meet me here at five thirty. I will call Biloxi and have them send an officer with you two. And you can have your warrant back when you and Myerson walk out the door. Now go do something constructive."

Jolene Hadfield was hoping she could remember the names of the decent council hopefuls when she voted next week. After having been waylaid the fourth time since the meeting let out by politico wannabes. The rookie captain stopped briefly in her office. She scanned the desk for recent post it notes and grabbed her purse. Making sure she had her new display pager and city cell phone. It was Friday night and she had plans. Harrellson might be a way back in the closet gay. But she wanted to see the inside of his house. Tire tracks, boot soles and Bowie knives were not on her mind.

"Welcome Captain Hadfield how are you this evening?" Tucker Harrellson asked as he let Jolene in his front door.

"The captain hopes her pager doesn't go off. Wow Tucker this house is beautiful." Jolene answered as looked around the vaulted ceiling great room.

"Would you like a glass of wine?"

"Yes, thank you. But forgive me if I don't have more than a glass. I am on call."

"No problem. Look around enjoy yourself. I'll be right back."

Hadfield sat her leather purse by the arm rest on a large leather couch. That probably cost more than all the furniture in her house. She checked to insure the purse's flap was secured and her pager still clipped in place. Her attention was drawn to the museum quality photo art decorating the walls. Many of the pictures were obviously over fifty years old. Some dated back to the World War One era.

"The Gulf Coast where I grew up. Unspoiled by gaudy gambling dens," Tucker said handing her a wineglass. "Look around and enjoy the pictures, they show the place like it should be. Make yourself at home. I've got some more work to do on dinner."

She sipped the wine and examined the pictures. Jolene found her way into a den. She liked the lodge style furniture in this room. One photo caught her attention. It was the first gambling casino opened. It was actually a riverboat moored permanently onto a pier. In the foreground of the picture was a younger Theodis Cleckler leading a protest march. A large sheath knife lay on the table below the picture.

Sitting down her wineglass she cautiously picked up the knife and withdrew it from the sheath. Jolene felt a sudden sick feeling in her stomach when she saw the words 'Burns Made.'

Harrellson called to her, "your pager is going off!"

Jolene carried the knife back into room. Laying it between her purse and couch armrest she picked up her beeper.

...Cpt. Hadfield.... MBI Agent Tyler Cook called ... Will be serving search warrant on Harrellson residence Bay View. Harrellson suspect in Serrano Austin and Hoffman homicides.... Call Agent Cook ASAP on cell number...

The urge to vomit almost overcame her. The doorbell rang. Harrellson answered the door. An officer she didn't recognize was standing there.

"Tucker Lee Harrellson," Officer Mike Leigh said. "I have a warrant for your..."

Harrellson drew a Glock from his front pocket and shot Leigh four times before slamming the door.

Reaching in her purse Jolene realized her pistol was gone. Gunfire struck the house and front door. She heard voices outside yelling.

Lyle Thigman answered his phone. He was grilling a steak at that moment and didn't care for the interruption. "Chief, this Helen in dispatch. I've been trying to notify Captain Hadfield of another agency serving a search warrant in our jurisdiction. She hasn't called back. It's MBI and they're getting impatient."

"Where are they going Helen?"

"The Harrellson house on Bay"... She was cut off by the screams of an officer on the radio.

THIRTY-SIX! OFFICER DOWN ON BAY VIEW I NEED HELP! GET THE SWAT TEAM OUT HERE!

Several shots were fired before the microphone was cut off.

"Chief I've got to...."

"Helen do not hang up." He ordered calmly. "Where are they?"

"OH NO!" Helen cried. "That's the address MBI is going to! We sent thirty six over there with a Pass Christian officer to serve a warrant!"

"Helen call out SWAT and tell Don Smith I'm on the way."

Thigman looked longingly at the steak. It was a little rarer than he preferred. He removed it from the grill and stuck it between two pieces of bread. He grabbed his pistol and portable radio. He took a go cup of coffee to wash down the steak sandwich.

On the scene with a backdrop of emergency lights patrol sergeant briefed his bosses.

"Car thirty six was assigned to escort Pass Christian officers to serve a misdemeanor assault warrant on Tucker Lee Harrellson at this address. They knocked on the door. A large buffed up white male answered it. Officer Leigh announced he had an arrest warrant. The male subject drew a pistol shot Leigh four times and slammed the door. Our guys and the other Pass Christian officer returned fire and were able to drag Leigh out of there."

"Do we know Leigh's condition?" The patrol lieutenant asked.

"Very lucky. His vest stopped all four rounds. He was knocked unconscious when he fell down. The medics said he woke up in they were loading him in the ambulance and asked if he were in hell. That is the only good news so far. Captain Hadfield's unmarked car is parked in the driveway. As far as we know she and Harrellson are the only people in the house. We have two couples here who were supposed be Harrellson's dinner guests. They confirm he'd told them Hadfield was invited. Of course MBI is here with a search warrant. Harrellson is a suspect in the casino CEO homicides."

"Do we have any idea what Jolene's condition is?" Thigman asked.

"The sniper position reports she is alive and sitting on the couch in the main room. Harrelson is there with her and he is armed with a Glock pistol." Hildibrand said.

"Who is on the rifle?" Thigman asked.

"Peterson' Hildibrand sighed. He's all we've got. I've ordered him to observe and report only. He's not qualified to shoot. I'm going to take position with him now. Captain Smith will lead the entry team." The lieutenant had a Burns built sniper rifle slung over his shoulder.

"Chief we have a negotiator trying to make contact. But so far no answer." Smith said.

"OK, Jolene's safety is our priority. Mark you have a green light to shoot if that son of bitch even looks like he's going to hurt her. Don this situation is officially under SWAT control. Resolve it." Thigman ordered.

Harrellson's expression was what Hadfield would have envisioned on a maniac. Two things scared her, getting shot by him or accidently shot by the police. She silently prayed that Don and Mark were outside with SWAT.

Tucker stood in front of a picture window holding Jolene's Glock by his hip. Casually pointing it at her like some old time TV gunfighter. She had slid her purse over the Bowie knife hoping he wouldn't notice it. She wished she had taken the opportunity to attend hostage negotiator training when it was offered a couple years ago. Hadfield recalled the first time she'd gone to lunch with Harrellson and his saying he'd been snake bit. She remembered the pathologist saying Hoffman had been snake bit post mortem. It was an opening at least.

"The first time we went to lunch Tucker you said you'd been snake bit. That didn't happen on a construction site like you said. It happened when you dumped Nigel Hoffman in that lake in Alabama."

"Yeah but I got even with that little OJ nigger for running off. I stuck his Uzi up his ass. Do you think they will trade nigger preacher Cleckler for you?"

"What do you want Reverend Cleckler for?"

"So I can stick your pistol up his ass and pull the trigger."

"They are not going to trade one hostage for another Tucker. You let me go and I'll get Reverend Cleckler to call you."

"I DON'T WANT TO TALK TO THAT NIGGER. I WANT TO STICK THIS PISTOL UP HIS ASS AND PULL THE TRIGGER YOU DUMB BITCH!"Harrellson yelled his face red and contorted with rage. At that moment the phone rang again. Harrellson turned and fired at the phone silencing it on the forth shot. He spun back around and leveled the Glock at Jolene.

Officer Peterson saw the scene unfold through his rifle scope. An officer's life in danger overrode orders. That might have been correct if he knew what he was doing. He fired the re-barreled rifle for the first time and missed.

The thirty-caliber bullet shattered the double paned laminated plate glass window and separated into two pieces. The lead core missed Harrellson by three feet and struck a picture. The copper jacket tore through Jolene's ear. The sudden stinging pain caused her to fall sideways over her purse.

Harrellson turned and fired shots at the shattered window.

Peterson worked the rifle bolt chambering another round. He aligned the cross hairs on Harrellson's chest and jerked the trigger. This shot struck the foundation. Peterson saw stars and lost consciousness.

"GO DON GO!" Hildibrand yelled into his radio as he leveled his rifle. The entry team was already on the door step with a cop that bench pressed three fifty drawing back a battering ram. Don Smith was behind him with his submachine gun leveled. Three more SWAT guys were poised to follow him inside.

Jolene grabbed the coffin shaped handle of the Bowie knife and stood up. Harrellson turned back and aimed the Glock at her face. She lunged forward. The knife struck just below Harrellson's sternum and Jolene shoved it to the hilt. The blade deflected on the spine. The point ripping through the skin and the back of his shirt

He bellowed blood gushing from his mouth into her face and hair. Wavering his eyes wide Harrellson didn't fall. The front door crashed opened and Smith ran in aiming his submachine gun at Harrellson.

Hildibrand aligned the cross hairs on the back of Harrellson's head and squeezed the trigger. At that instant Smith pressed his trigger sending a three round burst into Tucker Lee's back. His head exploded like a melon blowing his face and brains onto Jolene.

Smith and Hildibrand's shots were unnecessary. The Bowie knife killed Harrellson. His brain hadn't gotten the message he was dead.

Jolene covered with blood and brains realized she was alive and screamed. She spun around and vomited on the couch.

Hildibrand turned his attention to the prostrate Peterson.

Officers Gresham and Graham found him later.

"Partner this is happening too often," Graham said.

"You got that right," Gresham answered.

Both officers looked at the recumbent Peterson. His hands were cuffed around a tree. The big fighting knife he carried on his SWAT gear belt was stuck into the ground next to him. Someone used it to split the seat of his trousers and bikini shorts. The muzzle end of the barrel he had lobbied DePiano for was stuck up his ass.

228

CHAPTER SEVENTEEN

HADFIELD shivered uncontrollably. Her face was pale and her lips were blue from the cold. She wasn't sure what she had wrapped around herself to cover her wet naked body. It was the doorbell and heavy knocking on the front door that compelled her to leave the cold water shower. Somehow Jolene managed to open the door. She saw the concerned faces of her father, Don Smith, his wife, Mark Hildibrand, his wife, and three women from Rev. Cleckler's church. Theodis stood at the back of the group with Lyle Thigman, Desmond Taylor and four uniformed officers.

"Jo, honey we're concerned about you." Joe Hadfield said. "All you say to callers is that you're OK and you hang up. Sweetie I don't think you're alright."

"I can't get clean Daddy." Jolene collapsed into his arms still shaking and cried.

The Smiths and Hildibrands went in the house. The church ladies stayed on the porch helping Joe Hadfield comfort his daughter. After a few minutes Don Smith came out and reported to Thigman.

Her shower was running cold water only. Both taps wide open. Mark checked the hot water heater and said it was empty. Apparently she ran all the hot water out and hasn't given the system time to recover. Wet towels all over the place no clean ones in the closet. She has had a breakdown. Jolene hasn't been by herself since Friday night. It's Monday afternoon. We left her alone and somebody needed to be with her."

"We offered remember. She was emphatic saying she didn't want anyone here. I will make sure she gets help." Thigman turned to a couple of the uniforms. "Get them to the hospital now."

"Yes Sir." They carefully escorted Jolene and her dad to their cruiser.

As they watched the patrol car leave, Smith looked at his boss. "How are you going reconcile this mess with the Chief when he gets back tomorrow?"

"That won't be a problem." Thigman answered.

"He threw a running fit over the rehab time with that mess DePiano caused her. Chief never has liked her. And you say it won't be a problem. If you've got something on him how about passing it on. You're retiring December Thirty First remember."

"It's not what I've got on him. It's what the FBI has on him. I wasn't planning on briefing you Mark and Jolene on this until five today. Jolene obviously won't be involved so get Mark out here and we'll talk now."

Smith raised his eyebrows at Thigman's statement. Then he saw Hildibrand walking toward them. The trio moved to the street by their cars. The old cop looked at the younger men. "At five PM today the FBI will start arresting a number of public figures on corruption charges. The mayor three council members and the police chief are among those indicted. After the election results are tallied tomorrow evening. Those elected will assume office immediately. Biloxi will be under new management and I hope better leadership."

Smith and Hildibrand shook their heads. Mark softly said. "Wow."

"Busby and DePiano have been indicted as well as the city manager. This has been an ongoing investigation. A much needed one. The media scrutiny from Friday will change as of the ten o'clock news tonight. There is going to be a lot of worry and rumor in the PD. You guys are going to have your hands full dealing with it. It's not really fair to you. You're in new jobs. Both of you can handle it. Jolene can handle it. We've got to get her past Friday night."

"She was close to an FBI agent during that last incident. That woman really helped. Jolene said one of her degrees is in psychology." Hildibrand said.

"That would be Special Agent Havelee Harris. I've got a call in for her. But it might be a day or two before I hear back." Thigman answered. "Let's go see how the women and the church folks are doing."

Andrew Burns looked at his caller ID. The incoming call was from Miles Cromwell Esq. Andy answered the phone saying, "What are you recommending I buy today?"

"Hassinger and Brown called. Biloxi is looking for a therapeutic rehab place to send Captain Hadfield when she gets of the hospital tomorrow. She wants to go back to Mentone. Counselors from Chattanooga can come there. We may wind up not getting paid with the city and its insurance carrier involved. The only reason they paid last time was a judge ordered it. Maybe the new folks running the city will be easier to deal with. But you will have to OK it before I give them an answer. And the main lodge has only one room left. It is totally booked for Thanksgiving week. Only one cabin is available for the entire month. And the manager reports numerous inquiries. So you may lose money dealing with Biloxi."

"Theodis called me the other day and said she was in really bad shape from that mess with Harrellson. The cabin is hers as long as she needs it. The lodge food service will feed her and any guest she may have as often as she wants. They will consider her a VIP just like last time. Bill the insurance and Biloxi. Take what they will pay and comp the rest. Comp her entire stay if necessary."

"That woman is blessed to have a friend like you."

"I'm not sure she considers me a friend. Handle it the usual way."

"I'll take care of it." Cromwell rang off.

Burns switched his phone to forward calls to his cell. He was expecting a call from a client whose new rifle was ready. The dogs followed him as he walked down to the lake and sat on the pier. That bench and one he'd build next to small corral he had erected around Major's grave was where he spent time when wasn't working. Andy watched the lake and thought about Desmond Taylor's visit the past Tuesday.

All the loose ends had to be tied up in order to close the investigation of Harrellson's homicide and those of the casino CEO's. A formal identification of the Bowie knife was required. A formal affidavit was drawn up for Burns to sign attesting to his having made the knife. Taylor would have to interview Jerry Cleckler and get a formal statement as well. Desmond had filled Andy in on the gory details of Harrellson's demise and the role the Bowie played in it. It was no wonder Hadfield was having such a time of it. Andy wanted to reach out to her and say how sorry he felt about what she'd suffered. It was something he didn't know how to do. The cell phone buzzing interrupted his thoughts. His client would be at the gate soon.

Andy reached the shop in time to open the gate for Larson Huffstutler's Lincoln Navigator. Soon the new mayor of Biloxi Mississippi was admiring his new rifle.

"Are the citizens of Biloxi allowing you enough time to shoot it today?" Burns asked.

"Yes I've been looking forward to it."

"Targets are up at one and two hundred yards. Here's the ammo it's sighted in with. Hearing protectors are on the bench be my guest."

Andy watched as the Mayor fired the fired the rifle. After shooting at both targets Huffstutler was happy. "I'm glad I took Mark Hildibrand's advice about getting you to build this. I've never owned this fine of a rifle."

"I'm glad you're pleased. It was fun to build."

"I understand you are somewhat familiar with our police department and the recent events involving it."

"That's an understatement."

"From what I've heard about you that's the answer I expected. I appreciate the help you've given our people. Your involvement is why I'm going to bring you up to date on what's happening."

Burns nodded.

"We have voted to extend Lyle Thigman's mandatory retirement date two years and appoint him Chief of Police. He will use those years to groom our new command staff to lead the department and one of them to take his place. This will be Captain Smith. He has the most experience in management rank. He is now Deputy Chief. Mark Hildibrand has been promoted to captain and he is currently assigned to patrol division. When Captain Hadfield returns from trauma leave she will continue heading up the detective and administrative division. Hopefully we will have her back before the end of the year.

"She has suffered enough from vindictive management practices. Hadfield is extremely smart and a capable police officer. She is new to upper management as is Hildibrand. That's why we need Thigman around for guidance. I just approved funding for Hadfield to spend time in rehab. She's going to Mentone Alabama. I understand it is near Chattanooga. I really want her back. She has a lot to offer. I hope she doesn't give up a police career for the women's professional bass fishing tour. Rumor says she's seriously considering it."

"I know Hadfield Smith and Hildibrand. They've all been over here at one time or another. Hadfield eyes my lake with a look of pure lust. She's never taken me up on fishing it. And she is welcome anytime. They are all good people. I've never met Thigman. I would like to. You have a good plan for your PD. It will work. I hope Hadfield makes it back. I really do."

"I'm going to recommend she spend some rehab time with her bass boat in your lake. Andy I appreciate your time and your workmanship. Thank you. I hate to go, but duty calls."

Jolene Hadfield stood at the window of her hospital room. There wasn't much of a view and it was a cloudy day. That didn't help either. The doctor had given her a mild antidepressant and anxiety prescription. She said it was used for people who lived in rainy environments and needed relief from cloudy days. Today was certainly a good day for it. Jolene wondered if they had planned her hospital discharge from to coincide with the depressing weather. Her father along with one of his fishing buddies and Havelee Harris were due to pick her up. They would travel to Mentone convoy style. The FBI agent had volunteered to take some leave time and travel with her. They would be driving Jolene's truck pulling the bass boat. Joe Hadfield and his buddy were bringing Havelee's car. They would return to the coast the following day. Jolene heard the door open and turned around.

"Captain Hadfield I'm glad to see you are well and ready to leave this place." Theodis Cleckler said.

"I don't know about the well part. And I'm not wild about the dark day I'm going out in."

"I believe the Lord gives us days like this to remind us that He walks with us. And He is our shepherd our guide through dismal days like these. And when He gives us a glorious sunrise on a beautiful day. We see His majesty and know He is with us always."

Jolene saw the peace and serenity in his eyes that she had seen when she first met him. The kind smile that spoke the sincerity of his words.

"Reverend Cleckler, I have never properly thanked you and your church members for what they did for me last summer. That meant so much. And to see some of those same ladies at my door last Monday. I can't find words that express my gratitude for all you have done."

"Captain Hadfield you don't have to. As Christians we serve others. And you serve us. Your calling is ordained in the Bible. You are a Peacekeeper. And you do your job well because you strive to do what is right. We see that. Most important is the Lord sees it as well. He was with you that terrible night last week. His Angels protected you. He has placed you in position of great responsibility. So that you can serve others and by doing that, you serve Him.”

Jolene felt tears welling up in her eyes. She could not answer his words.

“Captain, we shared adversity together a few months ago in court. The Lord allowed us to prevail. Because we did the right thing. That time was only preparation for what He has given you now. You will get through this with His help and move on. I understand it has been arranged for you to spend some time at a very beautiful retreat. He will be there with you. Ask for His guidance. I will tell you why.

“We are approaching the time of year where darkness prevails over daylight. People suffering from hard times have it worst this time of year. It was during the darkest of those days that God gave us his greatest gift. His Son. And in the spring, the time of grand days and rebirth of all living things. The Son gave us the gift of eternal life. Captain, He will be with you. You need to let Him be with you in these coming days.”

Jolene hugged the preacher. She leaned back and took his hand. “Thank you Reverend Cleckler. Thank you so much.”

“It’s darkest before dawn.” Havelee said as she carefully watched her step on the narrow path. Jolene was leading the way navigating by the narrow beam of a Mini Maglite. Both women were wrapped in blankets from the cabin. Hadfield wanted to see the sunrise over Little River Canyon. Their destination was her favorite gazebo.

“It’s also the hardest time to stay awake on third shift.”

“I wouldn’t know about that. I’m always getting up about this time.”

“So the FBI bosses can’t threaten you with third shift if they don’t like you.”

"Hey we're nine to five and dress professional."

"Let me get a picture of you right now so I can send it to your SAC."

They arrived at the gazebo and found a carafe of fresh coffee and a pair cups. Jolene poured a cup and handed it to the FBI agent. "Thanks for taking the time to come up here with me. I really need a friend right now."

The darkness was turning grey. Hadfield finished pouring her cup and took a seat. "Being here seems to help. The doctor said when the medication kicked in things would get better."

"It will help. Getting away and sorting it all out will do you a world of good. Girlfriend you wanting to get out of bed and come out here for sunrise tells me you're on your way."

"Something Reverend Cleckler said yesterday made me want to come here. Right now I need that reassurance."

Each woman sat quietly sipping coffee keeping their thoughts to themselves. Both watched the sky to the east. Slowly it grew brighter. Rays of light beamed through the trees and the yellow orange ball appeared warming them as it lit their surroundings. Tears rolled down Jolene's cheeks. Havelee put her hand on Hadfield's forearm.

After a week Harris returned to Mobile. She promised Jolene that she would come back to the cabin and spend Thanksgiving with her and her father.

Two and half weeks later Havelee returned to Mentone and an hour after she arrived Joe Hadfield showed up with his old buddy Lyle Thigman in tow. None of the foursome could recall a Thanksgiving Dinner as scrumptious as the one prepared by the lodge staff. That evening in front of a roaring fire the conversation turned to past events.

"Other words if we had all checked our voice mails that near disaster might have been avoided." Hadfield said.

"That sums it up nicely." Thigman answered.

"Everybody had a piece of the puzzle and they thought the other person had the rest of the pieces." Havelee added.

"While it scared the crap of me and damned near got my daughter killed. It was probably the best ending. Convicting that pervert on circumstantial evidence with his family's money would have been tough." Joe Hadfield opined.

"They have done a good job of sweeping it under the rug as it is. We're going to let them do it. I'm not showing their attorney's any of our work product on the case. Jolene your pocket tape recorder got turned on somehow. And it picked up every word he said. Desmond Taylor did a great job of interviewing Cedric Cleckler. The casino people are happy with us exceptionally clearing the cases. Primary suspect deceased. We dodged the bullet big time. So it is over. Our only loss is Taylor."

"What are you talking about Chief?" Hadfield asked.

"Our G-person sitting over there grinning like a Cheshire cat poached him from us. He's turned in his noticed to be a fed. Harris do they give you a bonus for stealing good people?"

"It's a notation in your file saying you have excellent recruiting skills. But I like the word poached better. When he showed me what he'd found on Busby I knew we had to have him."

"I hate to lose him. But I'm happy for him." Hadfield said.

"It's time to bring this up. Jo when do you think you're coming back? The Mayor is willing to give you to the first of the year. I don't know how long the bill will get paid on this place though." Thigman said.

"I have some things left to sort out. I will either be back by the mayor's deadline or I'll resign."

"Jo!" Her father said.

"The matter is not up for discussion."

"How's the fishing up here this time of year?" Thigman asked, changing the subject.

Hadfield had the cabin to herself the next night. She'd spent the day after everyone left in the gazebo looking at the canyon. The lodge staff would discreetly leave her food and drink. They were unobtrusive about taking care of her. For the first time she thought about who was paying for the place. She looked at the fire for a while then picked up the phone and dialed the main lodge extension.

"Would it be possible to get a thermos of coffee at 4:30 in the morning?"

"Yes ma'am do you want us to set it by your door?"

"That would be fine. I'm leaving in the morning. I'll get the thermos back to you somehow."

"No worry Ms. Hadfield. You are a VIP guest. Keep the thermos with our compliments."

"Thank you, thank you very much."

"You're welcome. You have a safe trip tomorrow. We enjoy having you as a guest."

Andrew Burns inspected the knife he held. It was a fisherman's fillet knife made from the last gun barrel steel. It was as perfect as he could make it. He would have to pack it and make sure it was mailed. It wasn't going far, but it needed to be there before Christmas. The phone rang.

"Burns this sign says call for admittance. I wanna fish. Open the gate."

He looked at the monitor screen and zoomed in on the driver holding the gate phone. It was Jolene Hadfield. "Burns I've been driving since 4:30 this morning. I need to pee and I want to get the boat in the water. Are going to let me in?"

"The code is pound sixteen December." He hung up the phone and watched. She got it the first time.

Jolene came in the shop door and squeezed his arm. "Gotta go be back."

A few minutes she was standing in the shop stretching. "I've been on the road from Mentone. It's good to get out of the truck."

"You made good time."

"Ran into traffic in Birmingham and Montgomery. Not real bad for the Thanksgiving weekend. Did you have a good Thanksgiving?"

"My usual. I went to a restaurant in Bay Minette and had dinner."

"By yourself I suppose."

"Yes."

Hadfield spotted the fillet knife laying on the bench. She picked it up.

"I didn't know you made knives like this. May I take it out and look at it."

"Be my guest." He watched as she pulled it from the sheath. Jolene gasped when she saw the engraving on the blade.

For Captain Jolene Hadfield

Burns Made

"Andy it's beautiful."

"I started making if before, uh you know. I wasn't sure how you would take it. It's a Christmas present. I was going to mail it to you."

She put the knife down and hugged and kissed him on the cheek. "Thank you. I wouldn't have been able to tell you how I would have taken it either. Today I like it. I like it very much." She kissed his cheek again.

"Walk down to lake stretch your legs. I'll drive your truck and launch your boat."

Jolene enjoyed the cool afternoon and playing with the dogs. She watched Burns launch her boat and tie it to the pier. He parked her truck and joined her on the pier bench. "How was fishing in Mentone?"

"It was pretty good for this time of year. It was better last summer. That place is incredible. They waited on me hand and foot the first time. This time they put me in one of the cabins. Everything I wanted they gave me. They fixed an incredible Thanksgiving Dinner for me my Dad Chief Thigman and Havelee Harris. Last night they said I was a VIP guest."

"It's a nice place I've been there. But I wasn't a VIP guest."

"What were you doing there?"

"A meeting, I know the owner."

"It was sold while I was there the first time. The staff was really happy about the new owner. Is that the one you know?"

"Yes. I understand you've had a rough time lately. How are you doing now?"

"OK I guess. I've got to decide if I'm going back to work or resigning. If I had been a better leader or manager it wouldn't have happen. We were lucky nobody got killed."

"Why are you questioning your leadership?"

"I had two detectives out of town at a school. One of them the detective lieutenant. The other one a sergeant. And the sergeant was the primary investigator on those cases. If I had made sure they followed up on what they were doing we would have known about Harrellson. I was too busy trying to be a captain and figure out next year's budget. Nobody checked their voice mails! Not even me!"

"And you're thinking about giving up your job because nobody checked their voice mails. I think it is admirable that you are willing to accept responsibility for your people. Mark Hildibrand is blaming himself about the voice mails too. But he is not thinking about quitting over it. He is trying to get up to speed on his new job. You've got a job, do it. Biloxi PD has the best people in the best places. Thigman knows it and your new mayor knows it. The learning curve will be tough. You can handle it.

"Jolene I wouldn't wish what you've been though on anybody. Nobody thinks any worse of you because you didn't suck it up and come to work the next day. There would be something bad wrong with you if you had. You have too much to give. Go back to work."

He saw the tears on her cheeks. "Get in the boat."

When she was seated at the control console the dogs jumped in. Andy untied the boat and shoved it into the lake. He said. "Fish."

She petted dogs while they licked the tears from her face. She hugged them. Soon the boat was in the middle of the lake. After a few minutes, Jolene removed a rod from the tackle locker and checked the lure. She cranked the boat and steered for a spot she picked.

Jolene maneuvered the Ranger beside the pier. She tied the boat up and carried a pair of bass to a nearby cleaning table. The new fillet knife was awesome. In a few minutes she had four nice sized bass fillets ready for a skillet. She put the fish in plastic bags she'd bought along for that purpose. Walking to the house she wondered where Burns was. It might be presumptuous to think he would let her use his kitchen. She decided she was cooking him dinner whether he liked it or not. After depositing the fish in the fridge Hadfield called out to Burns again. He wasn't in the house or the shop so the barn was her next stop. She found him in the paddock brushing a horse she'd never seen before. The small horse was eating from a bucket hanging from a fence post.

The horse jerked its head from the bucket as she approached. She heard Burns speaking to the animal. "Easy does it fellow. She won't hurt you." He was stroking the horse's neck. Hadfield stopped further down the fence than she planned. Soon the horse went back to eating. She watched Andy and the horse.

"Is it alright to talk?"

"Sure don't yell or scream give him time to get used to your voice." Burns answered.

"Is he new?"

"Yeah he's been here about four weeks now. He is a rescue horse. There is a filly and a burro in the pasture that came with him. Rabun called saying the human society and the sheriff's animal control officer needed to remove them from where they were living. If it hadn't of happened all three would have starved to death by now."

"He does look thin. I can see his ribs."

"He looks fat compared to what he looked like when he got here."

"Was he abused?" She asked.

"Yes, whoever had him didn't know what to do with him. He is a wild mustang. The people adopted him at one of those wild horse and burro adoptions the Bureau of Land Management holds. The BLM collects a fee and assumes that who adopts the animals knows what they are doing. And that is not the case here. The little filly is a registered quarter horse. She has bounced back real well. She will be a good horse. The burro, is a regular little jackass. He's mean."

"What's Major think about his new friends?"

With that question Burns turned his head away from her. A few seconds he wiped at his eyes with a bandana. When he turned back she saw the sadness on his face.

"Andy did I say something wrong?"

"No Major was shot six times that night the gang-bangers came. I should have checked on him after the cops got here. But I didn't. He was barely alive when I came out to feed him the next morning. At least I was with him when he died. He's buried out in that pasture he loved."

The mustang turned away and trotted across the paddock. Burns watched him for a moment. He went into the barn and came out with a pair of feed buckets and put them in the bed of the ATV next to a hay bale. He motioned Hadfield to get in the ATV cab.

"How was the fishing?"

"Fantastic I caught eighteen fish over sixteen inches long. I threw them back except for two six pounders. They are cleaned and ready to cook for dinner. I'll cook them for you if you let me take a shower first."

"Take your pick of the guest rooms Hadfield. Each one has a shower. You are welcome to stay as long as you want. And you are welcome back anytime. Police captains need a break every now and then." He stopped at the pasture fence.

Jolene reached over and squeezed his hand. "Thank you."

Burns gave her a sad smile. He got out and went to the fence. She followed him. A horse bolted from the tree line and ran toward them. It slid to a stop its ears straight up and head cocked looking at her. Like she was the most incredible thing it had ever seen. The little horse whinnied loudly shaking its head and black mane. There were four perfect black stockings on each of its legs and its black tail almost touched the ground. Instinctively Jolene reached across the fence. The young buckskin hesitated appraising her for several seconds. Then it stepped up and nuzzled her hand.

Burns removed the feed buckets and hung one the fence. The little horse moved to its bucket. He took the other bucket a ways down the fence line and hung it. Jolene saw the burro approaching that bucket. Andy put hay out near each bucket. He came back to where she was watching the small buckskin eat.

"He looks just like a little Major how old is he?"

"She," Andy said, emphasizing the word "is a year old."

"What's her name?" Jolene asked, looking at Burns and seeing tears in his eyes.

"Jo," He answered softly, tears flowing down his cheeks. He touched her shoulder and pointed toward the gate. "Walk with me please."

The pasture was bathed in late afternoon golden light. She saw the wooden fence around Major's grave. A bench near it. The place was tranquil. Jolene felt at peace being here. Burns stood by the bench. He was still tearful as he spoke.

"I really miss that big buckskin. Theodis told me God gave him to me for a purpose. And took him away for another purpose. Theo said one day God will reward me with a finer horse. I didn't realize how much I needed those rescue horses until till they got here. I believe God sent them for a reason. I used to wonder why things like that happen. I don't go to church on Sunday. I drink beer and I cuss. I'm certainly not the paragon of Christian virtue. But He has seen me through some terrible times. I looked over this place when I got back. It was at this spot where I removed my hat and gave thanks to Him for all my blessings."

Jolene saw Burns remove his cowboy hat while he spoke. He quietly held it in his hands and sat on the bench. She sat next to him. The little buckskin walked up and poked its head over her shoulder. Silently Jolene gave thanks.

At the end of the pasture the sun became a bright orange fireball hesitating before disappearing into twilight and darkness.

At that instant an Air Force fighter jet in low-level flight burst from the orange orb and thundered straight up. The wings rocked as it disappeared into the darkening sky the pilot saying farewell. Jolene could not stop her tears.

The two dogs lay at their feet and the horse nickered softly. Andy put his arm around her shoulders and pulled her close as darkness settled around them.